THE PROLIFERATION OF TALENT

Garda Nua Part 1

PALADIN SHADOWS SERIES, BOOK 10

A Novel by **Aidan Red**

To my wife for her patience, tolerance and encouragement. Many thanks to my family and friends for their past and continued encouragement and assistance.

The Proliferation of Talent...

Shara and Greg's world took an unexpected turn when Sedona and Sierra, their twin daughter's talents awoke years too early. The other seven children's talent followed quickly. When their worst fears were resurrected and old threats reborn, protecting the children was the first thing on Shara's mind, but there was suddenly a lot more that had to be done...

Chapters

One Hundred-Nine
Monday, September 4
Labor Day

"Come here, you two," Greg said as he bent down and grabbed his twin daughters, Sedona and Sierra, in a shared hug, squeezing them and their first-place trophies. "We're so happy you rode well today." He leaned back to admire the trophies. "Is that seven for each of you today?"

"Yeah," they answered together.

"Brickle and Strawberry were on top of their game," Sedona said, and glanced over her shoulder at Sierra, holding Strawberry's reins tightly. "Red and Ginger did good too."

"Did 'well,'" Greg corrected.

"What was your best day, Mom?" Sierra asked, and hugged Shara.

Shara caught both of them in a hug and said, "Seven." They laughed. "Where's Tayn?"

"Over by the judges' stand talking with Alyssa," Sedona said.

"Oh, anything in particular going on?" Shara asked.

"No," they said together. Then Sierra continued, "He likes talking with Alyssa but I think he likes Billie Baine better."

"Okay, let's get these critters unsaddled and brushed out," Greg said, and took the reins.

Shara turned the girls and started walking toward their trailer and hauler.

"Then can we eat?" Sierra asked.

"Eat? You just ate, what? Not an hour ago," Greg teased.

"An hour and a half. But competition ridin' is hungry work, Dad," Sedona said, and ran ahead with her sister to the trailer.

1

Greg pulled Shara close and slipped his left arm around her shoulders as they followed the girls, enjoying their energy and cheerful exuberance. The girls greeted their ranch foreman Hank and put their trophies away with their others in the sleeping end of the trailer, then quickly returned to collect their horses.

"Did you get to watch them ride, Hank?" Greg asked, noticing Hank had the other four horses loaded, watered, and fed in their trailer stalls.

"Shur did, Mr. Greg," he said, and smiled. "They look so much like their mama it takes me back a number of years."

Greg sighed and smiled, looking down at Shara, snuggled against his side. "I know just what you mean, Hank. Almost like when I first saw her."

"Was it here in Clay?" Sedona asked as she uncinched Brickle's girth.

"Yes, ma'am," Greg said, and pointed to the east end of the main arena. "I hung on that fence over there and on a couple of others. I watched her in each of her competitions that day."

"You were fifteen, right, Mom?" Sierra asked. "Ready, Dad."

"Yes, I was," Shara said as Greg hefted the saddle off Strawberry. He carried it to the tack storage compartment. "I didn't know your dad then, but I am glad I rode well that day and made an impression on him."

"We are too," they said in unison.

"Brickle's ready, Dad," Sedona said as she led the horse toward the front of the trailer.

"Hey. How're the Malones?" a familiar voice said from behind the trailer as Greg and Sedona stepped out.

"Hey, Aunt Jill," Sierra said, and gave the redheaded woman a hug. "Hey, Uncle Nick. Where's Chy?"

"She's gone to find something to eat," Jill said as she turned to hug Sedona. "Alyssa and Ridan are with her."

"I think she has a tape worm," Nick said, and smiled as he hugged the girls.

"Hey, sis. Nick," Greg said as he gave Jill a quick hug and nodded at Nick. "I thought Rose, Doug, and their twins were with you. Shara has some things for Rose and Kayli."

"They left about an hour ago," Jill said absently. "Rose said she needed to help Eddie and Carole get ready for tonight."

"We saw Chy ride," Sierra said as she began brushing Strawberry. "Too bad Bucky stumbled going around barrel three."

"Yeah," Nick agreed. "But she'll do better next summer. I'll bring Cheyenne up to your place to practice earlier next year."

"A heated arena does help, Uncle Nick," Sedona admitted as she bent to help Sierra with the brushing.

"Eddie brought Billie down this morning to see the girls ride," Jill said. "But they went back early to get things started for dinner. We're meeting them for a brat and a beer when we get back in town. Wally and Carole are coming and will pick up Alyssa and Ridan there. Rose and Doug are coming. You guys ought to stop by; you know you're welcome. Bring Hench and Leeana."

Greg looked at Shara and smiled. "We'll definitely think about it."

When the girls had finished bushing both horses, they put the tools away and quickly turned to Greg, stopping squarely in front of him.

"May we go find Chy and get a snack?" Sedona asked.

"Again? You won't be hungry for dinner," Greg teased.

"Yes, we will," they said in unison.

"Do you have any money left from lunch?" They both shook their heads. "Okay. Try not to spend it all in one place," he said, and handed them some folding money. "Now, shoo."

When the girls had disappeared around the bleachers, heading for the concession area, Greg turned to look at Shara's and Jill's concerned expressions.

"I gather you heard STSX's report this morning," Greg asked, and sat down on a folding chair beside Shara. Jill took the third chair and Nick squatted beside her in the shade cast by the trailer.

"Doug and I were speculating on the ramifications. Do you think the successor they've installed for that tyrant Prince Kiese will be as vile?" Nick asked softly.

"Yes," Shara said sadly. "I understand it's a grandnephew, recently dubbed Prince Wilmet Kiese Lukré by the Cellystoan courts, and I'm certain part of the delay has been the search for the right, shall I say, disposition? And like the message said, he was officially installed as Lord Regent of Knobaal two days ago, and now we wait to see what he does."

"And does the director think he'll follow in Prince Kiese's footsteps and try to rebuild the Traders' Union?" Jill asked.

"His footsteps, yes, but not the Traders' Union," Greg corrected. "The director says intelligence indicates he's already spent the past six or eight months setting up his own collection system to make it harder for the Peace Force to infiltrate and discover their shipments."

"I guess," Nick said, "they won't be using any of the Merchants' Guild's facilities for shipping. So all of the surveillance the Force has put into place over the years won't be useful."

"The only thing we have going for us is the few in Apache Squadron that can sense where and who people are, like you Jill, Shara, Cheral, Franni, and Ani Tigs," Greg said. "And there are the few that the Force has planted in the receiving places in the slavers' markets, like on Angrilat and in the mines in the Greel System, at Dangcee and Tissl. But I think the one in Angrilat is the only one that has any chance of finding out where the shipments originate."

"There aren't enough of us to find, follow, and check out all of the freighters crisscrossing the galaxy." Jill sighed. "We've always had the Force tell us where to look, and with the kids as old as they are now, it'll be hard to hide it if we have to leave and go searching."

"I know," Shara said with a sigh. "At least we got a good eleven years with only a few boarding and surveillance missions."

"We're grateful you found and stopped the prince," Jill admitted, "so we could have these precious eleven years."

Shara blushed but forced herself to not look away. "The girls are starting to question how they seem to know what the other is getting ready to do. I caught their surprise the other day when they realized they were both quoting something one of them had to memorize for school."

"Wow, Shar," Jill said, and looked at Shara. "Aren't they a little young to be starting? You were late in your twenties when you first started *hearing*, and I was twenty-two."

"There's no set time, Jill," Greg said. "I think it has something to do with 'need.' I started when I was fourteen or fifteen, most likely because I was already in the Force and had a need. I think our three and Tayn will feel a need sooner than most. You might want to keep an eye on Cheyenne."

Nick nodded. "Jill will have to watch her since I'm still not hearing a thing."

"I'm glad you've been okay with that, Nick," Shara said.

Nick smiled. "I know you tried, letting STSX try his magic to jump-start any latent ability that I might have, and I thank you again for the attempt. But I'm resigned and perfectly comfortable with having normal capabilities while living with and among extremely talented people—one in particular."

Jill poked his shoulder playfully and smiled. She looked up and nodded at the six kids walking back toward the trailer.

"I think Sedona and Sierra are starting to take after Greg, getting taller and lanky," Jill said, gesturing with her hands at the noticeable height difference of the two raven-haired girls compared to the others. Tayn stood second in height and her redheaded Cheyenne was third, slightly shorter. Alyssa and Ridan were next. "They're starting to fill out a little too."

"Yup," Shara said, and smiled. "I was fourteen when I stopped 'filling out.'"

"You know," Jill continued with a smile. "Even though we've all known they are identical twins, it's uncanny how identical they really are. I'll bet it drives most people batty trying to tell them apart."

"Yes, it does," Greg admitted. "I think the scar on the back of Sierra's left thigh is their only physical difference."

"Aah, the barbed wire," Jill said. "I'd forgotten about that. She was, what? Six?"

"Yeah," Shara said. "Meara fixed her up, told her to wait a couple of days for it to mend a little—"

"Only, Sierra was back on Strawberry before Meara was back in the house." Jill laughed. "Must be nice, though, having your own live-in medic."

"It is, but you know, they've never questioned that," Shara admitted.

"How much do they know?" Nick asked, changing the subject.

"Very little," Greg said. "We've kept their lives as simple as we could, for as long as possible. But in all fairness, it's time we start enlightening them."

"Next year we have to take them and Tayn to get registered," Shara said. "Greg's going to start them in physical training in a couple of weeks." Shara changed the subject as the children got closer. "Hey, Alyssa, Ridan," she greeted. "Have you enjoyed the day?"

"Very much," Ridan said with a huge smile. "Mom says I can ride in some of the events next year."

"That'll be nice," Shara said. "I thought we might've seen you ride today, Alyssa."

"I was planning on it," Alyssa said, "but Jack was off his feed this week and Mom didn't think it would be a good idea. He did really well two weeks ago in Hawthorne."

"Yes he did," Shara agreed. "I remember you got seconds in two events."

Shara noticed Tayn stood patiently, a step back and to one side of Alyssa, quietly listening to the conversation. She thought he was showing a lot of his parents' diplomacy and tact lately, and since Tayn was only six weeks younger than the girls, figured Hench and Leeana had probably started preparing him for registration.

"Well," Greg said, and stood up. "The horses are loaded and secure, and it looks like you kids are fed and watered, so we ought to start back north. Anyone that needs the Necessary before we start, now's the time."

As he started folding the chairs, the horde ran to the portable facilities near the show corral. When they regrouped beside the trailer, Sedona and Sierra hugged Jill and Nick and turned to the hauler. They waved to Cheyenne, Alyssa, and Ridan.

"We'll drop the horses and the rig at the ranch," Greg said to Nick as the girls climbed into the back seat of the hauler with Hank, "and then we'll see you at Thom and Eddie's. Is Thom grilling?"

"I believe so," Jill said as she corralled their half of the horde. "He got a new, oversized grill and is going to try it out."

"We'll bring something to put on it," Greg said and helped Shara in, followed by Tayn.

"See you there," Nick said and led his group to their truck.

▲

After climbing the approach to the Buck Mountain Ridge north of Clay and slowly descending the switchbacks, Greg took Shara's hand and thought about the first time he visited the switchbacks, when he borrowed her sports coupe and then crashed it into Buck Hollow, fleeing the sheriff's ambush just weeks before the Traders captured her and Jill. He glanced at Shara and she squeezed his hand in response.

'That seems like such a long time ago,' she said in her mind, and smiled. *'A whole different lifetime.'*

Thinking of the rapid changes in their lives after he rescued them, they watched the tall pine forest that crowded the highway's very verge as it straightened and led them the nearly seventy miles north from the switchbacks, through the gap between the two buttes to Riggin, near the top of the long, forested valley.

She knew he was watching her as she absently looked east

into the dark forest, thinking about the captured traders' complex and how lucky they all had been. Shara turned back, *hearing* him share her thoughts and *felt* his happy feelings for their life together.

⋏ ⋏ ⋏ ⋏ ⋏

'Do they know we're coming?' Shara asked Greg silently as they buckled in and Greg started the double-cab pickup truck. They had settled the horses, parked the trailer and the hauler in the shed off the west end of the enclosed arena, and were starting into town.

'I had Five tell WL-One and he relayed the message to Thom and Wally,' Greg answered as they drove around the apartments, renovated years ago from the old bunkhouse just west of the main house. *'I told them Hench, Leeana, and Tayn will be a few minutes behind us and that we're all contributing to the menu.'*

"What were you guys talking about?" Sedona asked as they drove through the ranch's front arch and started into town.

"When was that?" Shara asked, glancing at her in the back seat of the truck.

"Just now and when we all went for drinks and a snack before we came home," Sierra said, explaining Sedona's question.

"In Clay, you seemed concerned or worried," Sedona added, "but not just now."

Shara looked at Greg and he held her eyes for a long moment.

"What did you hear?" Shara asked, and turned in her seat to look at the girls.

"In Clay," Sierra said, "I think you were talking about some prince or something. I don't think you like him very much. You sounded worried. Just now we could tell you were talking but the words seemed muted, garbled."

'Do you hear me now?' Shara asked silently, and looked

straight at Sierra, then at Sedona.

'*Holy cow!*' they thought together.

"Yeah." Sedona stared at her mother.

"Me too," Sierra said. "What's going on, Mom? Is this something to do with us being twins?"

"Not specifically, but it is a very closely guarded secret that we can *hear* each other," Shara said and held their eyes for a moment. "You can't let just anyone know you can *hear* each other or us."

"Dad can hear too?" Sierra asked.

"Yes, girls," Greg said. "Normally this talent waits until you've grown out of your teens before it manifests itself. For descendants of my family and of the Hawkins family, this is a normal but very secret ability."

"This is really important," Shara said. "You must not let anyone know you can talk to or hear anyone this way, and you have to be on your guard when you do, so other people don't notice you're doing something odd."

"Okay, Mom," they said together, then giggled because they had.

"School starts on Wednesday, so you have one more day off," Greg said. "We'll talk about this when we get home and first thing in the morning. Can you hold your questions until then?"

"We'll try," Sedona said.

"If not, ask me or Mom in private. We'll set down and start explaining some things you need to learn first thing in the morning." Greg asked, "Can you hear anyone else besides Mom and me?"

Sedona looked at Sierra and then looked sheepishly at Greg in the rearview mirror and nodded. "Sometimes."

"When did you notice you could?" Shara asked softly.

"At your birthday party, Mom," Sedona admitted. "We heard Uncle Paul thinking about how pretty Cousin Cheral was."

"And Leeana telling Hench how wonderful she thought Annie's cake was," Sierra said.

"Well." Shara forced her expression to be firm and devoid of emotion, "You know you shouldn't eavesdrop on other people's conversations, especially when they don't know you're listening."

"Yes, Mom," they both said.

"Thank you," she said, and glanced at Greg's efforts to keep from smiling. "And please remember, your classmates in school and friends outside of our family must not know you can do this."

"Yes, Mom," they said again in unison.

"Who can hear us, Mom?" Sedona asked. "How many in our family can hear?"

Shara glanced at Greg and saw his slight nod, hearing him say, *'I'll have to teach them, soon.'* Then she said, "Let's see. There's us, my uncle Paul, my cousin Cheral, your aunt Jill, and your grandma Coleen."

"Grandpa Henry?" Sierra asked.

"No dear," Shara said and shook her head. "Grandpa Henry can't. And neither can your grandpa Brendan and neither can your uncle Nick."

The ten-mile drive to the main highway passed quickly with Shara and Greg contemplating the sudden challenges they were about to face and the girls quietly eyeing each other, pondering the unusual secret they were suddenly sharing.

When Greg pulled in and parked the truck in the lot in front of Thom's Furniture Repair and Refinishing shop, Sedona and Sierra quickly jumped out, closed the truck door, and hurried off to find Thom and Eddie's daughter Billie. Greg went around and helped Shara out and closed her door behind her.

They walked toward the small crowd surrounding Thom's new grill, positioned just off the kitchen in the grass beside the porch that wrapped around the front three sides of the house. Greg handed Thom a sealed package of two full racks of precooked pork ribs in greeting.

"Hey, Thom," Greg said as Shara snuggled up beside him. "Warm these up and throw on some sauce. How's Deputy

Baine, Eddie, and young Billie doing?"

"Thanks, Greg," Thom said in return. "We're doing great. Rose, Carole and Mandy and Blaire are inside with Eddie. I think Billie and Kayli saw your girls and they've all slipped off somewhere. There's a cooler up on the porch. Help yourself."

Greg saw Doug and extended his hand. "Sorry we didn't get a chance to say 'hi' to the McIntire clan today."

Doug smiled and returned the greeting. "You were very busy rooting for your girls. We certainly understand."

"I'm going to see what the women are up to inside," Shara said, squeezed Greg's waist, and turned to the house. *'Keep an ear on the girls. I'll listen as well.'*

'Okay,' Greg answered, and watched Shara climb the steps and slip into the house. He was amazed at how their lifestyle and activities kept her in shape. She shed her pregnancy gains in a few months and her chasing the girls around and their persistent training and horse work kept her as pretty and shapely as she was when they got married. He was so enthralled watching his mate that he almost did not hear Thom.

"So?" Thom asked. "Eddie said the girls did well this morning. How was the afternoon?"

"Yes, they did. Cheyenne placed second in two events, reining and penning, which is not bad for her first season competing," Greg said, smiling at Wally, Ted, Dan, and Doug. "And I really feel odd, like I'm bragging about my girls, but Sedona and Sierra both took seven first places. I want to be the proud and happy dad, but I don't want to sound too over the top."

"Well," Dan said, "I think you have a right to be a little proud of your girls. Blaire's been riding with Carole out at their place, but she hasn't shown any desire to compete. She spends a lot of her time following me around and talking to Wally about one aspect or another of police work."

"She's what? Eighteen or nineteen now?" Greg asked, thinking out loud, and saw Dan's nod. He stayed on the subject of horses and continued. "She'd have to ride in the adult classes."

"Carole told me a long time ago," Wally said, "that Shar was quite the star in the competition events. I'm glad your girls are able to follow her lead and do well."

"Thanks. Like their mom, they've been riding since before they could walk," Greg said, and turned at the sound of a truck slowing on the highway. "And there is our second-place winner now."

They watched as Nick pulled in and parked his truck beside Greg's and the kids piled out. Alyssa and Ridan went straight to Wally and began telling him about their day. Nick added to the menu and Jill hurried inside to see what was going on. Cheyenne seemed a little reserved and waited beside Nick, listening to the men chat around the grill when Alyssa and Ridan went looking for the girls and Kail.

Hench and Leeana pulled in right behind them and parked the ranch's truck in line with the others. Tayn and Leeana met Hench as they rounded the front of the truck and made their way to the group guarding the grill. In greeting, Hench handed Thom a vacuum-sealed package and smiled.

Wally looked at Tayn and pointed down the drive past the garage. "Tayn, they went that way."

"Something different, Thom," Hench said with a sly smile. "Grill them or bake them. They're a nice side for any meal. After you taste them, I may have to import more."

Thom thanked him and pointed to the house and repeated his explanation of who was inside.

"I understand you did well today, Cheyenne," Wally said. "Alyssa was very put out this morning when Jack wasn't up to the events."

"Thank you, sir," Cheyenne said. "I know Alyssa had her heart set on riding today. We talked about it on the way down this morning, and if we'd known sooner she could've practiced on one of our other horses. But thank you for letting her and Ridan go with us anyway."

"You're very welcome," Wally said.

Thom tended to the grill, adding the additional offerings,

and Greg stepped up onto the porch. He checked the cooler and asked, *'Do you want anything, Bren?'*

'Sure. Is there one of those spiced beers?'

'Yes, there is.'

Greg picked a beer for Shara and a ginger beer soft drink for himself and listened for Sedona and Sierra. At first he was puzzled; he could tell *where* they were, but no one was saying anything and it was dark. As he *listened,* he saw someone pass a beer can around in the dim light. He was about to say something when Sedona passed and told the group "No," explaining they would not tell. He smiled when Sierra followed her lead and they both sat back and watched Billie, Tayn, Alyssa, Ridan, Kayli, and Kail sample the can.

Greg straightened and opened the kitchen door as Cheyenne stepped up beside him. She looked up at him and said in a matter-of-fact tone, "They shouldn't be doing that, Uncle Greg."

Still *listening* to the girls, Greg stared at Cheyenne as she entered the kitchen and calmly stopped at the peninsula counter beside her mother. He closed the door and stopped beside Shara and handed her the beer.

He smiled at Cheyenne and asked, "Can I get a hug from my favorite niece?"

Tuesday, September 5

"Thanks, Matti," Shara said to her head house girl as she set a carafe of coffee and another of juice on the dining room table. "How's Dusty this morning?"

"He's fine, Mrs. Shara," Matti said. "He took two of the hands out to the stone quarry early this morning."

"What're they working on?" Greg asked as he poured a cup for Shara and for himself.

"Hank's adding stone gateposts to that gate west of Meara's and our apartments," Matti explained, and then turned back to the kitchen. She stopped at the door and asked, "Will the girls

13

be joining you for breakfast?"

"Yes, Matti," Shara said.

Matti nodded and slipped into the kitchen.

Shara was reaching out to see where the girls were when the heavy wood back door opened. Hench, Leeana, and Tayn entered, followed quickly by Sedona and Sierra.

"Morning Shara, Greg," Hench greeted, and helped Leeana with the chair that had become hers over the course of twelve years of living and eating on the ranch.

Tayn settled into his customary place beside Hench and the girls hurried down the hallway.

"Morning to the Kooiches," Shara said in return. "How is everyone this morning?"

"Very good, I think," Tayn said, and poured himself a glass of juice.

"I think Tayn enjoyed his day at the rodeo," Shara said, smiling at Leeana. "And I hope you two enjoyed your time to yourselves."

"He says he did," Leeana said, and smiled at Tayn. "And we did very little. Rode up into the western hills and had a quiet lunch on that outcropping you showed us years ago. The views are still breathtaking."

Sedona and Sierra came back from their rooms and took their places beside Shara just as the house girls, Cara and Kym, began setting platters of eggs, assorted breakfast meats, potatoes, biscuits, and fruits down the middle of the table. Serving had switched from individual plates to family style when the family suddenly grew beyond the four adults with the arrival of the children and Meara.

Shara smiled at Greg, remembering when Kym had joined the family. The girls were five when she became their third house girl. She had a troublesome, now humorous, first few months of adjusting to the odd routines and comings and goings around the Malone household. Matti and Dusty had married and moved into one of the new apartments Greg had built, and Kym took over Matti's old room in the main house.

"Good morning, girls," Greg said as he began serving himself and Shara from one of the platters. "Where have you been so early this morning?"

"Checking on Brickle," Sedona said.

"And Strawberry," Sierra added. "We put them out in their paddock to enjoy the beautiful morning."

"It isn't going to stay nice and warm much longer," Sedona commented, then poured a glass of juice and handed the carafe to Sierra.

They looked up when the back door opened again and Meara came in and took her place at the end of the table between Sierra and Tayn.

"Morning, all," she greeted, and poured herself a cup of coffee. "Sorry to be running a little behind. Took a walk to watch the sunrise and went a little farther than I thought."

"Morning, Meara," Shara said. Everyone else greeted her as Shara passed the platter of biscuits her way.

Shara thought about how fortunate she, Leeana, and later Jill, had been to have Meara and her medical talents available to help in the preparations and delivery of the four children. Still assigned to Kiile's marine detachment at Obscure when hers and Leeana's babies were born, Meara, one of Kiile's Medics, had no specific home to return to when she was up for retirement that fall. Meara had fallen in love with the beautiful valley and the surrounding mountains, and being only forty Terran years old, she was having a difficult time deciding whether to retire and stay or to reenlist for another thousand days of duty and risk possible reassignment at some time in the near future. Shara offered to hire her as their resident nanny and medical staff if she retired, and Meara quickly accepted. Three days after her official retirement, Meara moved into the new three-apartment wing just west of the main house. With Matti and Dusty moving into the second apartment when they married, they had one left for guests, like Greg's mom Coleen and her husband Brendan when they visited. Besides, Shara smiled to herself, it was nice to have another non-family female opinion from time to time.

As they ate, Greg interrupted the casual conversations concerning the warm and pleasant weekend just past and expectations for the coming school year.

"Hench, I was wondering if I might borrow Tayn for part of the day today," he said in the tone of a question.

Hench and Leeana looked up, sensing the more serious feelings of his accompanying thoughts.

"We had a talk with the girls last night," he continued, casually eating between words and phrases. "And I'm going to reintroduce them to an old friend of ours and give them a history lesson." He looked up and connected with their silent look.

"Yes," Leeana said softly. "I agree. It probably is time."

"Yes, I think it is," Greg said, and sipped his coffee. "There's an event coming up next year and there have been some recent changes that make us feel some preparation must be started."

"Dad?" Sedona asked. "Why are you being so cryptic? Is this about what you said we don't know very much about?"

Shara chuckled and looked at Greg, "Good question."

Leeana laughed softly.

"Okay, okay," he said, and laughed at himself. "I am being too cryptic. And yes. Cheyenne is coming and they will be joining us. They've left their ranch and are almost to the county road. The issue is, all three of the girls have started to show a talent for *hearing*, and they need some instruction and they need to hear the whole background, the whole story, so they understand what's happening and what has happened." He looked at Tayn, and asked Leeana, "Has Tayn shown any signs?"

Tayn looked surprised and then glanced at his folks. Greg watched as Leeana silently asked the focused question like Shara had with the girls, and he saw the same startled expression.

"I see he has," Greg said, and put his cup down and refilled it. "How much have you explained?"

Leeana slowly shook her head. "Nothing, actually."

"I know," Tayn said sheepishly, "that Mom and Dad and you both are in some kind of a military service, but they haven't explained what kind or where they serve. I've never seen them in any kind of uniform and I don't know what they do, but I know you four disappear from time to time without explanation. Sometimes for a couple of days. I think we've all noticed that." The girls nodded when he looked at them. "Meara's always taken care of us and told us you'd be back soon, but we always worry and wonder why you keep things so secret. Is an explanation of this part of the 'whole story'? To tell us what is happening to us? To tell us why we hear and feel the strange things we hear and feel?"

All four of the adults nodded, and Greg continued. "Yes Tayn, it is. It's because you are all maturing early in a talent I will simply refer to as *hearing* that we must start explaining what you don't yet know." He looked at Leeana and Hench, asking silently. When they nodded, he said, "I would like you to join us and the girls this morning. We'll start as soon as Cheyenne gets here."

"What about Rose and Doug's twins?" Leeana asked. "They'll have to know too."

Greg nodded with a sigh. "Neither Kayli or Kail have shown any talent, which is expected since neither have Rose or Doug. I gave Doug three recorder cubes last night and asked him to play them for Kayli and Kail so they listen to the story at the same time as you three kids and Cheyenne. Since they can't *hear*, it would be unfair to have Kayli and Kail come here to listen."

One-Ten

"Please sit down on the edge of the porch," Greg said as he stepped down off the back porch and into the wide yard between the main house and the barns. He turned and knelt down in front of Sedona, Sierra, Cheyenne, and Tayn. Hench and Leeana and Jill and Nick and Meara and Shara arranged themselves behind the children on the porch. Greg smiled. "I'll start by admitting what you have surmised, that we—myself and your parents—have two lives. One is the life you've known as far back as you can remember: horses, ranching, school, calm and casual days in this beautiful valley," he said. "And the other is one that has to be kept very secret. We've tried to give you a normal childhood with all of the normal joys and opportunities that we could give you, to keep you from having to grow up too soon, but your hereditary gifts have chosen to awaken early and force us to explain—now, rather than later—our secret world. One that you are about to begin sharing in."

Sedona and Sierra glanced back at their mom and then at Jill.

"Can we ask questions as you explain things?" Sierra asked.

"Certainly," Greg said. "You can ask me or any of us. You will certainly have a number of them." He smiled and looked deep into Sedona's eyes, then held Sierra's, extending his warm pleasure that this moment had come. "I also want you to know we are all very proud that this is happening. In a few minutes, we will let an old friend of ours tell you the story from when Shara's cousin Cheral and I landed in Pitcarthy, Pennsylvania just over thirteen years ago, roughly a year and a few months before Shara and I got married.

"Tayn, you said you figured out that we are in a military organization and you are correct, but the truth is far different than what you might have surmised. I came here following a group that was stealing people and selling them into a slave market. After Cheral and I had followed the trail here to the valley and we had been here a little while, I discovered that two people they were specifically trying to steal were Shara and Jill."

"Mom and Aunt Jill?" Sierra asked, disbelieving. "Why?"

"Because we have the same talents you are just now beginning to experience," Shara said. "And a few more that were anticipated by a relative of mine that ran the local branch of the slavers' group."

"Tayn," Greg continued, "your father is a colonel and my campaign lieutenant in command of my Fighter Wing and all flight operations."

"Fighter Wing?" Tayn asked with a chuckle at the same time the girls silently mouthed the same question. "Like flying fighters?" He made a gesture with his hands, one leading another in a chase.

"Yes. We are all fighter pilots," Greg said, and smiled, "among other things. Your mother Leeana is a captain and co-commander of the wing and is a talented navigation and communications officer as well as a highly decorated fighter ace. Jill and Nick are captains in that wing and are also both fighter pilots." He smiled at Cheyenne and then at Sedona and Sierra.

"Your dad, girls," Shara continued, "is the campaign commander and the head of a flight training school. I am a captain and co-commander and we are both decorated fighter pilots. Collectively, we are part of a secret, undercover group known in the Force as Shadows. Cousin Cheral is a Shadow and a fighter pilot. Kiile is a marine captain and squad leader in command of over a hundred marines. Meara is a retired marine captain and medic, who graciously accepted our offer to have her live and work with us here on the ranch after she retired."

"What is the campaign, sir?" Tayn asked, glancing at his dad and then back to Greg.

"When we rescued Shara and Jill from the slavers," Greg said, "I went back to headquarters to update my superiors and to receive my new assignment. That assignment was to train a new group of cadet pilots and all of the nav-coms under my command to be fighter pilots and then to go after the slave traders wherever they were. When I got back, your parents were assigned to my command along with many others."

"Others?" Sedona asked. "I mean, you said Kiile has marines and you have fighters, but we've never seen any of them or anything flying around."

Greg smiled and looked at each of them. "Well, Sedona. If you did see any of them, they wouldn't be secret, would they?" Slowly he straightened up and stood. "Any comments, Hench, before we show them the answer to that question?"

"No, Greg," Hench said, also trying to keep his smile from showing his pride for the moment. "We'll help provide answers and explanations as needed."

"Very well," Greg said, smiling as he turned toward the open meadow just past the west side apartments. "If you will follow me, please."

Greg stopped at the narrow, man-width opening in the low, three-rail fence that stretched west northwest from the apartments to the gate that separated the main ranch yard from the open meadows. "The reason you haven't seen anything flying around is because you can't see what stands in front of you, like ours or Hench and Leeana's heavy fighters sitting in this part of the pasture."

"What? You always said to keep the horses out of this area was because—" Sedona said.

"Something about the grass not being good for them," Sierra interrupted.

"Maybe there was really a little more to the story than that," Greg admitted, and stood the four of them side by side along the pasture side of the fence. Greg took Shara's hand and stood at one end of their line, and Hench and the others stood at the other end. At his request, they took seven steps forward and suddenly stepped through STSX's cloaking veil. Tayn and the girls stopped suddenly, completely stunned, mouths agape, staring at STSX's aft portal and entry ramp. Their eyes scanned his form from one engine pylon to the other and took in every detail they could.

"Hench," Greg said softly. "Please drop KKLC's veil."

Hench passed the request along and suddenly KKLC14's sleek shape coalesced beside STSX, his nose facing the group.

"These are two of our heavy fighters, fondly known as Q-Ships," Shara explained, "and officially known in the Force as recondite corvettes. Ours is Q-STSX1 and Hench and Leeana's is Q-KKLC14. Jill and Nick fly light fighters, call signs Apache Fifteen and Sixteen. Please follow me inside."

"Why are they called 'Apache?'" Sedona asked.

Hench chuckled. "Because your mom's half Apache. Someone once called her your dad's 'renegade Apache Lieutenant,' and he liked it so much he named the squadron after her."

"Sounds like Uncle Kiile," Sierra said half out loud as they turned to follow Greg. Sierra and Tayn snickered and nodded.

Shara and Greg led the way up the ramp and Hench veiled KKLC, then he and Leeana followed and settled on the left side Medical couch. Shara gestured the girls to the two double-wide cushioned chairs and pulled the stowed table into place between them. Tayn took a folding stool that Shara handed him and set it in the aisle. Jill and Nick took two folding stools from the equipment bay and set them in the opening at the back of the sleeping bay.

"I know this is a little cramped," Shara said, "but we can take breaks as often as you need to. Any questions?"

"Yeah. Lots of them," Cheyenne said as she looked around the compartment and everyone laughed. "But I don't know where to start."

"Okay," Shara agreed. "Children, this is STSX. He will provide you with a history of everything that has happened here since Greg arrived in Pitcarthy. STSX, please say hello to our children."

"GOOD MORNING," STSX said in a soft, congenial voice, "SEDONA MALONE, SIERRA MALONE, CHEYENNE JORDAN, AND TAYN KOOICH. I WILL CONDUCT

A QUICK TEST TO ASCERTAIN YOUR EMPATHIC CAPACITY. IT IS HARMLESS AND SHOULD NOT BE FEARED."

STSX focused on each open-mouthed child's mind and asked silently, *'IF YOU UNDERSTAND THIS REQUEST, PLACE YOUR RIGHT HAND ON THE TABLE IN FRONT OF YOU.'*

Startled by the new voice and message in their minds, the children looked at each other and slowly put their right hands on the table.

'IF YOU SEE AN IMAGE IN YOUR MIND, PLEASE PLACE YOUR LEFT HAND ON TOP OF YOUR RIGHT HAND.'

Again, the children looked at each other and slowly put their left hands on top of their right hands.

"THANK YOU. TAYN KOOICH. WHAT WAS THE IMAGE YOU SAW?" STSX asked out loud.

"I... saw you," Tayn said, "a Q-Ship with double red stripes, flying before a field of stars. I was looking from inside a glass dome, a little behind you and on your left side. The pilot was wearing a red headband and the feeling was anxious, as if something important was about to happen. I… think the pilot was Shara… There was a smaller ship tucked up under you, like you were carrying it."

"VERY GOOD, TAYN. CHEYENNE JORDAN, WHAT IMAGE DID YOU SEE?"

"I...saw Mom," Cheyenne said, "with Aunt Shara and Rose McIntire standing in a room—smelled like a basement, maybe—with five people sitting against a wall in front of them. There was something familiar about the two on the right, but I don't think Mom or Aunt Shara or Rose had ever met them. The other three seemed wary, dangerous, maybe threatening."

"VERY GOOD, CHEYENNE. SIERRA MALONE, WHAT IMAGE DID YOU SEE?"

"I...saw our mom," Sierra said, "digging an arm out of the snow. Someone was under the snow beside a large rock. It was very cold with very strong winds and blowing, blinding snow. Aunt Jill was digging beside her. She felt like she was in a panic, a combination of guarded relief and pent-up foreboding." Sierra looked around suddenly. "It was Uncle Nick under the snow."

"VERY GOOD, SIERRA. SEDONA MALONE, WHAT IMAGE DID YOU SEE?"

"I...saw a large person standing in the front driveway beside a fancy car. A heavyset woman," Sedona began slowly, softly. "She was a judge, a circuit judge or something. A Judge Bernice Reeds, and there was a man beside the car with her, a...a Harold Danley from Clay. It was snowing heavily, blowing and foggy. There was something floating behind the car, a dark gray orb of some kind, waiting. It felt like it was a guard or something. Mom and Aunt Jill and Mom's uncle Paul and grandpa Jack and Shelly Woods' husband Jim and Hank were there, facing the judge and the man, blocking the drive. The air was filled with tension, apprehension, and Hank was carrying his sawed-off shotgun."

"VERY GOOD, SEDONA. YOUR EMPATHIC CAPABILITY IS MORE MATURE THAN EXPECTED. WOULD THE CAPTAINS LIKE TO EXPLAIN THE IMAGES OR SHALL I?"

"Thank you, STSX." Leeana looked a Tayn. "I won't speak for the others, but I'd like to explain Tayn's."

Tayn looked at her and waited.

"These images are all from before any of you were born. The one STSX gave you, Tayn, was from our squadron's first off-planet mission to find and release slaves being shipped to a place called Angrilat. It was before we reached our rendezvous with another Q-Ship called a Watcher, and the patrol cruiser Brigstoan, where we would release the patrol fighters in preparations for an engagement. Shara was pregnant with you two—" She smiled at Sedona and Sierra. "—and she was piloting STSX. That was her cousin Cheral's fighter underneath STSX. The image was from KKLC14's cockpit and I was flying. I was pregnant with you, Tayn. The red headbands and the red stripes are symbolic of the Apache Squadron. Only the female pilots and female Shadows of Apache Squadron wear the red headbands, and only the commander's ship has two red stripes.

All of the other ships have a single red stripe. The fact that you see so much and can feel the atmosphere of that moment is incredible."

Pleased, Tayn smiled back at Leeana. "So, I was there?"

"Yes. Technically," Leeana said with a wide smile, "you and Sedona and Sierra were on every off-planet mission we flew before you were born. You flew in every combat encounter we met."

"Wow. Off planet," Tayn said softly and smiled at Sedona and Sierra. "But how? There aren't any real spaceships. We just have rockets that put satellites in orbit or send probes out into the solar system."

"Good questions, Tayn," Greg said. "But I think I'll let you hear the history before we answer the 'how' question. You'll discover that, even though most of us were born here, there is a lot more to our ancestry. And our equipment."

"Okay," Tayn said, filled with resignation, forcing himself to hold his curiosity as he glanced at his dad. "Thank you."

"We'll explain more after you listen to parts of the story," Hench said with a wide smile.

"Cheyenne," Jill said to catch her attention. "Your image was the morning we found your uncle Greg's mother. She was stolen when Greg was ten, and he spent a lot of his life looking for her without success. The three of us were leading an attack on the slavers' main data collection complex in Virginia and had followed the Persons-of-Importance tags of the two that you felt were familiar—the ones on the right. We'll discuss the POI tags after the history lessons.

"The three men with them had led them into a dead end with no way to escape, hoping to lure someone from the Force to come and try to rescue them. Your uncle Greg, Doug McIntire, and your dad—with some of Kiile's marines to help—entered the complex through two other points and were waiting for us to interrogate the five in the basement and give them a signal. Two of the men did not survive and the two familiar people were Greg's mother Coleen and her husband Brendan, Sedona and Sierra's grandparents that still live in Florida. Your dad and I weren't married yet when that happened."

Cheyenne looked at her mom and then slowly looked at the other adults, her mouth open to speak, but no words came out.

"The image you saw, Sedona, came first," Shara began. "Judge Bernice Reeds was my great aunt on my mother's side of the family, my grandmother's sister. After I met Greg, I found out that she led the local slavers' operations. Mother was half Reeds and half Hawkins, and as you will soon learn, the judge thought she had killed me and Jill and then came to take control of the ranch. We surprised her by being alive and she fell into the wash under the bridge in the front drive. From her, I was able to get the information that led us to find your uncle Nick, which is Sierra's image.

"Judge Bernice had your uncle Nick taken with the intent of letting him die in a blizzard up on the reservation. Your dad was away at headquarters updating our superiors when we discovered Nick was missing, and with the information I got from Judge Bernice, Jill and I went to find him. Your image, Sierra, was when we found Nick, nearly frozen to death. Many more details, and the whole story, STSX will give you now that he has measured your capability to learn. The best method is to give you the information verbally and empathically at the same time. You will assimilate the information fully while you sleep tonight and the next couple of nights."

"Mom?" Sedona asked. "What was that floating behind Judge Bernice's car?"

"That was Remote Two," Shara said. "It was guarding the road to stop Bernice if she tried to escape. I should've had it stop the car, but that's hindsight."

"What's a Remote Two?" Sierra asked.

"When you have finished listening to STSX and we break for lunch," Greg said, "we'll introduce you to some of the remotes and explain what they are and what they can do. Okay?"

"Okay," Sierra and Sedona said together.

"STSX?" Shara asked. "Break the sessions as you need, but please explain the whole story from Cheral and Greg's arrival in Pitcarthy up through Jill and Nick's wedding. Will you please begin?"

⋀ ⋀ ⋀ ⋀ ⋀

Dinner passed quietly with the four children mentally reviewing the things they had learned during the day and eating without their normal conversation and banter. Even the adults kept the conversation to a minimum and the subjects light.

"Greg," Hench said as he refilled his water glass and offered some to Leeana. "Are you going to come to the patrol briefing tomorrow?"

"I'll come after breakfast." He glanced at Shara. "Unless you have something I need to do."

Shara shook her head. "You need to visit with the new cadets and see how the remotes are working out as target generators. The kids will be in school, so a session tomorrow will have to be shorter and in the evening."

"Okay. I'll be down mid-morning," Greg said.

"Where's *down*, Dad?" Sedona asked, pulling herself out of her thoughts to hear his comment and realizing he hadn't hidden it from them.

"In today's session, you learned about the slavers' facility, the one they called Point Obscure," he said, and looked at each of the children. When Sedona nodded, he continued. "In tomorrow's sessions you will learn that we occupied Point Obscure and turned it into a secret fighter base and a landing site for supply transports and others. Kiile and his marines and Cheral and the other pilots live there. That's where *down* is."

"Will we get to see it?" Tayn asked, and looked at his dad.

"Soon, son," Hench said, and smiled.

"Dad?' Sedona asked when Tayn settled back into his thoughts. "I know you explained the remotes and what they do, how they levitate or float about following your commands, like a program..."

"How many do you have?" Sierra asked, finishing her sister's question.

"Lots, if you consider all of us," Greg said. "Hench and Leeana have six, your mom and I have ten, and Kiile has somewhere around fifty. Actually more, I think."

"And they've been here, watching us since you and Cousin Cheral came," Sedona said, half question and half statement.

"Cheral and I only had three left when we first arrived," Greg said.

"And you ride them?" Sedona continued. "And they're armed to fight and they can cloak, is that what you called it?"

Greg nodded.

"And you're going to teach us how to talk to them."

"Yes," Greg said, and smiled. "You'll learn about everything as quickly as we can teach you, but right now we need you to focus on the lessons."

When everyone had finished dinner, Jill and Nick thanked Shara and Greg for the day and said Cheyenne could ride to the ranch with Sedona, Sierra, and Tayn after school. Jill would come by after she got off work, see how things were going, and take Cheyenne home afterwards.

Sedona and Sierra excused themselves and retired to their rooms, down the hall and across from Greg and Shara's room.

When the girls left, Tayn asked to be excused and started out to his apartments. Leeana got up and went out with him, and Greg spoke briefly with Hench before Hench followed them out.

"Well that went better than I expected," Meara said as she stacked the dishes for Cara and Kym. "I wasn't sure you were doing the right thing this morning, but Medical reported they handled the surprises very well. I was impressed with their questions."

"Yes, I felt like they handled it well. And the questions were good ones," Shara said. "Have you heard the story before?"

"Some," Meara said. "Mostly just what was passed around the ranks about you two after I was assigned here and met both of you. It's nice to get a little background to fill in what isn't common knowledge."

"I'm glad you're getting to hear it," Shara said, and smiled. "I was worried a little also. We each have different things to fill in for each of the kids. Tayn will hear details from Hench and Leeana's past, before they came to help us, their relatives and family that Tayn will someday get to meet. Cheyenne will see our story through different eyes, seeing Jill and Nick as they grew up, the mistakes and successes they made; Jill's and my fights, arguments, misunderstandings, and make-ups. Jill's discovering she has a brother. Nick's concern watching Greg's brother try to kill them. And Sedona and Sierra will see how shallow and narrow my world was before Greg found me and I became part of his world."

"I'm sure they'll understand," Meara said. "They are four very bright children and have extremely good role models to follow."

"I hope they think we're good models," Greg said softly, "and not a couple of overly strict, narrow-minded adults trying to impose our wishes on their lives."

"I certainly doubt they feel like that," Meara said, and turned to the door. "You two get a good night's sleep and don't worry about this too much. Even under the best of situations, something like this will take a little while to settle and soak in. You've had years to grow accustomed and they've had one day. Goodnight, you two."

"Goodnight," Greg said, and watched the door close behind her. He turned to Shara and saw she was pushing the kitchen door open. "Come sit with me, Bren?"

"Yes," she said, "in just a minute. Get settled and I'll be right there." Shara smiled and slipped into the kitchen.

⋏

Greg added a couple of small logs to the fire in the fireplace and settled into their favorite overstuffed chair. He kicked his boots off and set them neatly under the side table, wriggled his shoulders into the cushions, and stretched his feet out on the hassock. Shara came out of the kitchen with a tray holding a short decanter of red wine and two stemless glasses. She set the tray on the end table and poured the two glasses before she handed him one and then settled crosswise on his lap, facing the fire.

"A toast, love," she said softly and kissed him. "And a prayer that we can always make the girls feel loved and that everything is going to be okay."

"To our children, Bren," he said in return and clinked his glass against hers. "And to the best mother they could possibly have."

After a sip, Shara kissed him again before she snuggled to watch the fire. Greg set his glass on the tray and held Shara close, both of them feeling the warm thoughts of the other, the pleasure of being together. The spell lingered uninterrupted for nearly a half an hour before Greg looked up and saw the girls, dressed in their two-piece sweatpants-style pajamas, as they came out of the hallway.

"Mom, Dad?" they asked together.

"Hey girls," Greg said, and Shara started to get up.

"Don't get up," Sedona said. "We like seeing you two together in your chair."

"It's very comforting to see you love each other," Sierra added. "But we would like to talk to you."

"We also wanted to tell you we don't think you're overly strict and narrow-minded," Sedona said.

Shara got up and crossed to the loveseat, and Greg followed her lead and settled beside her.

"Well, I'm glad for that. Come here," Shara said, and glanced at Greg, thinking about Sedona's reference to them overhearing Greg's comment. She reached out to the girls as they came around the end of the sofa. Shara pulled Sierra onto her lap, facing Greg, and Greg pulled Sedona onto his lap, facing Shara.

"I can't hold all three of you at one time anymore." Greg squeezed Sedona and reached for Sierra's hand. "But there's always space for you if you need it or just want it."

"What's on your mind?" Shara asked, and repeated Greg's gesture by squeezing Sierra and reaching for Sedona's hand.

"I was...well, we were surprised today when ST...STSX showed us images, and not just words," Sierra said. "We haven't seen images before when we *hear*. Is that normal?"

Shara chuckled. "Yes, loves. When I felt very alone, when Judge Bernice was trying to find me, your dad would send me images, thoughts, moods of encouragement to keep my spirits up, to give me hope and determination."

"But can sharing images be useful?" Sedona asked.

"That wasn't useful?" Shara teased.

"They certainly are," Greg said. "Many times when we're working, we share things we see to get the other's input, ideas on what we're seeing. We did that to find ways into the complex where your mom found your grandmother."

"Are we going to be surprised with other strange abilities?" Sedona asked.

"Thinking about what might happen is a little scary," Sierra admitted.

"They shouldn't be scary, but I'm certain you will develop other talents as well," Shara said, and squeezed Sierra. "For an example, your dad and I have the ability to know where people are, to sense them and see where they are, what they're doing." Shara glanced at the clock and smiled. "I was going to show you what your grandmother is doing right now, but it's late back there and they went to bed a while ago."

Sedona smiled and winked at Sierra. "I'll bet they're not asleep yet and doing something we shouldn't see."

"What?" Shara looked at the two of them and chuckled. "Why would you say that? Maybe they don't do anything but go to sleep."

"Maybe, but you and Dad don't go right to sleep when you go to bed," Sierra said.

"Oh we don't? Have you been eavesdropping on us?" Shara was still smiling, knowing they would know.

"Not really, Mom," Sierra said.

"You keep your thoughts tightly controlled and blocked," Sedona said, "but we feel your feelings, your warmth when you two love, the security of feeling you are near us all the time. We can tell when something bothers you, and after today and thinking about what the story may reveal, I think we understand that your feelings of concern and tension come from your secret jobs and not because you are upset with us or each other."

"Like the concerns you had in Clay yesterday," Sierra admitted. "As we learn, will we be included so we know what makes you sad or concerned in the future? And not have to guess so much?"

"Unfortunately," Greg said, "you will probably be more involved than you want to be. At least I will tell you that you will be very involved."

"Did everything...? No, I know it did," Sierra said. "But it's hard to believe Aunt Jill was almost shipped away, almost sold as a slave and lost, that you were poisoned by your own great-aunt and almost died and were rescued by Dad and STSX. None of us would be here now if Dad hadn't found you, if you hadn't gotten Dad and Aunt Jill out of the emissary's frigate before it exploded, if you six hadn't attacked and captured the facility, ah, Obscure, if—"

"I know," Shara interrupted. "We try to not dwell on what might have happened and to celebrate what did. You'll get yourselves lost worrying about what didn't happen or what could've happened. Your dad taught me that sometimes you have to act on your passions and instincts and not think things to death. To focus on the one thing you have to do, do it, and then think about the next thing and do it, and repeat the steps until you're out of things to do next. The rub is that you have to be sure you're on the right path, that your passions and instincts are right, and that is where training comes in. You'll see how that works as you hear more of the story."

"What is the event that is coming in a year that we have to be prepared for?" Sedona asked.

Both of the girls waited in silence.

"The service that we belong to is called the Galactic Peace Force," Greg started explaining. "We are like undercover policemen or soldiers. When a child of the Force reaches twelve Terran years of age, about four thousand, three hundred and eighty turns or days old, they are registered and identified at headquarters in a place called the Rings. They officially receive a Peace Force identification that lets anyone else in the Force know they belong to the Force."

"As soon after your twelfth birthday as we can," Shara said, "we will go and you will meet the director for registration."

"What happens when we get registered?" Sierra asked.

"Normally," Greg said, and quickly told Shara what he had in mind, "like when I was registered, you become a student and learn how to be an agent or a Shadow. Part of that training is how to protect yourself, how to work undercover, how to analyze information, and many take flight training in the academy."

"Wow," they said together.

"That takes a long time, doesn't it?" Sierra asked.

"I said 'normally.' And yes, normally it is a four-year study, and then you get assigned wherever the Force needs you," Greg said.

"But we don't want to go wherever—" Sedona started to say.

"I said 'normally,'" Greg interrupted with a firmer voice. "But I happen to run a school here. The Academy takes four years to train a cadet, and we take three months."

Their eyes grew wide as they heard what he was saying.

"As soon as the story has been explained to you so you know 'who' you are and 'why' we're here," Shara added, "you'll start physical training and learn how to be a Shadow. You will also learn navigation and communications and piloting."

"All of us?" Sedona asked.

"Yes," Greg said. "Hench and I have already talked about Tayn, and do you think Cheyenne is going to be left out when her mom and dad are Shadows and fighter pilots?"

"We don't want to be left out either," they said together.

33

"I should hope not." Greg squeezed Sedona. "I'll let you in on a little secret, but you can't tell the others until they've heard it in the story. When you two were born, your mom, in less than a year of training and combat, was the highest scoring fighter ace of this campaign—maybe in the whole Force—for a first-year. Her cousin Cheral was second, Franni was third, and Leeana was fourth. You'll have to listen to the story to know how many each scored. So, ladies, as you'll find out, you have a family honor to uphold." He winked at them.

"Our plan is to have you fully trained and pilot-qualified before we go for registration," Shara said. "If your teenage years and hormones don't cause you to hate us, we want you to be here, with us and your aunt and uncle and my cousin. I'm not ready to let you strike out across the galaxy on your own. Not yet, anyway."

"What about Kayli and Kail?" Sedona asked.

"They are hearing the story," Shara said. "But they may wait a year or two to train since they are still three years younger than you two."

"And as for your talents," Greg said, "they are good, but people outside our secret world can't understand our talents and tend to fear them, so we hide them. We're always here to help you learn and adjust. Remind me, tomorrow night before we start our story session—I want to teach all four of you how to mute your thoughts so no one can hear you unless you want them to."

"Does that include blocking you two out?" Sierra asked with a giggle.

"Not yet, young ladies," Greg said, and tickled Sedona. "Any more questions?"

"No," they said together and Sedona hugged Greg's neck, Sierra hugged Shara's, and they got up. The girls quickly hugged the other and scurried off down the hallway.

Greg smiled after them and Shara wrapped her arm around his waist. "They're growing up too fast," she said with a sigh.

"I know," he said, and then bent to her and scooped her up in his arms. "Catch the lights, Bren. I think we should give the girls some warm, loving feelings to help lull them to sleep."

Wednesday, September 6

"I thought you had a student this morning," Greg said as he and Shara stepped out onto the back porch.

"Not until ten," Shara said as he stepped down and turned in front of her.

He pulled her to him, nearly at eye level with each other due to the height of the porch, and he gently kissed her.

"I should send a message to the director," Greg said as he helped her down, "and let him know what I've started. At least, I should alert him to the early awakening of the children."

"Hmm. I wouldn't tell him too much just yet," Shara said, and started toward the stable. "He might not approve of what you're about to do. They are too young in the Force's eyes." She stopped and looked back at him, nervously slapping her open left palm with her riding gloves. "Greg, did you feel a presence yesterday?" she asked. "New, but not really. Vaguely familiar in an unsettling way?"

"Yes, I did," he said. "It's an old prescience that I haven't felt in many years. Someone has returned to the valley."

"Yeah," Shara said, and turned to look east, toward town, toward Riggin. "And he's coming across the county road toward the ranch."

'TWO IS MONITORING THE PROGRESS. MARINE FIFTEEN AND A SQUAD OF THREE ARE WAITING TO INTERCEPT,' STSX said softly in their minds.

Suddenly, they both saw Remote Two's images of the road—the approaching pickup truck and the four men waiting in the brush beside the road. They recognized Marine Fifteen when he stepped out, even though he was dressed in jeans, boots, a plaid shirt, and a western hat. He started casually walking toward the ranch, and turned to wave at the truck as if to ask for a ride.

'Can you identify the person in the truck?' Shara asked.

'YES. DON NIKLE, THE LAST OF JUDGE BERNICE REED'S COUNCIL OF ELDERS. HE HAS BEEN MISSING FROM THE VALLEY SINCE MARSHAL LIMA RESCUED THE CAPTIVES AT THE FARMSTEAD EAST OF GRANTS ELEVEN AND A HALF YEARS AGO. JANUARY 23, GALACTIC DATE C.3482.407.'

'Damn!' Shara was about to ask another question when the truck in Two's image suddenly swerved, turned around, and sped back toward town.

'Two!' Shara shouted silently. *'Follow that truck and tell us where he goes.'* Shara looked back at Greg, her expression suddenly concerned. *'This is not good, love.'*

'I agree, Bren,' he said. *'At least we know he's back in the neighborhood, and he doesn't know we know.'*

Shara half smiled, feeling some comfort in Greg's words and his endearing use of the nickname 'BrenCara,' that he had given her so many years ago.

'Maybe you should start carrying your Kaaspr again,' Greg said as he turned back to the main house.

'Never stopped, love,' she said, smiling at him and patting her front jeans pocket.

⏶ ⏶ ⏶ ⏶ ⏶

Greg was sitting on the long log bench on the back porch of the main house, looking at STSX in the pasture beyond Meara's apartment, when Hench stepped through the back door and stopped beside him.

"They've settled into the next session?" he asked, knowing they had as he sat down on the end of the bench.

"Yeah," Greg said. "Shara and Leeana handled their questions and got the story rolling again." He looked at Hench. "Were you inundated with questions last night?"

"Yeah. Quite a few." Hench smiled. "When you suggested we tell them, it was a bit of a relief and a little frightening. I think both Leeana and I felt the same way." He paused a moment. "We weren't involved in a lot of Tuesday's part of the story, but it helped Tayn understand what brought us here and why we've stayed. It also let him ask a lot of questions we didn't know he had, about us, our families, how we grew up, what he might expect."

Greg nodded. "Questions about family. That's good."

"Yes. Good questions. We had a long discussion," Hench continued, "on how his responsibilities will change and how he'll see things a lot different than his school friends from here on. How he'll see people doing a lot of things they shouldn't, but how he'll need to continue to help them, maybe even guide them without their knowing. I explained how we do that and that it's part of what being a Shadow is."

"There are times," Greg said, "that I've thought it might have been easier to raise boys. Not that the girls have been hard to raise, but sometimes I think I would know how to handle certain situations, answer certain questions better because I would know how boys think, feel. But then Shara reminds me that if we just listen, give them the best answers we can, and show them how much they mean to us, it doesn't matter if they're boys or girls." He looked at Hench and smiled. "I love the girls without question. But sometimes they are so different."

"Leeana tells me the same thing about Tayn," Hench said with a chuckle. "Boys have to be difficult for mothers for the same reasons." He sighed. "Tayn told me about them sneaking a couple of beers out of Thom's house Monday night."

"That's good," Greg said, and nodded again.

"He said that after yesterday, he figured we already knew," Hench said, and Greg nodded at him again. "I asked him what he thought about it, and he said he thought about it afterwards, and after Ridan and Kail and the girls had gone in the house, he sat down with Billie and talked about why they shouldn't have done it."

"How'd that go?" Greg asked.

"Surprising," Hench admitted. "He said Billie broke down in tears. He said he didn't know what to do so he followed my example, what I do when Leeana feels badly or uncertain.

He hugged her and held her until she could collect herself. It turns out she stole the beers thinking it would impress Tayn, show him somehow that she wasn't just any little girl." Hench chuckled softly. "I wasn't happy that he was a participant in the first place, but I think in the end, he grew up a little Monday night."

Greg was about to comment when he felt Jill pull up in front of the main house.

"I'm glad he did the right thing, Hench," Greg said. "I've noticed he's paying a lot of attention to manners and appearances lately. I think our kids are maturing much earlier than we did—at least earlier than I did."

"Thanks," Hench said, and turned at the sound of voices in the dining room behind them.

"Jill's here," Greg said, nodding toward the house. "I need to talk to both of you before she gets involved with the history."

Greg got up and opened the back door just as Jill reached it.

"Oh, thanks," she said as he pushed the door open for her. "Good timing, or are you coming in?"

"No," Greg said, and smiled. "I need to talk to you and Hench for a minute. Come and have a sit. How's the mill today?"

Jill sat down on the bench and Greg dropped down on the edge of the porch in front of them.

"The mill's fine," Jill said, and then waited, absently remembering when she had returned to work at the mill after she and Nick married, to fill her need for a job everyone could see, letting her work with the Force remain hidden in secrecy. She started working in the Finance Department under her father, handling the orders and invoicing while she went back to college and finished her delayed final year just before Cheyenne was born.

"This morning we had an unsettling incident," Greg began, bringing her back to the moment. "Around eight thirty or quarter till nine, Shara and I felt an old, slightly familiar presence close by." He explained that as they were trying to identify it, they realized it was coming across the road toward the ranch and STSX put a name to it.

"Nikle?" Jill asked sharply in disbelief. "He disappeared when Wally and Kiile's men attacked the farmstead. Back before any of us had kids."

"That's right," Greg confirmed. "We didn't go looking for him because we never had a positive identification on his sense before."

"You know where he is?" Hench asked.

"Yeah," Greg said. "Two followed him into Riggin. He drove along Poplar towards the elementary school and turned north on Cleary. Basically, he went around the block and then north to Birch and out to Mann, like he was looking for something or, more likely, someone. Then he went north to that little motel north of town. The curious part is that when Fifteen waved to him, like he wanted a ride, he acted like he suddenly realized he had been seen and quickly turned around and hurried back to the highway and then into town."

"He could've taken the road by mistake," Jill supposed.

"I doubt it, Jill," Greg said shaking his head. "Nikle knows exactly where this ranch is and who lived here. The name's changed since he was here, and I guess there is the possibility that he thinks it has sold or changed owners, but we think he might have been trying to see if one specific thing was still here."

"What?" Jill asked, and Greg just looked at her. "Nooo, not Shar?"

Greg nodded. "He'll go and do some research, if he hasn't already done some, and he'll know she's here and that she's married and has daughters. He'll also find out that you and Nick married, where you live, and that you have a daughter."

"Oh, shit! That's all we need," Jill swore and slapped her leg.

"You still have Remote Three, and I've alerted Four to watch the traffic that goes south past Doug and Rose's place. I don't know how much he knows about Doug and Rose's involvement, but Four should have given them a full briefing by now. Shara and I are going in to see Wally in the morning and we'll be sure Doug and Rose know all that we know. Five is still tracking Wally and the deputies, and One and Two are still running surveillance around town. I've also set Six out to help One and Two watch over the kids at school and as they travel to and from."

"Are there any of the old Councils left?" Jill asked. "I'll bet he'll try to reconnect with anyone that's still around."

"That's part of why we're going to see Wally," Greg said. "As you know, he has permanent deputies assigned in Clay, Hawthorne, and Grants, and one that covers the farmstead east of Grants out to Community, and one that covers the ranch east of Hawthorne. I understand they occasionally run into some of the old Family attitudes down there."

"I can set out a couple of our remotes, Greg," Hench volunteered. "Just show me where you need them."

"Thanks," Greg said, and nodded. "You and I can sit down later and work out the details." He looked at Jill. "Do you still carry your Kaaspr?"

Jill hesitated and then answered sheepishly. "Not all of the time. I sorta got out of the habit in the last couple of years."

Greg shook his head but smiled. "I thought I told you to never let your guard down?"

"No. You told Shar and she told me." Jill smiled. "But I have it. It's in the truck and I'll tell Nick."

"I'd also suggest Blues under daily clothes," Greg continued. "I don't know what Don might try, but I don't like the feeling I have and I don't want to lose anyone due to carelessness on our part. I have to assume Don still thinks you and Shara are valuable to him, and when he realizes we have daughters, I think he'll think they're valuable to him as well."

"Can't Wally pick him up for his past deeds?" Jill asked.

"I'll find out if he can and if he can make those old kidnapping charges stick," Greg said. "But even if he can, we all know Don is slippery. For the moment, maybe we have an advantage. He doesn't know we know he's here and he doesn't know we can track him."

Greg leaned back against a porch post and glanced at STSX

in the evening half-light.

"You might also want to be sure the shields are working at your ranch," Greg said absently.

One-Eleven
Thursday, September 7

Abe Brownly was just finishing his breakfast when he was startled by a knock on his front door. He glanced at the clock over the dining room buffet and wondered who would be calling on him so early on a workday. He crossed the living room, opened the door, and stared dumbfounded at the face that greeted him.

"Don? Don Nikle?" he finally stammered. "Where did you come from? What are you doing here?"

"Hello, Abe," Don said softly. "May I come in? It has been a long time."

Abe stepped back and let him enter. "Can I get you a cup of coffee?"

"Sure," Don said, and followed Abe to the dining room table.

Abe set a cup in front of Don and poured. "Where did you go? You just disappeared."

"Yeah," Don said, and sipped the coffee. "My world sort of blew up in my face. Actually more than just my world."

"What happened? I did not hear any more from you after Chief Parks and one of his deputies had the shootout with the local Deputy Thom Baine."

"Shootout?" Don asked in surprise. "What happened?"

"No real details. It was pretty well known that Parks did not like Deputy Baine, but Parks was doing something down by the elementary school and Baine found them," Abe explained. "Parks' deputy drew down on him, and Baine killed him and wounded Parks. Parks wounded Deputy Baine and slipped away and died later at Sheriff Black's old house. Some said Deputy Baine was badly wounded, but he was back on the streets in a week."

"Always knew Parks would screw things up," Don said, and took another sip of coffee. "When was that?"

"Eleven or twelve years ago, late in January," Abe said after a little thought.

"Makes sense," Don admitted. "I had finally collected a shipment for the Traders. First gathering of perishables since the judge died. Parks was collecting the last two I needed to make my quota, but he never showed up. I did not know why. The day the freighter was to arrive, Monday the twenty-third of January, everything came apart. Suddenly, soldiers in winter camouflaged uniforms overran the farmstead. They surrounded the main houses and the alarms went off all over the place. The soldiers entered the buildings and the underground facility, disabled our security, and released the perishables. I heard later, the fighting was over in eight or ten minutes.

"I got away and it took a few days to make my way back to Grants on foot. Parks was gone and Chief Russell was at the underground facility when the attack happened. No one has heard from him since that day."

"So what have you been doing for twelve years?" Abe finally asked as he refilled their cups.

"I went back to my sister's place," Don said. "She was a widow with a different last name. So I figured staying with her would buy me some time. After a few years, I made contact with someone I knew from the Traders' Union and learned their shipments had been regularly intercepted and boarded. Nothing had been getting through to the Traders' client, a powerful prince that bought most of the people they collected and shipped.

"I understand he started setting traps for those doing the intercepting and boarding, all to no avail. Finally, he took the matter into his own hands and personally led a huge battle fleet to clean out the interceptors."

"Wow," Abe said softly. "Bet that sent them running."

"The prince's battleship, all of his cruisers, and all of his fighters vanished," Don said, and took a longer sip. "I do not remember the number of ships involved, but the number was large and they were all destroyed by the intercepting force."

Abe stared at Don. "Who was this intercepting force? They must have had a massive fleet to defeat the prince."

"By the time the prince was lost, he had already lost over three quarters of his battle fleet trying to stop them." Don shook his head. "Some organization called the Galactic Peace Force. My contact said the only reports they got were sightings of what they called a single heavy fighter with a diagonal red stripe on the forward body. No one ever reported a large fleet of ships."

"Wow." Abe stared at Don. "That must have been one hell of a fighter. So all of the slaves that were collected and shipped never got through?"

"I do not know how many got delivered or how many were intercepted," Don said, "but two months ago I heard they were about to install a suitable replacement for the prince and they want new shipments. The Traders think enough time has gone by that they might be able to get a small freighter close enough that we could send a ship up to it and not be detected. Possibly rendezvous on the back side of the moon."

"Really?" Abe asked in disbelief. "And how would you 'send them up' if you had any?"

"I made contact with two pilots," Don said, "that flew from the second launch facility, and they said they hid two converted fighters when the Indian Ocean facility was captured a few months after the farmstead attack. They checked on the fighters five years ago and again last year, and they are still operational and hidden."

Abe smiled. "I guess that explains why you are back in the valley."

"I need to know if Bill Copper and Jack Wilton are still around," Don said by way of agreement. "They were the last of the Family Support Council when I had to leave."

"They are getting old," Abe said, "but I heard they were still living near Hawthorne and are in good health. Without a Council of Elders, there has not been a need for the Family Council."

45

"That is about to change," Don said with a rueful smile. "Second, tell me what has happened in the valley in twelve years, and specifically with the Smallwood and Thomas women."

▲ ▲ ▲ ▲ ▲

Marshal Wally Lima looked up in surprise as Greg pushed the back office door open and let Shara enter ahead of him.

"Good morning," Wally said as he stood up. "I wasn't expecting you this early." He absently glanced out into the parking lot but wasn't surprised when he did not see their truck.

"Morning, Wally," Greg said, and extended his hand and nodded to Thom seated at his desk. "Kenny isn't in?"

Wally gestured to the meeting room in the corner of the office and shook his head. "Coffee or a soda?"

Greg silently asked Shara and then said, "No thanks. I think we're fine for now. How's life in the new big house?"

Wally smiled sheepishly. "Actually wonderful. We really like the space and the incredible view. I can shove Alyssa and Ridan outside and barely have to watch them. Carole is content to work the horses and fix up the, let me see if I get this right, corrals, paddocks, stables, and feed barns. Oh Shar, she asked if you could visit sometime over the weekend. She has questions on something about cutting and reining pens, positions, layouts, or something that I know I am getting wrong here."

"Sure." She cocked her head as she took a seat at the round table next to the inside wall. "Do you mind?"

"No, go ahead," Wally said.

'WL-One,' Shara said. *'Tell Carole I'll come by Saturday after our training with the girls. Maybe just after lunch. Tell her if she needs to talk to me, just use the link to Five and ask. It's better than a phone.'*

"Carole still has her headset, doesn't she?" Shara asked as a second thought.

"Yes. Many thanks," Wally said. "Having them for Carole and Eddie—and Mandy, when she wants to be included—has made the world so much easier."

"That's why I started including Shara in everything from the beginning," Greg said.

"Okay, now what can I do for you?" Wally said, and leaned forward on the table, clasping his hands in front of him.

"Does Thom have to be in the office at his desk?" Shara asked.

Wally sat up and glanced through the doorway into the office. "Well, not really. Is he a problem?"

"No. Sorry," Shara said. "If he doesn't have to be visible in the office, I think he should be included and listen in."

"Oh," Wally said, and smiled. "I misunderstood. Hey, Thom. Join us. You can keep an ear open for the phones, but join us."

"Sure," he said, and slipped his files into a drawer, got up, and casually walked to the meeting room. "Good to see you again so soon."

"Maybe not," Greg said as Thom settled into a chair by the door.

Greg had Wally and Thom's full attention and quickly launched into the recent events. With a glance at Shara and her subtle nod, he explained that they were accelerating the training of the girls and Tayn and were preparing for a resurfacing of the old threats. He explained they were increasing surveillance around the Jordan ranch and had alerted Doug and Rose.

"If something breaks, I've offered Doug and Rose and their kids a place at the ranch," Shara said. "If Don is doing what I suspect, our kids are in the most danger."

"So he's here, in Riggin?" Thom asked for clarification.

"That's what I said," Greg said watching Thom's changing expression as he considered various options. "At the old motel north of town. You could go and see if you can pick him up at the motel, but he won't be there."

Thom looked at Greg and started to raise an argument, but stopped. "You're right, he won't be. He left a crumb to see if we know he's here."

"Yeah," Greg agreed. "Don's not smart, but he isn't dumb. He has an instinct for slipping out when things get tight. Wally had him boxed in at the farmstead, yet he slipped away—probably camouflaged or visually altered so the troops didn't notice him, but the fact is, he slipped away. We've alerted Kiile, and One and Two are watching what he does. I'll have Five keep WLOne and WL-Two up to date. Right now, I think he's trying to reestablish the old business. He wants Shara and Jill and once he knows about the girls, I think he'll want them too."

"Wally," Shara added quickly, "I think he's going to do something soon, unexpected and quick. He doesn't know we know he's here, so he'll probably try to snatch and run. We're pulling the kids up as fast as we can without overloading them, but I'm sure this will break before we're ready."

"You're serious," Thom said, suddenly thinking about the ramifications.

"Yeah, Thom," Shara said. "You, Eddie, and Billie are not immune either. Blaire's old enough, maybe, but she has never been trained to defend herself." She looked at Wally and saw that he thought of Carole and Alyssa. "Have Billie, Alyssa, or Ridan shown any tendencies toward *hearing?*"

Thom shook his head and Wally rubbed his chin.

"I know," Wally said softly, "we all have backgrounds in the Force, but I never thought about the kids having any talents."

"If you suspect any talent," Shara continued, "run some checks with WL-One or bring them out and we'll run an empathic evaluation. Have Dan bring Blaire out too."

"Thom," Greg said, "this valley has always been girl-heavy. By that, I simply mean there are more girls than boys, always. Girls are prime targets for the slavers, and if Don's trying to reestablish the collections, he'll be going after the girls first. And since he's here, I'm pretty sure he's made contact and set something up with the Traders."

"Okay," Wally said slowly. "I'll get a report from the deputies in Hawthorne and Grants and alert them to the situation. If there's something happening down there to support

Don's activities, maybe one of my guys will know." He looked at Shara and shook his head. "Shoot, Don already has a plan. He has to already have people lined up to help him. He may already be in place and ready to strike. It might already be too late."

"Greg and Hench have set up a surveillance mesh using the remotes," Shara said, "and we have extra monitoring your place, Wally. Please don't let Alyssa and Ridan run around unattended for a while. With Kiile's help, we have forty-eight remotes in a low-altitude stationary carpet over a large portion of the northern valley. The hope is they will detect suspicious movements and alert us." Shara forced herself to slow her speech and calm her thoughts. "We'll get a warning, but it may only be minutes. Hench has placed two remotes outside to assist you. If we get an alert or something happens, each remote can carry two of you to the scene. WL-One will coordinate. Oh, and he and WL-Two can also take two of you a piece. Seconds could be precious."

Friday, September 8

The children were quiet. The storytelling had brought them up to Nick and Jill's wedding, and yet they seemed almost eager to hear more about their family's past. They walked down STSX's ramp and followed Meara to the main house and the heavy back door. Jill and Nick followed the children and spoke softly to each other as Hench and Leeana trailed close behind them. Shara sighed and took Greg's hand. She told STSX to close up and secure himself as she and Greg stepped off the ramp together, they took their time following the group back to the house.

"I think we have to tell them about Don Nikle," Shara said softly.

"Yeah," Greg agreed, "but how, without scaring them?"

"I guess we'll see what questions they ask first," Shara said, and squeezed Greg's hand. "They probably already know something is brewing."

Greg nodded and they walked the rest of the way to the

house in silence. When they pushed the door open, the children were standing around the table, waiting. Meara, Jill, Nick, Leeana, and Hench stood behind them, facing the door with wide smiles.

"Thank you," Tayn said when Shara and Greg stopped in the archway to the dining room. The three girls repeated the "Thank you" and Tayn held out two large pieces of Annie's famous double chocolate cake. "For everything you have done and continue to do for us, and our family."

Shara smiled and composed her thoughts as she accepted the plates from Tayn and passed one to Greg. "You are all very welcome. And thank you for helping to make us a family."

With that, everyone turned and took their normal chairs around the table, and Jill, Nick, and Cheyenne sat down at the rounded end opposite Meara. Cheyenne quickly took the chair next to Greg.

"Uncle Greg?" Cheyenne asked softly between a bite of cake and a sip of her milk.

"Yes," Greg said, and paused to listen.

"Is it okay if we hear strangers talking in our heads?" She took another bite of cake.

"What do you mean, strangers?" Greg asked, and turned his body slightly toward her. "Can you tell me what it was like?"

"I don't know why I heard them," she said, and sipped her milk again, "but yesterday after we got to school, I heard two men talking. I looked for them and didn't see anyone. Then I realized I was *hearing* them like I hear you, Aunt Shara, and Mom and Dad. In my head."

"Well, I do know that sometimes we do hear other people unexpectedly," Greg said. "Some people broadcast their thoughts or voices and can't receive, and sometimes people with talents can hear them when they do. Sometimes those people can also *hear*. That's why we showed you how to control your broadcasting."

Cheyenne looked up at him and finished swallowing the last of a bite. "Then it's okay to *hear* them?"

"I guess so, unless what they are saying or thinking should be private or is inappropriate," Greg said, and smiled. "Everything people say and think shouldn't be heard."

"Good," she said, and took another bite, then looked up at him. "Because I think one of them is interested in finding Mom and Aunt Shara. Mom was Thomas before she got married, like Grandma Amy and Grandpa Jack, and Aunt Shara was Smallwood like her dad before she got married to you. One of the men was asking the other about the Smallwood and Thomas women."

Everyone at the table had stopped and was watching them, listening to Cheyenne. Sierra turned and looked at Sedona and Sedona looked back, a knowing expression on their faces.

"I figured from the story, you should know he was asking," she continued.

"Can you show me what his voice felt like?" Greg asked softly.

Cheyenne skewed her expression, twisting her mouth to one side, and squinted before she said, "I'll try. I've never sent anything to someone before."

"That's okay," Greg said. "Just talk to me first and then remember the voice and the rest will happen by itself."

"Okay," she said, and the conversation between the two men suddenly drifted into Greg's mind. He smiled at her and she beamed at his approval.

"That was very well done, Cheyenne," Greg said, and squeezed her shoulders.

He glanced at Shara's curious expression and said softly, "She heard Don Nikle and Abe Brownly."

"That's the name in tonight's story," Cheyenne said, her eyes suddenly wide. "STSX said he escaped when Marshal Wally and the others tried to capture him. He was a bad man." She stopped and looked at Sedona, Sierra, and then Tayn. "Did I hear the same man? The one that was stealing people?"

"I'm afraid so, dear," Greg said, and gently squeezed her shoulders again. "And if you hear him again, keep your mind

51

closed so no one hears you and be sure to tell your mom, dad, or any one of us that you can *talk* to."

"Does this mean the trouble is starting again?" Cheyenne asked, concern filling her face.

"Yes, dear," Greg said. "I think it may be."

Then he smiled and looked at Jill and Leeana and then at Shara.

"But to help cheer you up and also prepare you for possible trouble," Shara said as she got up, "your parents and us have something for each of you."

Shara went through the coatroom by the back door and retrieved four carrysacks she had hidden in the ranch office. When she returned, she checked the contents of the first carrysack and handed it to Cheyenne. Then she checked each of the other carrysacks and handed the appropriate ones to Tayn, Sierra and to Sedona.

"Wow," Cheyenne said in surprise. "Like the ones you wore in the story," she continued happily as she pulled the blue-black body suit out of the carry sack.

"There are two suits each," Shara said, trying to speak over the clamor of squeals and 'thank-yous.' "There are boots, a utility belt, and a wool-like head mask and hat. I want each of you to go and put one of your suits on with your belt and boots so we can be sure they fit right."

Cheyenne was off her chair and halfway to the hallway before the rest of them started moving.

"Tayn," Shara continued, "you take the hall bath and the girls can all use one of the girls' bedrooms."

Suddenly the room was quiet, and the adults looked at each other and sighed.

Jill looked at Greg. "Did she really hear them?"

Greg nodded. "She did. What we don't know is whether Don *hears,* or if he can knowingly *speak.*" He looked at Jill. "You will have to listen and see if she hears him anymore, and be sure she doesn't say anything back that he might hear."

Jill nodded and took Nick's hand as Tayn came out of the

hallway and stopped in front of Hench and Leeana. He slowly turned around for them to see.

"Even has my name on it," Tayn said proudly. "Just like yours."

Leeana was beaming and Hench was down on one knee looking at the fit when the three girls came out of the hallway and stopped for inspection.

"It fits great, Mom," Cheyenne said, and turned for Jill and Nick to see.

Sedona and Sierra spun around for Shara and Greg and bent and squatted, testing the stretch in any way they could think of.

"Okay, okay," Shara said, slowing the girls down and pulling them to a stop so she could look at the fit.

"They feel really good, Mom," Sedona said, and stretched the fabric across her chest to show she had room for filling out.

"Thanks, Dad," Sierra said, and hugged him. "These are wonderful."

"Oh Lordy," Matti said as she stepped out of the kitchen and stopped, suddenly seeing the children in the flight suits. "The kids now too?"

"Look, Matti." Sedona happily ran and hugged her. "Aren't they grand?"

"Yes, yes, they are, Miss Sedona," Matti said, regaining her composure. "Complete with your names and everything. All of you do look just grand."

Matti took a deep breath and looked at the empty plates. "Are we all finished here, Mr. Greg?"

"Yes, Matti," Greg said, and smiled. "Thank you, and please thank Annie again for us. The cake was wonderful. And I think the kids will be sufficiently wired for another hour or two."

When Mattie returned to the kitchen, Shara took Sierra to the middle of the living room and stood her between the foyer and the dining room.

"There are a few secrets about these suits that you need to know about," Shara said, and tapped the pad on the side of

Sierra's utility belt.

The room filled with shouts of 'oh!' and 'what happened!' when Sierra suddenly disappeared.

Shara smiled at the open mouths and the awed utterances. "She's still here, but she is inside a veil, what we call Cloaked. Like STSX and KKLC14 were." Shara tapped the pad again and the empty space shimmered and Sierra reappeared. "Each of your suits has this capability, but I must caution you, you cannot see one another if you're both cloaked unless you're standing right beside each other and the veils join. That means, until you can tell where each other is with out seeing them, be very careful when you use the cloaking capability. I know it looks cool and a lot of fun, but these are not toys. Cloaking is for your protection, and only for your protection.

"I've shown you this capability because of our previous conversation and the possibility that trouble might be starting again." Shara smiled to ease the seriousness of her words. "Remember this. If you have to hide and use your veil for protection, Hench, Leeana, Jill, Greg, and myself still know where you are and can find you. And of course, you can *talk* to us and tell us where you are."

Tayn laughed and the girls giggled softly.

"There are other benefits the suits have, but we'll save those for another time," Shara said when she noticed the time. Jill nodded and said they should think about going.

"Okay," Greg said. "Tomorrow is field trip day. We are going to go for a ride on the remotes and visit Kiile, Cheral, and the others at Obscure. Wear your Blues with your regular clothes over them." He turned to Cheyenne. "We'll arrive at your house and pick you three up at about nine. Is that okay?"

She nodded and crossed the space to hug Greg. "Thank you, Uncle Greg. Thank you very much." Then she hugged Shara and thanked her as well.

"Go collect your clothes," Jill said, and watched the kids scurry into the hallway. "Thanks Greg, Shar. This will certainly help the transition," Jill said and hugged Shara.

They followed Cheyenne, Jill, and Nick out, and Hench

and Leeana turned toward their apartment. Tayn stopped and hurried back to Greg and Shara. "I know my dad and mom helped a lot, but thank you both. These are really great."

"You're welcome, Tayn," Greg said, and put his arm around Tayn's shoulders and pulled him close. "Wear them proudly."

⋏

Greg, Shara, and the girls watched the truck's taillights disappear over the crest a mile down the road, then they turned and started up the drive toward the house and its large portico.

"I'm glad Chy told you about what she heard," Sedona said, holding Greg's hand as they walked.

"I am too," he said.

"It made her very uneasy," Sierra said, holding Shara and Sedona's hand as they walked. "I think it makes both of you uneasy too."

"Very much so," Shara admitted.

"But you know how to defend yourself," Sedona said. "Hearing and seeing the story, I was amazed at how well you can fight, how quickly you can decide what you need to do. There's no way that Don Nikle can hurt either of you."

"Thanks for the vote of confidence," Greg said, and smiled, "but there is nothing certain in a fight."

"Oh...you aren't worried about yourselves," Sierra said, suddenly realizing his thought, "are you? You're worried about us. You think he wants us too."

Shara stopped, turned to Sierra, and pulled her tight. Sedona quickly joined them and threw her arms around both of them, and Greg stepped closer and pulled Shara to him with the girls between them.

"Yes," he said, "we are afraid he will try to take you two, and Cheyenne, and Billie, and maybe Alyssa and Ridan and maybe Kayli and Kail too."

"Not Tayn?" Sedona asked without moving.

"They may not know about Tayn," Shara said, "but maybe him too."

Slowly Greg relaxed and picked Sedona up. "Man, you're getting heavy. And big too. Let's get inside and think about a nicer day tomorrow."

He set her down at the front step and opened one panel of the heavy, double front door into the foyer. When his three girls had gone inside, Greg closed and bolted the door.

Saturday, September 9

"Chy," Jill called from the kitchen as Cheyenne went back out onto the front veranda for the third time in as many minutes. "Don't be so anxious. They still have ten minutes before they are supposed to be here."

"I know, Mom," Cheyenne said. "But I can't help it. Uncle Greg said we'd be riding on remotes and I want to see them coming."

Jill pushed the screen door open and stepped out to stand beside her.

"They'll be cloaked, Chy," Jill said softly. "They can't let anyone see them when they go by remote. Do you have your Blues on?"

"Yes, Mom," Cheyenne said, and looked sideways at her. "I'm even wearing my belt and the boots that go with." She sighed and sounded a little exasperated with the questions.

"Don't sound that way," Jill said as Nick stepped up on the end of the veranda and walked over to them. "Your uncle Greg will ask you, and I just want you to be ready and him to be proud of you."

"I am and he already is, Mom."

Nick gave Jill a quick kiss. "You both ready?" he asked, and leaned down and squeezed Cheyenne's shoulders.

"Yup."

"Greg said he's bringing extra remotes. One to help Three watch the ranch," Jill said, and glanced around the yard stretching to the stables and the road to Nick's Dad's house, "and the other for Chy and me to ride. He said you would need to ride with Tayn."

She looked up and said, "They're almost here, Chy. Over the stables and a little to our right."

Cheyenne searched the area, and just as they came over the stables, they unveiled.

"Calm yourself, young lady," Nick said before Cheyenne could start jumping in glee.

"Yes, sir," she said, and stayed in place as the remotes with people suspended beneath them slowly drifted down in front of the house. Cheyenne was waving exuberantly, but she remained in her place on the porch until Greg stepped off Seven and walked up to the steps.

"Are you ready, young lady?" he asked with a quick smile at Jill. When Cheyenne nodded vigorously, he continued. "Blues under your clothes?"

"Yes, sir," Cheyenne said firmly. "Boots to match and my belt."

"Okay then," Greg said, and turned sideways and gestured to the group in the yard. "Better bring your mom so we can get you mounted."

Cheyenne quickly caught Jill's hand and started pulling her down the steps.

Greg led the way and stopped beside Shara and Sedona on Eight as another remote drifted up to him and stopped. Cheyenne smiled at Sierra standing on the stirrup under Seven with Greg's empty stirrup dangling beside her.

"Nine," Greg said, "please extend a stirrup for Cheyenne." Greg moved Cheyenne beside him, and Nine descended so she could grasp the handhold on the remote's underside as it lowered the stirrup.

"Now just step on and hold onto the shaft with one hand and the handhold with the other," Greg said, and showed her where.

"Thank you, Nine," Cheyenne said as she slipped her foot into the stirrup.

"I'll hook his safety cable on your utility belt so you'll be okay if you slip," Greg said as he pulled her shirttail out and clipped the hook through an eyelet on the utility belt.

"Okay, Nine," he continued. "Stirrup for Jill."

"Whoa," Cheyenne said, smiling from ear to ear as Nine lifted up so Jill could step into the longer stirrup.

"That's very good, Chy," Nick said as he checked her foot and handholds quickly and then went to Tayn's remote. Hench stepped off and joined Leeana on hers.

"Everyone ready?" Greg asked as he stepped back into Seven's stirrup.

When everyone nodded or said they were ready, Seven lifted them up over the house and the other remotes followed. Greg called for them to veil and heard Cheyenne's "wow" when everyone except Jill disappeared from her sight.

⋏

Cheral was already on a run for the curved corridor of steps leading up to the clearing outside the south lip of Obscure's large launch portal when Kiile got Surveillance's alert that the commander and others were arriving. When she reached the top of the stairs and stepped out into the clearing, the four children were already stepping off the remotes and their parents had them in a loose but respectful cluster.

Cheral reached the group and hugged Shara first and then hugged the girls. Cheral stopped and looked at Tayn. "Do you accept hugs or just handshakes?"

Tayn stepped forward and hugged Cheral with a wide smile. "I like hugs," he said as he stepped back.

"Me too," Cheral said.

"Good morning Commander, Captain," Kiile said, greeting Greg and Shara. "And Colonel and Captain and Captains," he continued, greeting Hench and Leeana and then Nick and Jill.

Then he smiled at the girls and nodded to Tayn.

"May I speak with you a minute, Kiile?" Hench asked, and led Kiile away from the group. "I would like to talk to you about a situation that is brewing."

"Dad?" Sedona asked as Hench and Kiile walked away.

"Yes, dear. What is it?" Greg replied, and turned to face her.

"Is this the clearing?" she asked. "Where you had the big fight and captured the facility and where the frigate crashed?"

Greg caught her hand and then Sierra's hand, called Cheyenne and Tayn, and started walking toward the southeast and the wide depression in the ground. He stopped at the edge of a deeper depression with a rock outcropping on the east side.

"Yes, this is where the frigate crashed and exploded," he said, and pointed to the various trees still standing. "We had to clear away a lot of broken and splintered trees, but this was a forest, just as dense as that over there." He pointed to the west. "That rock outcropping in the middle of the depression is where I put your mom and Jill, hoping to shield them from the explosion."

Greg turned and saw Tayn standing a few feet behind them.

"Come closer, Tayn, and ask any questions you might have," Greg said.

When he had answered their curiosities and they were satisfied, he led them back toward the closed portal.

"That area ahead of us that looks like a big pasture," he said, and pointed to the area just beyond the rest of their group. "That's a great big door that opens to let ships in and out. Over there, the smaller ship is a Class 1 patrol fighter that the students use to start their flight training. And the longer, sleeker one behind it is a Class 2 patrol fighter like Cheral, Nick, and Jill fly."

"Wow," Sierra said. "The other two look like STSX and KKLC." She twisted her mouth and looked closer. "No. Actually, they look like KKLC. STSX has a different canopy and shape up front."

"Is that what we'll use to learn in?" Tayn asked, his expression full of awe.

"Most likely, but we'll see," Greg said, and led them back to the others. "It'll depend on what is available when we get to that part of your training. You and Sedona and Sierra will train this winter and into next year. Cheyenne, you'll start training next fall, after your next birthday. I'm bending the rules and starting training at eleven instead of waiting until you're twelve, but I want you all trained as early as I can train you."

"Can't you say I'm almost eleven?" Cheyenne asked, knowing he wouldn't.

"Cheyenne," he said, and put his hands on his hips. "I have to teach a lot of serious things—things more serious and adult than you have been exposed to. Besides, I'm not sure any of the pilots' chairs will adjust to your size." He tried to make his concerns sound light and not be too stern with her.

"If I can't learn the flying part," Cheyenne persisted, "can I learn the rest with Tayn and Sedona and Sierra? I know I'm almost a year behind everyone else, but I'm smart. I can do the work. Even if I have to do it all over again when I'm older, I'd like to learn with them."

Greg stopped and looked down at Cheyenne's unwavering, serious expression.

"Okay," he said. "Tell you what I'll do. No promises, but I'll talk with Hench and with your mom and dad and see what everyone thinks. Then I'll let you know."

"Okay. Thanks, Uncle Greg."

He turned and led them back to the group.

"Are we ready to take this crew inside for a tour?" he asked.

"Sure," Cheral said, and gestured toward the hatch into the corridor of steps.

One-Twelve

"Is Aunt Shara really someone 'special'?" Cheyenne asked as she took another bite of her supper. She had showered and dressed for bed early, after spending most of the day with them and her aunt and uncle at the secret facility Obscure.

"Well, of course she's special." Jill said, and refilled her tea glass.

"No, not that way," Cheyenne continued. "I mean, everyone at Obscure was extra nice to Aunt Shara and Uncle Greg."

"They are the commanders and are in charge of everything," Jill explained.

Cheyenne stared at her mom, her fork with a piece of meat stabbed on it poised in front of her, and sighed. "No. I know they're the bosses. I mean, like 'famous' or something? The story was full of the 'hundreds' of things Aunt Shara did. Was all of that really true? Did she do all of those things?"

Jill smiled and glanced at Nick, seeing his guarded laughter.

"Yes, Chy. I'm afraid she did," Jill said, and smiled. "Your aunt Shara and uncle Greg are almost legends. They are 'very special' people in that way."

"But you and Dad can fight like they can. Why aren't you someone famous?"

"That's the way it works sometimes," Nick said softly and smiled at her. "We don't need to be famous, and I'm sure your aunt and uncle aren't doing what they do to be famous either. Sometimes the people around you treat you nice because they are respectful and that is their way to say thank you for doing what you do. They don't know what else to do. Your aunt and uncle have helped a lot of people—many, many that they don't even know."

"Wow," Cheyenne said, and scooped up another spoonful of

61

potatoes. "Will I get to be like them?"

"What? Famous?" Jill teased.

"No. To be treated nice because I did things good?" Cheyenne sipped her tea, obviously thinking. "That's better than famous, isn't it, Dad?"

"Yes, dear." He smiled. "It certainly is."

She hesitated a moment and then asked, "Has Uncle Greg talked to you about me yet?"

"About you?" Jill asked, suddenly wondering what her daughter might have done. "What about you?"

"Training. I want to train with Sedona, Sierra, and Tayn, but at first he said I was too young."

"You are a year younger, dear," Nick added.

"I know," she said softly, "but I told Uncle Greg I really wanted to train with them and I would repeat it later if I had to. He said he would talk to Hench—I mean Colonel Kooich— and then he would talk to you and see what you thought." She looked at them with a hopeful expression. "Please Mom, Dad. There must be a reason my talent has awakened...awoken... started now. Even if I can't learn the flying part yet, I still want to start training."

"We'll see," Jill said. "Let me and your dad talk about this a little before Uncle Greg asks us. Okay?"

"Oh, okay, Mom."

Cheyenne quickly finished her supper and asked if she could be excused, saying she wanted to watch the stars for a little bit before going to bed.

"Sure," Jill said, "but would you mind helping Piper and take your dishes into the kitchen for her?"

"Sure, Mom," Cheyenne said, and slipped out of her chair and stacked her dishes.

"Make a second trip for your glass, Chy," Jill said as Cheyenne started to try and stack the glass on top of the dishes and utensils.

Cheyenne made the trip into the kitchen and quickly came

back for the glass.

"Are you going to stargaze from the upstairs porch?" Nick asked as she stopped and gave him a hug.

"Well, yes," she said in a matter-of-fact manner. "It's closer and the view is better."

Jill chuckled as Cheyenne scampered up the stairs. "Take a shawl. It's starting to get chilly after the sun goes down."

Nick collected their plates and utensils and was about to get up when Piper stepped into the dining room and took them from him.

"Now, Mr. Nick," Piper said, and gave him a stern look. "You know this is my job." Then in a milder tone, she added, "Thank you, though, for the thought." She chuckled. "That little Miss Chy is really keyed up tonight. It's always nice to see her so happy."

"Thanks, Piper," Jill said. "Dinner was very good."

Piper nodded and smiled and carried the dishes into the kitchen.

Jill got up and went into the living room. Nick followed and sat down beside her on the long sofa in front of the fireplace and the fire he had started when they got home. It had settled to a comfortable amount of flame and embers.

"Well, well," Nick sighed as he slipped his arm around Jill. "So she's all hot to trot and start training. We can't even get her to do her homework without a bit of an argument. And now..."

"Yes," Jill said, "but with her *hearing* in full bloom, she's suddenly found herself equal to the others, just out of sync by a little time. It's obvious she's eager, but I'm not sure she can simply move ahead a year and be okay."

"If Greg asks Hench and they both agree to bend the rules and let her in two years early instead of one, they'll have their reasons. We'll ask him why he wants to try, if he comes and asks."

"Okay." Jill smiled and snuggled down and rested her head on his shoulder.

▲

'Sierra, Sedona?' Cheyenne focused her mind and called softly as she scanned the stars with her binoculars. She was reclined in a chaise lawn chair on the deck outside her room, wrapped in a soft blanket and studying the heavens.

'Hey, Chy,' the two voices answered in unison.

'What's up?' Sierra asked. 'What did you think about that place? Wow.'

'I know. Wow is right. Wasn't it great?' Cheyenne said. 'And riding on a remote was pure heaven. Have you gotten to do that before?'

'No. Mom and Dad have been just as secretive as yours have been,' Sedona said. 'Today was the first time. What's up? You feel troubled.'

'Two things, I guess,' Cheyenne admitted. 'Uncle Greg said I may not be old enough to train with you and Tayn. I know you heard me plead with him and he said he'd talk to Hench, but I'm not sure he will if he thinks I'm too young.'

'Chy! If Dad said he'd talk to Hench,' Sierra said sternly, 'you know he will. He wouldn't say he was going to do something and then not do it. Especially to us or to you. You are his favorite niece.'

'Thanks. I'm his only niece.'

'Still his favorite!' Sedona added. 'And you're our favorite cousin! Be patient, I think Dad and Mom have a lot on their minds right now. And hearing this Don Nikle really has them thinking.'

'Did you tell them?' Cheyenne asked bluntly.

'No. Not yet,' they said in unison.

'You gotta tell them so they don't think I'm the only one.' Cheyenne hesitated.

'What is it, Chy?'

'I heard him again this afternoon, right after we left the dining room, ah, the Mess, in Obscure.'

'We didn't hear him then. Are you sure?' Sedona asked. 'Why

64

didn't we hear him?'

'You were talking to that Colonel Mooren and his wife, mate, Franni,' Cheyenne said. 'He sounded soft, hushed, and being busy and in a conversation, his voice was probably too soft to get your attention.'

'What did he say? What was he talking about?' Sierra asked.

'Something about a fire and getting bees to leave their nests,' Cheyenne said.

'What does that mean?' Sedona asked.

'I think he's going to set something on fire, maybe a distraction,' Cheyenne added.

'Do you know who he was talking to?' Sierra asked.

'No, but that man was a lot louder, maybe closer or something. No, Aunt Shara said distance doesn't normally make the voices louder or softer,' Cheyenne said, thinking to herself. 'She said something else did, something...Underground does! Either it was because we were underground or because he was.'

'Hmmm.' Sedona thought a moment. 'There's nowhere around here where you can be underground, other than Obscure. We'll tell Mom and Dad that we heard Mr. Nikle in the morning and ask where he could be and be underground at the same time.'

'Thanks,' Cheyenne said. 'I'll talk to you in the morning. It's late and Mom's coming to check on me. Goodnight.'

''Night, cuz. In the morning,' they said in unison and broke the link.

The bedroom door opened behind her and Jill stepped out onto the porch and knelt down beside the chaise.

"Time to come in, Chy," she said, and helped Cheyenne up out of the chaise.

"Thanks, Mom," Cheyenne said as she picked up the bottom of the blanket and went inside.

When the door closed behind Tayn as he headed out to

his apartment to get ready for bed, Greg picked up his cup and took another sip of coffee. He looked at Shara and then at Leeana and Hench, then he gently *touched* the girls in their rooms quietly snuggling into bed themselves.

"I know you must feel as strange as I do, Hench," Greg said. "It was one thing to plan and train when it was just ourselves, and a slightly different other thing when we married strong, capable women who happily trained with us. But thinking about actually starting the kids in physical training makes me think of the many dangers they may have to face in the future, and frankly those possibilities scare me more than any encounter I've ever faced."

Hench nodded. "We feel the same way, but we don't have any choice with their talents starting to show so early. We have to teach them what's necessary."

"I know I'm not ready for this," Leeana admitted, "but I don't see any way out of it."

Greg turned to Shara and she smiled weakly.

"I'm almost afraid to say what I've been thinking," Shara said.

"I think," Greg said, "we should start with physical hand-to-hand combat exercises and strength training. Physical training and rope climbing. Maybe as early as Monday or Tuesday."

"Physical and hand-to-hand training will be regular with each session," Shara said, thinking about the options. "How long will you wait before you introduce them to the nav-com and Ship Knowledge training syllabus?"

"I'm not sure. I think I will focus on the personal defense aspects first," Greg said, "and let the testing tell us when they are confident and able enough to add new subjects."

"Fair enough," Shara said, and looked at Leeana. "We'll probably see Jill tomorrow, and I'll explain what we're planning to her and Nick then."

"Kiile said he has a young marine that can help," Greg said. "He can be here in the afternoons when the kids get home from school." He looked at each of them, hesitating briefly. "Okay," he continued, and pushed himself away from the table. "Let me know if any of you have any other ideas. I think now, we should get some rest and see what tomorrow brings when it gets here."

"All right," Hench said, and stood up. "I'll put a routine together tomorrow and then see what Kiile's man thinks when he gets here. We can do some training here in the enclosed arena, and then later move down to Obscure for things like the long ropes."

He helped Leeana up, gestured a goodbye, and they left for their apartment.

Greg walked around the living room and switched the lights off while Shara secured the back doors and checked the kitchen.

When she came back into the dining room, Greg hugged her and then turned her toward the hallway.

Sunday, September 10

"Greg! Wake up!" Shara shouted, and shoved him as she threw the covers back and started grabbing her clothes. She absently noted it was dark and not long after midnight. "We have intruders approaching the shields."

'Sedona! Sierra! Wake up!' she shouted in her mind.

'What...?' they said groggily as they shook the sleep out of their eyes.

'Wake up! We have intruders! Tayn! Wake up! We have intruders. Get your Blues on and wake your folks! Hurry! Girls, get your Blues on. Now!'

Greg was beside her and slipped into his Blues. He could hear the rustling in the girls' rooms. *'No lights, girls! Tayn. Keep it dark!'* Then he refocused his mind. *'STSX, Ignition ready now! Release Two from recharge, and remotes Seven through Twelve! We have intruders. Tell Hank!'*

"Okay, Bren," he said as he checked the hilt indicator on the Kaaspr and slipped it into the backup pouch on his utility belt. "Let's go."

Greg stepped into the hall and pushed the girls' door open. *'You two dressed?'*

'Yeah, just,' they said together.

'Wow! There are a lot of people!' Sedona said.

'Sedona, where's Tayn and his folks?' Shara asked as she felt the area around the ranch.

Hank was up and had roused the hands, and she felt movement in Hench and Leeana's apartment.

'Tayn says they're just ready to slip outside,' Sedona answered.

Shara stopped and reached for Leeana, and when she felt the soft touch, she showed her where the intruders were creeping closer to the shields, unaware that they were there.

'STSX, distribute the remotes in a circle around the structures,' Greg said. *'We're going to let the intruders in and then reclose the shields. Tell Hank and Meara where they are.'*

Shara slipped into the house girls' wing and woke them, telling them to stay in the inside commons area and stressed no lights. Then she hurried back into the dining room.

"One of you, grab hold of my utility belt and the other grab Mom's," Greg commanded. "Whatever happens, do NOT let go of our belts. We're going to go outside and cloak. There's going to be a fight, so stay quiet. We don't want them to know where we are. Okay?"

"Yeah," the girls said together, and Sedona grabbed his belt.

Sierra grabbed Shara's belt as Greg gave Shara a quick kiss. "Let me know if you have any trouble."

"Who else?" she said, and the girls felt the warm emotional exchange between their parents as they heard them repeat the phrases the history told them they had used so long ago when they were going into a battle.

'STSX, we're going out the front,' Greg said, *'and Shara is going out the back. Show Hench and Leeana where we are and tell Hank and Meara.'*

Greg slowly pushed the heavy front door open and felt

Shara open the back door. He turned the lock as he slipped out and gently pulled the door closed behind them. The lock clicked as he felt the intruders' locations and switched their veils on.

'There's twenty-six, Dad,' Sedona said.

'Good work, Sedona. That's the number I got. STSX, raise the shields and let them slip past. You and KKLC14 better stay cloaked and hover. Stay silent until they are close in. Once they are all in, reset the shields and help the remotes contain the intruders.'

'DAD!' Sedona shouted in her mind. 'Chy says there's a fire at their grandpa's place and lots of men there too!'

'STSX, alert Kiile and Wally and get some help over to the Jordans'. Contact Four and Doug and Rose. Jill! We're a little busy right now, but we'll come as soon as we're finished here.'

'We're taking the north side of the barns,' Shara said, 'around the paddocks and near the arenas.'

Greg knelt in the middle of the wide front yard, about halfway to the stone fence. 'Sedona, watch the fence. The shield reaches just to this side of the fence, and we should see them climb over and come inside.'

'Why are you letting them in?' she asked.

'I want to catch them and find out who they are,' he said, 'and if we're lucky, Nikle will be with one of the two groups.'

'Dad,' Sedona said softly, 'he isn't.'

Greg looked at Sedona under the joined veils. 'What?'

'He's...he's not here. Mr. Nikle is somewhere underground, waiting for the men to bring him whoever they are trying to capture.'

'How...? Never mind, we'll talk about that later,' Greg said, and refocused his mind. 'STSX, tell Kiile to check the tunnels from Obscure north and over to Clay. Nikle is somewhere in the tunnels and has access to a road.'

'Dad, they're coming over the fence,' Sedona said calmly.

'I see them. Thanks. Look for a wide spot between them. With only twenty-six, they'll be spaced out a lot. We'll go through a gap and get behind them. Then we'll have them between us and the remotes.'

'Tayn and his mom and dad are waiting for the ones coming from the east,' Sedona said. 'Mom's northwest of the barns by the arenas, and Hank has the northeast behind the arenas and bunkhouse covered.'

'Let's go,' Greg said, and slowly started walking toward the line of shadows creeping toward the house. As they got close, Greg stopped and let them pass. 'Let them make the noise,' he said, and felt Sedona watching them, the closest about fifteen feet away.

When they were past, Greg moved to the west and stopped south of the new apartments.

'Meara knows where we are and she's letting them pass as well.' Then he refocused.

'SHIELDS ARE REACTIVATED.'

'Bren, are you in position?' Greg asked, and she said she was.

'Tayn says they are too. Leeana told Mom and STSX told Hank,' Sedona said.

'Okay,' Greg said. 'All remotes—draw a circle in front of the men. Trap them between the circle and the shields. Neutralize any with weapons or any that attack.'

Suddenly, bolts of white-hot light streaked down in front of the intruders and Greg knelt and aimed his Brekshiir 710.

'Stay behind me,' Greg said softly, and felt Sedona's silent agreement.

He picked the two men nearest him, and when they turned in fear and confusion he yelled for them to drop their weapons. One fired in the general direction of his voice, and Greg returned a volley; the Brekshiir dropped one and his Kaaspr dropped another.

▲

Shara led Sierra between the paddocks, stopping suddenly when Sedona shouted, 'Chy says there's a fire at their grandpa's place and lots of men there too!'

'You're listening to your dad and Sedona?' Shara asked.

'Yeah,' Sierra said. *'I heard Chy. I heard Dad.'*

'Come on,' Shara said.

'Are we going to find a gap in between the men and get behind them too?'

'No. We're going to keep them away from the buildings,' Shara said, and moved toward the western end of the open arena.

'There they are,' Sierra said, pointing to the advancing shadows.

Shara waited until they heard STSX reactivate the shields, then she said, *'Let's wake them up, love.'*

They heard Greg's call to STSX, and suddenly white-hot streaks speared the ground in front of each man, and then followed as they tried to turn. Three charged for the open arena and lit flares as they ran.

'Stay behind me,' Shara said as she knelt and fired a volley from her Brekshiir 710.

Three brilliant flashes threw the men backwards and the flares fell harmlessly on the ground.

Some of the men ran in retreat only to slam into the invisible, active shield, stumbling backwards, staggering. They turned and saw the spears moving closer, closing in on them, squeezed against the electrified air blocking their retreat. Shara saw someone run forward, scoop up a fallen flare, and charge past the paddocks.

Her Brekshiir flashed and he tumbled head over heels and slumped in a limp pile.

'Come on. There are two between the barns and the house,' Shara said, and started back toward the main house.

As they reached the west end of the barn, she saw one of the men light another flare. Two flashes caught him simultaneously, one from Shara's Kaaspr and one from the dark gap between the main house and the apartment. The second man turned and Shara's second shot knocked him to the ground.

'Tayn says his dad helped get the first one,' Sierra said when

Hank's shotgun boomed twice in short succession from the other side of the bunkhouse, and Sierra felt a sudden sadness.

Shara felt the area in front of the main house and saw two men wither and fall. She turned back in time to see Seven eradicate a line of five intruders with flares racing back to the house from the shields.

Suddenly marines in dark brown and green camouflaged uniforms began to flood out of the darkness, over the perimeter, and after a number of short scuffles, STSX gave a tally: *'EIGHT INTRUDERS PENNED IN AGAINST THE SHIELDS ON THE EAST AND THREE PENNED IN AGAINST THE SHIELDS ON THE SOUTHWEST. FIFTEEN INTRUDERS DEAD. ONE RANCH HAND, TOMMY, DEAD.'*

Shara hugged Sierra and felt for Greg and Sedona, sensing the girls' sad reaction to the new reality.

'Jill? Are you all right? Do you need us to come?' Shara asked, and turned to look southeast.

⋏

"Mom," Cheyenne said as she stopped beside her parents' bed in their dark bedroom, shaking her mom awake. "Mom! That man is talking again and there are a lot of men around grandpa's barn. A lot of them are coming this way."

Jill shook herself awake and heard Cheyenne explain her message again.

"Nick! Intruders!" she shouted. Seeing Cheyenne's images, she threw the bedcovers off and grabbed her clothes. "Chy, put your Blues on. Quick! Nick! Hurry."

Jill was in her Blues and fastening her utility belt by the time Nick started dressing.

'MOM! Grandpa's barn is on fire! Hurry!' Cheyenne shouted, and then stomped her last boot on and ran down the stairs.

'STOP!' Jill shouted. *'STOP, Chy! It's a trap!'* Jill was down the stairs and caught Cheyenne standing frozen in the doorway. She grabbed Cheyenne in a hug and clutched her tight. *'Thank you, honey. Remember what you told Sedona and Sierra you*

72

heard. We're the bees. Don't run outside by yourself—not now.'

Nick stopped beside her. "The shields are active and cloaking is active."

"Okay, let's make them play in our court. Greg says to bring them inside and hold them," she said. "Let the remotes contain them, and if any attack us or the house, it's fair game."

Nick nodded. "I'll warn Piper."

"Chy," Jill continued, "grab my utility belt and don't let go." Then she shifted her focus, *'Three, raise the shields and let them in. As soon as they are in, lower the shields and don't let them out. Use Six to help stop them.'*

'I'm ready, Mom,' Cheyenne said, and Jill heard the deep concern in her thoughts.

'Okay, Chy. Turn your cloaking on. Daddy will be invisible, but we'll know where he is. Let's go,' Jill said, and slowly swung the front door open.

"Nick, we'll go right and you go left," Jill whispered as he rejoined them. She turned and crossed the veranda to the north. *'Wait and see what they are going to do,'* Jill said to Cheyenne as the men crossed the unseen perimeter and Jill and Cheyenne heard Remote Three.

'SHIELDS ARE ACTIVE. REMOTE FOUR HAD ALERTED CAPTAINS MCINTIRE AND IS COMING TO ASSIST. THE CAPTAINS ARE TWELVE MINUTES AWAY.'

The men began to move more quickly, and some lit flares as they ran. Jill's Brekshiir 710 fired a volley into the rushing line of men and Nick's Kaaspr flashed from the opposite end of the veranda. Cheyenne looked up where she knew the remotes were as spears of white-hot light dropped in front of the running men.

Some yelled and screamed and a few tried to retreat, slamming into the invisible, unyielding barrier.

'There are more coming around behind the house,' Cheyenne yelled, *'and two behind Dad.'*

"Nick, behind you," Jill shouted, and turned to look for the shadows east of the house.

'*I see four,*' Jill said. '*How about you, Chy?*'

The yard filled with bright laser bursts and then fell dark.

'*Not anymore,*' Cheyenne said soberly as they saw flashes from the other side of the house. '*Dad's okay,*' Cheyenne said before Jill could say the words.

Suddenly it was quiet, and as Jill rose up out of her crouch she saw Kiile's marines flood the yard.

'*Mom?*' Cheyenne asked. '*How can they get through and the other men couldn't?*'

'*We each have an access code implanted—you as well—and the shields know us, the Friendlies, and let us in.*' Jill refocused as she felt the area around the house. '*Three, status please.*'

'*TWENTY-FOUR ATTACKED, SIX CAPTURED, EIGHTEEN NEUTRALIZED. FOUR RANCH HANDS KILLED AT THE BARN,*' Three replied.

'*Damn! Thank you, Three. Chy, we can drop our veils now,*' Jill said, and they stepped up onto the veranda, shimmering visible again. '*Are you okay?*' Jill asked as she turned and knelt down and looked at her daughter.

'*I think so, Mom. Are four of Grandpa Bob's men really dead?*' Cheyenne asked, and hugged Jill.

'*If Three says so,*' Jill admitted, and squeezed Cheyenne tight and sighed. '*Then they are.*'

"Shadow Jordan, Cadet Jordan," a marine said as he stepped up onto the veranda and greeted Jill and Cheyenne.

Jill quickly turned and stood up, holding Cheyenne's hand.

"I'm sorry we didn't get here soon enough to help you this time. We were not posted to watch your ranch."

"Twelve? Yes, it is. Thank you for coming anyway. I'm sorry to always seem to need late-night assistance."

"The last time was many years ago," Twelve admitted as Nick stepped up beside them. "At least this time your mate is not in need of Medical. Any ideas what prompted the attack?"

"Yes," Jill said, and explained the situation. "Colonel Kooich explained it to Kiile this morning, but we didn't expect Don

Nikle to strike so soon."

"The commander thinks Nikle was trying again to abduct you and the captain, and now the children?" Twelve asked, to be certain he had the facts straight in his mind.

"Yes. Or more. Remember Don was the last one of the Elders responsible for filling the slavers' quotas. Did Kiile get the commander's message? Don is somewhere waiting for these and the ones that attacked headquarters to bring their captives to him."

"I don't know if a message was sent to Squad Leader Kiile," Twelve said, "but I heard a request from Fifteen calling for backup troops. He's guarding the commander's place."

He reached for his earpiece to call and inquire, but Cheyenne interrupted him.

"They're mostly okay," she said. "They neutralized fifteen and have eleven in custody, and...and one ranch hand is dead." Tears began to roll down Cheyenne's cheeks. "They had two QShips, six remotes, and thirteen on the ground waiting. Aunt Shara heard them coming. Fifteen's troops were late also." She inhaled and straightened her shoulders. "We only had two remotes and three on the ground waiting." She exhaled slowly. "There were no other attacks tonight—just them and us."

Twelve stared down at Cheyenne, realizing the discrepancy she pointed out and was unable to say anything.

"And Mr. Nikle is somewhere that way," she added, and pointed north toward town. "Uncle Greg says he's in a tunnel somewhere."

Twelve shook his head quickly and asked Jill, "Who alerted you? Did you see them coming, Captain?"

"No," Jill said with a wide smile and squeezed her daughter's shoulders. "Cheyenne did."

Jill, Nick, and Cheyenne had thrown their regular clothes on over their Blues and were in their front yard when Wally's patrol car pulled away from Bob's barn and started down the drive to their place. Wally stopped at the gate in the low stone fence and got out.

"Morning, Wally," Nick said, and extended his hand. "I figured only your deputies would be working the night shift."

"Hey, Nick," he said, and nodded to Jill and Cheyenne. "We were about to call it a night when WL-One alerted us. Thom and Ted are still checking things around your dad's place."

"Carole's here?" Jill asked, and looked at the patrol car.

"Yeah." Wally pointed back over his shoulder. "When Shar, Greg, and the girls arrived, she wanted to stay and talk to them. And Doug and Rose were already there."

"Do you need to talk to Cheyenne or me?" Jill asked, and stepped toward the gate.

"No," Wally said, and smiled. "I'll talk to Nick now and talk to you later."

"Thanks," Jill said, and she caught Cheyenne's hand and started trotting up the drive.

"Greg says you think it was Nikle," Wally said when he looked back at Nick.

"It was. No thinking about it," Nick said firmly. "Cheyenne heard him planning it, and then again just before the men attacked."

"Cheyenne did?" Wally asked, as if he might have heard Nick wrong.

"Yeah. She woke us just before the men set fire to the barn," Nick explained, "and told us a lot of men were coming before we even got out of bed. Jill confirmed it once she was awake enough."

"Kiile's marines collected them?"

"Yeah. Twenty-four hit us and eighteen died." Nick sighed and looked through the trees where they blocked his view of the partially burned barn. "Four of dad's hands were killed. Cheyenne said twenty-six hit Greg, which makes it an even fifty if you count both attacks. She said they killed fifteen of the intruders also and lost one of their hands. The rest, Kiile's men will interrogate, but Nikle wasn't with them. Cheyenne said he was underground somewhere in town."

"I see," Wally said, and rubbed his chin. "Is Kiile checking the tunnels?"

Nick nodded. "Wally, haven't your men in the south seen anything?" he asked. "Nikle couldn't pull fifty men together and send them up here without someone seeing them, knowing they were there, getting ready for something."

"They should have," Wally said. "I've sent an inquiry asking those very same questions. But I do have to say things have been very quiet for the past eleven or twelve years, and we've certainly become too complacent. Greg told me Don was back, but I don't think he expected him to act so quickly."

"At least we saw them at the last moment," Nick said, and glanced northwest at the trees.

"Have you checked your property?" Wally asked as he started along the fence. "To see if Kiile's men left anything behind?"

"Not yet," Nick said. "Three—spotlight on, please, and follow us."

Suddenly a bright light flooded the spot where they stood, centering them in its twenty-foot circle.

"Three, drift around the yard. We're looking for any signs of the intruders and anything that might have been left behind." Nick gestured for Wally to lead and follow Three's moving light.

⋏ ⋏ ⋏ ⋏ ⋏

"I hear you were a real trooper this morning," Greg said after Cheyenne and Jill passed Bob's paddocks and stopped beside him, Carole, and Shara.

"She was sad, but as calm and composed as I've ever seen her," Jill said with a wide smile. "She woke us up and told us what was happening."

"And I hear you heard Mr. Nikle again," Greg said, and

ruffled Cheyenne's hair. "Sedona and Sierra said you heard him planning the attack."

"Yes, sir," Cheyenne said. "I'm sorry I wasn't smart enough to know what he was planning when I heard him. I'm really sorry, Uncle Greg."

"Don't be," he said, and smiled at Shara and then at Jill. "None of us were listening like we should've been, and you wouldn't know...since you haven't been trained what to look for."

Cheyenne looked up at him, her face smudged where she had wiped her tears with her sleeve, and stared.

"From what I saw tonight and heard about how my untrained, favorite niece handled herself in a major life-or-death crisis," Greg said, and took a deep breath, "I think training is essential." Aside, privately to Shara, he added, *'I think weapons use training is also essential.'*

Cheyenne's mouth dropped open. "Do you mean...?" she whispered.

Greg looked at Jill. "If your mom feels it's appropriate for you to learn how to protect yourself and to better understand what you can or need to do to help in this time of need—" He looked back at Cheyenne. "—then I'd like to include you in an accelerated learning class."

Cheyenne spun around and looked at her mom, her expression pleading. "Mom? Can I?"

Jill looked at Greg and smiled a tight smile. "She's certainly been exposed to the real facts of life and the life-or-death reality of this situation. I think I have to agree she'll be in less danger if she's trained. And with her talents waking up all over the place, she needs to learn how to handle them as well."

"Thank you, Mom. Thank you," she said, and hugged Jill tightly. "I promise to learn really, really good." Then she turned to Greg and glanced at Sedona and Sierra's wide smiles. "But Uncle Greg, I'm still really too young and you said—"

"Let me put it this way," he said. He knelt down in front of her, took her hands, and looked at her. "I won't lie about your age, but I will 'forget' how old you are for now. Whether your age becomes a problem will be determined by how well or how poorly you do in your training and scoring. There are tests, just like in regular school, to see if you are learning. And with each test, you will have to show you've earned the right to proceed and to keep up."

"I will. I promise I will," she said, and hugged him.

"It will be more difficult at times than you imagine, but just ask for help if you need it. No one will give you the answers or do your work for you, but we will all help teach you and help you."

"Thank you, Uncle Greg," Cheyenne said. She straightened and wiped her eyes once more and looked at Shara. "I'm so sorry Tommy died, Aunt Shara." She sighed. "It really didn't look good for a while."

Shara smiled tightly. "No, Cheyenne, it didn't. Thank you." Shara bent and hugged her.

"I think these cadets need some rest after a full night of unexpected crises," Greg said, and looked at Jill and then at Shara. "The colonel will prepare a syllabus later today and classes will start tomorrow after school. Can you come to the ranch, Cheyenne?"

Cheyenne looked at her mom, and when Jill nodded, she said she could.

"Very well," Greg said. "We'll bring you home after dinner." He stepped forward and hugged Jill quickly. "Chin up, Sis. Bring one set of her Blues over later today."

Then he turned and said goodnight to Carole and Wally, and to Rose and Doug as two remotes settled above them.

"A few minutes longer, love," Greg said to Shara as he gently pulled Sedona to the remote. "Then we will go home. Sedona, Sierra, you can use the bunks on board STSX until we get you home." Then he refocused his mind. '*STSX. Alert Kiile that I'm coming. I have some things I need to discuss with him, immediately.*'

One-Thirteen
Saturday, November 18

"Stow your loose stuff in your bins," Shara said as she led the girls through the equipment bay on her way to STSX's central chamber and the ladder to the upper deck. "Then come up to the cockpit."

Greg followed Sedona and Sierra in and helped them stow their utility belts and a change of street clothes.

"STSX, please secure the aft portal and the airlock," Greg said, and led the girls forward.

"Dad?" Sierra asked, pointing to the two bunks across from the double-wide cushion chairs. "Are those going to be our bunks when we travel and need to sleep?"

"Yes," Greg said, and smiled. "Unless you want to start sleeping together again."

"No," Sedona said. "That's okay. We can sleep together sometimes, but we like having our own beds."

"Up the ladder," he said, and shooed them ahead of him. "Mom wants to get started. It's three hours later in the morning at grandma's place and they're probably wondering where we are."

On the flight deck, they turned forward and Sedona slipped into the older jump seat on the left and Sierra stopped and looked at the right-hand jump seat.

"Where are you going to sit, Dad?" Sierra asked, and looked back at him in the nav-com chair.

"You take the jump seat," he said. "I'll use the instructor's seat when I come forward."

He turned back to the panels and started the preflight checks as Sierra took her seat and buckled in.

"Ignition is ready," he said when he came forward. He unfolded the instructor's seat and secured it in the cockpit portal, and then settled and buckled in as Shara started the familiar litany.

"Sensor status," Shara said as she toggled the row of switches on the pilot's chair's right-hand armrest.

"CLOAKING ON, SENSOR BLOCKING ON, SHIELDS ARE FULL, PASSIVE SCAN INDICATES NO LOCAL TRAFFIC."

"Thank you, STSX," she said. Then she glanced at Sedona and then at Sierra. "Secure?"

"Yes, Bren," Greg said softly, and winked at the girls. "We are all three secure."

Greg noticed the girls were watching Shara's every move as she added thrust and slowly lifted STSX up from the pasture to drift west away from the main house and the other buildings. Slowly Shara lifted the nose and accelerated into the bright morning sky.

"Mom," Sedona asked, "we were wondering why your flight suit says Casi Ge...Geaardt and Dad's says Stran Geaardt on them."

"Gee, like 'geese' and 'art.'" Greg pronounced it for them.

"Did they belong to someone else?" Sierra asked.

"No, dear," Shara said as she settled STSX into the climb. "They are our registered names in the Force. Dad's family heritage goes back a long ways in the Force, and we are registered as Geaardt. Your grandma is also a Geaardt. I am known as Casi, your dad is Stran, and Grandma Coleen is Moira."

"Will we get Geaardt names?" they asked together.

"Yes you will," Greg said. *'Shall I tell them?'*

'Why not?' Shara asked. *'Maybe they'll be used to them before they are registered, instead of surprising them like they did you.'*

"You actually do already. You, Sedona, will be Caiti Geaardt," Greg said, and watched Sedona's smile. "And Sierra, you will be Dani Geaardt."

"Like a boy, Danny?" she asked, and turned to look at Greg.

Shara chuckled. "I told you she'd question that one."

"No, dear," Greg said, and smiled. "It's like my ancestor, Great Grand Matron, registered as Daniela Geaardt."

"Ooh," Sierra said softly. "Was she nice?"

"I'm sure she was," Greg said, "but I never actually met her. But I know you will be, unless someone picks on you too much."

"That's right," Sierra agreed. "But why can't I have a 'C' name like Mom and Sedona?"

"A 'C' name?" Greg asked.

"Yeah," Sierra said, and looked at him as if it should be obvious. "Mom's named Shara, and we're Sedona and Sierra—'S' names to everyone else—and she's Casi to the Force, a 'C' name. You gave Sedona a 'C' name, Caiti, so why do you want me to be different?"

"Okay," Greg said softly. "I see your point and I don't want you to be different. What name would you pick?"

She thought a moment and then smiled. "I like Coli, after Grandma Coleen."

Greg smiled. "What do you think, Bren?"

"I think it's a lovely choice," Shara said without turning to look. "And I think your grandma will be pleased."

"All right, Sierra," Greg said. "You will be known to the Force as Coli Geaardt."

Sierra smiled and started to say something when she suddenly felt a change and her eyes slowly grew in size. "What's happening?"

Both of the girls looked at each other and realized they were floating up against the seat straps.

"Oh, you've just discovered weightlessness," Greg said. "You've been talking so much that you didn't realize you are in space now. Look outside."

They looked over the canopy sills and squealed in delight.

"You'll miss too much looking that way," Shara said, and

slowly rolled STSX so the earth hung above them.

"Wow," they said softly in unison. "Is this really happening?"

"Yes, it is," Greg said. "You can now honestly call yourselves 'space farers.' You're actually traveling in outer space. Now, you're both good at geography. See how many places you can recognize."

For the next twenty minutes, the girls pointed at and identified the many landmarks they had only seen in atlases and in pictures or videos. They had to orient themselves and their thinking; since inverted relative to the earth and heading east, north was to their right instead of its normal position on their left.

Sedona noticed immediately as Shara reduced thrust and pulled STSX's nose toward the globe in the beginnings of their descent, and they watched closely as she manipulated the controls and how STSX responded.

As they approached the upper edges of the atmosphere, Shara rolled STSX to his normal attitude and slowed to keep their speed within limits. Over the Florida panhandle, Shara dropped STSX to a lower altitude and drifted toward a city growing ahead.

"That's Gainesville, Florida straight ahead," Shara said, and pointed. "Grandma's place is just past it and to the south."

A few minutes later, STSX stopped in a low hover over the wide backyard of a large patio home. Shara locked STSX's controls and swiveled the pilot's chair to aft facing.

"Okay, girls," she said as she stood up. "Let's go and get your grandma and grandpa boarded."

The girls were down the ladder in a heartbeat, and Shara hurried to keep up. They stopped in the open aft portal and tenuously leaned out to look down, seeing their dad on the patio behind the house talking to his mom.

"Safety straps on," Shara said, and pulled a strap from the sides of the portal and snapped one on Sedona's utility belt and the other on Sierra's. "If you slip, these will catch you and you can climb back up and inside. You know how to do that."

"Yes, Mom," they said together.

"Dad will send their cases up and you two can put them in the equipment bay," Shara explained again, "and Dad and I will bring them up. Ready?"

"Sure," Sedona said.

⋏

"Hurry up, Brendan," Coleen said as she rolled her suitcase out onto their back patio. "Shara says they're here."

When she turned back to face the backyard, Greg stepped out of STSX's veil and greeted her with a hug. "Hey, Mom," he said, and grabbed the suitcase. "Is this all you've got?"

"Yes," she said. "Brendan has one too." She turned back to the door. "Come on, dear."

Brendan pulled his case through the door and then stopped and locked the door.

"Hey, Brendan," Greg said, and gave him a quick hug. "Let me get that. Seven, down here."

Slowly, a single stirrup slipped out of Seven's veil and Greg tied the luggage handles to it.

"Take these up to Sedona and Sierra," Greg said as Shara stepped out of the veil and hugged them both. "Brendan, you can ride with me, and Mom, you ride with Shara."

Brendan stepped through the veil and mounted the remote with Greg, and they watched as Coleen joined Shara on hers.

"Did I hear you say the children are with you?" Coleen asked as they started up, following Greg and Brendan.

"Yes, they are," Shara said, and watched Brendan step onto STSX's partially extended ramp and then step inside. Greg released the remote and stepped inside to make room for Shara as they drifted up to the ramp. Coleen hurried through the open portal and Shara followed her inside.

"Grandma! Grandpa!" the girls shouted in unison, and hugged Coleen before she could get farther than the equipment bay. Then they hugged Brendan.

85

"Just look at you two," Coleen said. "All dressed up in your own flight suits. You must fly a lot with your mom and dad."

"A little," Sedona said.

"But today was our first time in space," Sierra added.

"My, my," Coleen said. "I hope it was as thrilling for you as it was for me."

They nodded vigorously and pulled Coleen and Brendan further into the main aisle.

"Okay, you two," Greg said, and gently moved them to the cushion chairs. "You can visit here for a few minutes if you want, but we need to get going. Grandpa Henry is waiting for us also."

"Can we still come up and watch?" Sierra asked, suddenly torn between visiting and riding in the cockpit.

"Mom?" Greg asked, and turned to Coleen. "Can you climb the ladder up to the flight deck?"

"I think so," she said, and smiled at the girls.

"Okay, girls," Greg said as Shara moved through the crowded aisle. "Take your grandma and grandpa up to the flight deck. Brendan and I will stand behind the jump seats and grandma can use the instructor's seat."

Quickly, the girls helped Coleen up and led her to the ladder; Sedona scurried up first and held a hand to help Coleen as she reached the top. Sierra was immediately behind her.

Brendan came next and Sedona had him stand behind Sierra's jump seat, and then she slipped into the left jump seat as Greg led Coleen into the cockpit, lowered the instructor's seat, and locked it into place. When he had her strapped in and checked the girls, he took his place behind Sedona.

"We're secure, Casi," he said, and Shara turned to the switches on the armrests.

"Ignition Ready. System status," she said.

"IGNITION IN FIVE SECONDS, CLOAKING STILL ON, SHIELDS ON, ALL SYSTEMS GREEN. PASSIVE SCAN IS CLEAR."

"Hover at two hundred feet, please," Shara said, and STSX responded, lifting them as requested.

The indicators on the panel changed to green, and Shara eased the thrust levers forward and pulled STSX's nose up and away from the patio home.

▲ ▲ ▲ ▲ ▲

When weightlessness interrupted Sedona and Sierra's conversation with their grandparents, Sierra turned and looked over the cockpit sill and then at the position of the sun.

"Mom," she said. "Why are we over water? Antelope Springs and home are back the other way."

Sedona quickly looked over the sill on her side to confirm Sierra's observation.

"They're this way too," Casi said, and smiled. "Honestly, I thought you two would be more adventurous, more curious and eager to see all you can see on your first trip around the world."

Casi rolled STSX inverted, again to soar beneath the planet as they approached the west coast of Africa. Sedona and Sierra pointed out seas, islands, countries, deserts, and notable landmarks for Coleen and Brendan, and Stran smiled at their enthusiasm.

"Greg?" Coleen asked. "When did the girls start *hearing*?"

"Started in June," he said. "We didn't realize how much their talent had matured until Labor Day. They started asking all sorts of questions, and Casi confirmed they could receive a direct question and could reply empathically. Since then, along with Cheyenne and Tayn, they have blossomed, *hearing* and *feeling* people and objects. After the attacks on the two ranches, we've started the four of them in physical, strength, self-defense, and recently, in nav and com training."

"Have there been any other attacks?" Brendan asked.

"No," Stran said, and shook his head. "We've only sensed Nikle in the valley a couple of times since. Before the attacks, after we found out they were *hearing*, we had STSX tell the four of them our history and explain who we are and why we're here, then we gave them their flight suits and started getting them ready for Registration."

"Aah, yes." Coleen smiled. "That is coming rather soon, isn't it?"

Stran nodded and turned his attention to the back of Casi's chair when Casi queried STSX.

'STSX, contact Kiile and find out when they last checked on the Indian Ocean facility,' Casi said. *'I'm sensing functioning power systems. Ask him what operations he's conducting.'*

Stran glanced to their left and felt for the facility.

'Maybe we ought to drift over that way,' Stran said privately, *'and show the girls some of Australia before we cross the Pacific.'*

With the barest of a nod, Casi altered their course so they would cross over Somalia and go directly to Australia, with a slight southerly jog to pass over the captured launch facility, a thousand and sixty miles west of Perth. They were just off the east coast of Somalia when STSX repeated Kiile's answer.

'CAPTAIN KIILE REPLIES HE HAS NO OPERATIONS ACTIVE AT THE LAUNCH FACILITY. THE FACILITY WAS UNMANNED, UNPOWERED, AND SECURED WHEN THEY VISITED AND CONDUCTED SYSTEM CHECKS FOUR MONTHS AGO ON JULY 10.'

Casi turned and looked at Stran, deep lines of concern evident on her face. *'Doesn't Kiile have a remote stationed there?'*

A long moment passed and then STSX said, *'CAPTAIN KIILE REPLIES THE NEED FOR A FULL-TIME REMOTE WAS RESCINDED SIX YEARS AGO AND REPLACED WITH SIX-MONTH RECURRING VISITS.'*

'Tell Captain Kiile he needs to get a force together and investigate immediately. I think the previous tenants may have returned.'

"Mom, Dad?" Sedona asked, feeling the sudden tension. "What's wrong?"

Casi looked at Sedona and then at Stran. He nodded and Casi sighed.

"Okay, girls," Casi began. "Can you see the image in my mind?" Casi focused on the spot in the ocean ahead of them and just beyond the arc of the planet.

"Yes," Sierra said.

"What does it look like to you?" Casi asked.

"Like an island under a bowl, a domed cover of some kind," Sedona said, wrinkling her mouth and nose like Cheyenne did when she was trying to do something difficult.

"I see people in the island," Sierra added. "Thirty-five men and one woman. There's a submersible under the island, between a series of legs that reach waaaay down to the ocean floor."

"Is that a problem, Mom?" Sedona asked, *sensing* the concern showing on her face.

"It is, when no one is supposed to be there," Casi said, and pulled STSX's nose toward the planet.

"It isn't a real island at all. It's man-made," Sierra said softly.

"How are you two doing back there, Coleen, Brendan?" Casi asked.

"We're okay," Coleen said. "Just a little puzzled. Is this something to do with your work?"

"Yes," Stran said heavily.

"CAPTAIN KIILE," STSX said out loud, "SAYS TWO TRANSPORTS WITH THIRTY MARINES EACH, THREE QSHIPS, AND THREE PATROL FIGHTERS ARE EN ROUTE TO INVESTIGATE. ETA TWENTY MINUTES FROM THE NORTHWEST."

'Where are you going?' Stran asked when they began to skim the upper reaches of the atmosphere.

'To take a closer look,' Casi said, and rolled STSX back to a normal attitude. *'Kiile might need another ship for backup.'*

'Bren!' Stran said sharply. *'Be Casi! Stop! Remember you have civilians on board. You are not in a position to engage in combat. Leave it for Kiile.'*

Both girls and Coleen had turned to look at Stran's stern

expression, and the girls heard his words. They felt Casi abort STSX's descent.

'Bren,' Stran continued privately in a softer tone. *'You've alerted our troops to the threat, and they have immediately responded. Like they should. Let Kiile do his job. We can listen while we look around the west coast of Australia for anything else we can sense that shouldn't be there.'*

Casi's shoulders sagged a little. *'Okay, love. I know you're right.'*

'Kiile will give his commanders a report when he gets back to the Ranch.' Stran turned his attention to the girls. "Can either of you two feel something *different* about the men in the facility?"

"Yes," the girls said in unison.

"But we don't know what it is," Sierra said.

"I don't know how to explain it," Stran said, "but it's like the feeling you got when you heard Mr. Nikle and the men that attacked our ranch and Aunt Jill and Uncle Nick's place."

"Yeah, it is," they said together.

"Now we're going to *listen* for that feeling wherever we go," Stran said, and smiled.

"CAPTAIN KIILE ASKS," STSX said out loud, "IF YOU KNOW HOW MANY ARE IN THE SUBMERSIBLE VEHICLE?"

"Two," Sedona and Sierra said together.

Casi smiled. "STSX, please tell Kiile we sense two persons in the submersible."

Casi guided them on and conversation fell silent. They felt the facility and Kiile's position as he got closer.

"Kiile's five minutes out," Casi said softly as they passed over the invisible spot in the ocean where the launch facility lay under its veil.

STSX was somewhere between the facility and Australia's west coast when Kiile dropped two underwater teams and then maneuvered his transports through the cloaking veil and into the open launch portal. Both Casi and Stran felt the sudden confusion in the facility and glanced at the girls in their jump seats. They knew the girls were hearing it too.

"Mom," Sierra said suddenly. "There are two ships of some kind powering up someplace farther east, ahead of us. They have that same 'different' feeling."

"They feel about as big as Cousin Cheral's fighter, but different," Sedona added.

"Thank you. I *see* them too," Casi admitted, and smiled again. "You two are getting pretty good at seeing things. They are still on land in Australia, somewhere around the gold mines in the western Gibson Desert." Then Casi focused her senses on the presences. "STSX, please tell Kiile there are two fighters powering up—"

"One's moving, Mom," the girls said in unison. "Coming this way."

"One of them," Casi continued, without hesitating, "is lifting off and coming their way. Size comparable with our Class Two patrol fighters."

Coleen stared at her granddaughters for a long moment and slowly smiled. She did not want to interrupt, but was very surprised at their obvious ability and self-control in the face of the realities of the moment.

"Grandma?" Sierra asked when she turned to look at Coleen. "Can you *see* them too?"

Coleen smiled and slowly shook her head. "No, dear, I didn't get that blessing. But I am very glad all four of you have."

"The last fighter and one person," Stran said, "probably its pilot, seem to be waiting for the first to report back."

"Are these the last of their planet-side fighters?" Casi asked as she guided STSX closer to the coast.

"Intelligence thinks they lost their last freighter when Wally freed the captives at the Farmstead twelve years ago," Stran confirmed. "And the latest info we received indicated they still had a way to take captives from the planet surface to a waiting transport. These may be all that's left, or they may have other ships scattered and well hidden."

"We could go looking for them," Sedona said with a wide smile.

"Yes, dear," Casi said. "We could, but we'll know if they come out of hiding and fly."

"And unless they fly," Stran said, "we don't need to know where they are."

"Why not, Dad?" Sierra asked, and looked at him, puzzled. "I thought you wanted to stop them."

"I do, dear," he admitted, "but if they leave the planet, I want to get the transport so we can find out where it is supposed to go." His expression saddened a little. "My dilemma is that unless I can find a better way, I have to let a few people get captured so I can find out. I don't like that, but the Force needs to know what the slavers are going to do, now that they have a new prince in the picture."

"Okay, girls," Casi said, changing the subject. "Kiile says he has things under control, so let's see what other sights Australia has to offer."

▲ ▲ ▲ ▲ ▲

"Seventeen, Thirty-six," Kiile shouted as he stepped into the cargo bay of the transport. "Two underwater teams, on the double. At the left-side hatch."

There was a scurry of activity as Seventeen and Thirty-six disappeared into the throng of troopers. Four men in wetsuits and air tanks emerged and stopped beside the hatch.

"Thirty feet, half mile east of the cloaked facility," a voice said over the internal address system. "Fifteen-foot swells and winds out of the southwest."

"Disable the submersible," Kiile said as he approached Seventeen, Thirty-six, and the divers. "Rig the coupling so it cannot disconnect and neutralize all thrusters. Two remotes will provide top cover and recovery once the facility is secure."

Seventeen swung the hatch open and counted down. On his mark, the first diver stepped out and disappeared from sight;

the rest followed in quick succession. Seventeen acknowledged their wave and swung the hatch closed.

The transport rose up and Kiile readied his men. The second transport reported ready and fighters ready.

Kiile turned to the nav officer. "Shields?"

"No shields," he replied from the cockpit at the forward end of the short corridor. "Cloaked and the portal is open, possibly expecting an incoming vessel."

"Any incoming lit up?" Kiile asked.

"Negative. No response to any of the codes," the nav officer said.

"Okay. Both transports together," Kiile said. "Let's pay them a visit."

▲

Suddenly, completely unexpected, the two transports pushed through the veils from opposite sides, coalescing their impressive bulk as they crossed the open lip and settled quickly onto the bay floor. Marines poured out of the transport's opposing side hatches and rear portals, quickly filling the bay and charging into the various passages and hatches. They followed the confused cries from the startled workers and sentries.

The brief sounds of weapons fire drifted back into the bay from places around the perimeter, and Kiile touched his earpiece when his nav officer confirmed the approach of a single fighter from the east.

"Alert the fighter escorts," Kiile said, and glanced up, knowing they were cloaked above them. He turned back to the engagement at hand. "Thirty-six, status."

"South and east sides are being secured. Last cluster of four barricaded in the security billeting area have succumbed to the sleep gas canisters. Three have gone down to invite the submersible crew to join us."

Kiile smiled. "Seventeen?"

"Neutralized seven that were guarding a group of twelve captives," Seventeen replied. "Captured six more. We're bringing them up on the west side."

Kiile tapped his earpiece in acknowledgement, then heard his nav officer update the approaching fighter's position, slowing ten miles out."

"Withdraw the transports, cloaked, and let the fighter land," Kiile said. "Once he's inside, reposition above the portal and drop your veils." Then he refocused. "Forty-two, I need ten veiled troopers in the launch bay to greet our incoming."

Kiile turned at the sound of running boots, and watched the perimeter as the transports shimmered into the background and lifted out of the way. He waited as the nav officer gave position information in closely spaced intervals. Finally, the fighter slipped inside the facility's veil and dropped its own cloaking. It settled softly to one side of the launch bay, and after a moment the side hatch swung open and the pilot dropped to the floor. When he stepped forward, away from the fighter, Kiile's marines closed in around him and unveiled.

He saw the uniforms, grabbed his belt weapon, and instantly a stunning blast from three marines hit him. The pilot withered and fell in the center of the ring of troopers.

"Bring the transports back in," Kiile said, and tapped his earpiece. "Contact the commander. Inspection is complete. We'll debrief at headquarters at sixteen hundred hours, headquarter time."

⋏ ⋏ ⋏ ⋏ ⋏

Greg and Shara and the girls were just heading back to the main house from a casual tour of the arenas and the barns, showing Henry some of the improvements Shara had made to help her students, when STSX announced Kiile's transport was landing in the meadow just west of the two Q-Ships.

"I really think the girls enjoy these holiday gatherings," Shara said as the girls hollered a welcome and broke into a run around the stable toward the field where Kiile and Cheral's ships were landing.

"I can see that," Coleen said, and chuckled as they watched them streak around the pens and disappear.

Henry laughed softly. "They do seem happy when their extended family shows up."

"Why don't you three go on inside," Greg said, "and Shara and I will go and greet Kiile. We need to get his report on today's engagement, then we'll be right in."

"Sure," Brendan said, and took Coleen's hand and led her toward the house.

Henry fell in step behind them as Greg led Shara after the girls.

⚊ ⚊ ⚊ ⚊

"Afternoon, Kiile," Greg said, and extended his arm as Kiile jumped out of the transport's side hatch and Cheral approached from her parked fighter.

"Commander, Captain," he said formally, and took Greg's hand.

Cheral went straight to Shara and caught her in a hug. "Afternoon, Cousin," she said, and then caught Greg's extended hand. "Greg."

"Let's get in where it's warm," Shara said, and turned toward the main house. "Can you stay for dinner? Greg's mom, Brendan, and my dad are here."

Kiile looked at Cheral's nod and said they could.

"Matti," Shara called as Greg pushed the heavy back door open and guided her in. Shara crossed the dining room just as Matti opened the kitchen door. "Hey, Matti. Will you set two more places for dinner tonight? Kiile and Cheral are going to join us."

"Certainly, Mrs. Shara," Matti said, and then greeted them. "We can always make room for Mr. Kiile and Ms. Cheral. Can I get you anything to drink?"

"Not for me," Cheral said with a feigned pout. "I'm flying back tonight."

"Nothing for me either, Matti," Kiile said as he followed

Cheral into the formal part of the living room.

Greg took Shara's coat and hung it in the coat room as Shara followed them to the living room. Coleen and Brendan had settled on the loveseat and Henry on the sofa near the fire in the casual living room. As she sat down on the loveseat in the formal portion of the living room near the front windows with Greg beside her, Shara saw the girls come out of the hallway and hurry around to visit with their grandparents.

Cheral sat down on the other loveseat, and Kiile took a chair near her. Shara tried to hide her surprise that he had not sat next to Cheral.

"Okay, Kiile," Greg said softly. "STSX said your engagement lasted less than twenty minutes. What do you have to report?"

Kiile first explained that Cheral had already briefed Colonel Kooich at Obscure and then settled into a description of his approach and, based on Shara's information that there were only two in the submersible, his plan to disable the vessel before he surprised the entire facility. He described Thirty-six's squad and how quickly they overpowered the resistance, putting the last four to sleep with a non-lethal canister. He further described Seventeen's discovery of twelve captives—eleven men and one misused woman. They neutralized seven of the men guarding the captives, explaining that Seventeen's men were a little upset over their inappropriate handling of the woman. The six guards they took into custody seemed extremely penitent. He explained they had accounted for the twenty-three slavers and the twelve they were holding.

'Twenty-four,' Sedona's voice said in Shara, Greg, and Cheral's minds. 'They missed one hiding in the wave generator control room closet. Marine Nineteen just discovered him.'

Shara and Greg looked up and Cheral turned to look, but Sedona was in a quiet conversation with Coleen and Henry. Shara looked at Cheral and then told Kiile what Sedona had said.

"They told us there were twenty-four of the *different* people there when we were leaving Somalia," Shara said, covering her mouth to speak softly. "I guess you left a small contingency of troops there when you left."

"Yes," Kiile said, pondering what they were telling him. "I was just going to mention that."

"You should ask Nineteen whether the last man is able to give you any useful information," Greg said, and caught Shara's hand.

Quietly, shaking off his surprise at the news as quickly as he could, Kiile tapped his earpiece and sent an inquiry. His expression went pale as he received a reply. He looked at Shara and then at Greg. "The girls?"

Shara nodded slowly. "They're *hearing* and *sensing* more and more every day. And not just the Force."

"They're *hearing* almost anyone that broadcasts," Greg said with a smug smile. "We have our hands full trying to teach them when it's okay and when it isn't okay to *listen* to people."

"What about Tayn and Cheyenne?" Cheral asked.

"The same," Shara said, and smiled.

Cheral and Kiile just smiled.

"Okay," Greg said, and leaned back in his seat. "I think we've got the picture. How about some non-alcoholic refreshments and we join the rest of the family?"

Greg and Kiile got up and went to the kitchen where Greg asked Matti to get Kiile whatever he wanted. Cheral was slow to get up, and Shara caught her attention and she sat back down.

⬥

"Is something wrong, Cheral?" Shara asked as she sat beside her. "You seem guarded—sad."

Cheral let her shoulders drop. "I don't know, Shar. For the last few months, Kiile's been very distant. I know work's been almost boring over the last few years, and being a decorated combat veteran, I know he feels he should be doing more."

"But he can request a different assignment if he wants—"

"He won't," Cheral said. "He is committed to supporting the commander. They've supported each other since they were cadets together. You know that."

"Yes. Greg and I'll think on this and see if there's something we can do to help," Shara said, but she knew there was more. "All right, cuz. What's this mean between the two of you?"

"You know, two months ago," Cheral said, "I got word from the director to report to Headquarters in the Rings this coming week."

Shara nodded. "Greg said you're getting a permanent ship assignment. Is that a problem?"

"Not in itself," Cheral said, "but I'm to be assigned a Q-Ship."

Shara's face burst into a bright, wide smile. "Greg hadn't told me that. That's wonderful."

"Yes, it is," Cheral smiled. "But..."

"But?"

"Yeah, but," Cheral said, and looked at the floor. "With a Q-Ship, I suspect I will be assigned a nav-com, and that seems to upset Kiile. He hasn't said so in so many words, but he's certainly not happy that I'm getting a Q-Ship." Cheral sighed. "It isn't like he would ever be a crew member on a ship of mine, but suddenly it's like he doesn't want me to advance. And that has come between us.

"And on top of all of that, I've waited over twelve years for that man to propose and ask me for a mating. He always acted like that was going to happen, until this assignment came up. Now I can hardly get the time of day from him. I was actually surprised he was okay with me in the escort today."

"I wish I had good advice," Shara said.

"Thanks, cousin," Cheral said, and forced a smile. "You know as well as anyone, I have to go, and I'll just have to see how things are when I get back. I'm assuming I'll get back before I have to go somewhere else."

"When are you leaving?" Shara asked.

"First thing in the morning," Cheral said as she stood up with Shara. "Pti and Lori volunteered to take me on KCMM9."

"I'm sure it'll be a good trip," Shara said, and led her to the dining room. "We'll be listening. Now, how about a tea to soothe your concerns?"

One-Fourteen

"Will you pass the roast, Dad?" Blaire Lupis said as she sipped her hot tea and set her fork down.

"Sure," Dan said, and passed the platter to Mandy and she passed it on. "How was your day?" He smiled, pleased with how pretty his redheaded daughter had turned out.

"Pretty normal," Blaire said. "Went out to ride with Carole this morning, had a sandwich with Sam for lunch, and then went to the library."

"How's Sam?" Mandy asked. "We haven't seen him in a while. Is he doing okay?"

"Yes. He's still mad at me. You remember he's out helping Marty Davis, doing his part-time thing through the summer and fall," Blaire said, and poured a little more gravy on her meat. "Now he says he's thinking about finding other work, blaming it on the weather getting colder. He said he talked to Gary Woods about an opening they have in the offices at the mill."

"Yes, I remember. I thought he was happy at the Davis'," Dan said, and glanced at Blaire.

"I thought he was, too—mostly," Blaire admitted. "I don't know why he feels he needs to change. I honestly don't."

Suddenly, a sense of dread washed over Blaire and she quickly glanced around the room. It was unchanged, and her parents obviously had not noticed anything, or felt anything. Her gaze stopped at the kitchen and the back door, knowing the threatening feeling came from outside. But slowly she realized it came from farther away, and it abated as she wondered. Her shoulders twitched and a shudder ran down her back. She knew she'd felt it before, but could not remember exactly when.

"I'm sure he'll tell you," Mandy said without noticing her daughter's questioning looks, and buttered another roll, "when he decides what he wants to do and probably why. He's always been good about telling you how he feels about things."

"Maybe," she said absently, and returned her attention to the slice of roast and the last of her potatoes.

She was not sure Sam was telling her everything he was feeling anymore. Something had changed in the last couple of months, more than him still being angry with her. She remembered meeting Sam at a dinner with her mom and dad when she was much younger, and he had become the older, doting friend she felt she had grown up with. It was not long after she and her mother had moved to Riggin, but she could not remember the details of the evening, other than it was the first time she had felt the warmth and happiness she always imagined a close family would have.

"Mom?" she asked as she finished her food and wiped the plate with the last of her dinner roll. "Where was that big dinner we went to right after we moved here?"

Mandy looked up with a puzzled expression. "The first big dinner was Christmas dinner at the Davis'. You met Carrie Anne there."

"Ah yes," Blaire said, "I remember. I was what? Seven?"

"Yes, dear," Mandy agreed. "We arrived here early in Christmas week, and Wally brought Carole by on her way to work the day we unloaded."

"Whose house were we at the night I met Sam?" she continued.

"That was a month later at Thom and Eddie's house," Mandy said, and smiled softly to herself. "Well, it was Thom's house at the time, but I think that was also the night Eddie accepted Thom's proposal and a few days before Wally and Carole's wedding."

Blaire thought a moment and stacked her dishes. "I remember it was a wonderful and happy evening," she said, and reached for her mother's dishes. "But I don't think I've ever heard why Sam was there. Do you know?"

Mandy hesitated and glanced at Dan. Blaire noticed.

"Wally brought Sam and Glory back to their folks," Mandy said slowly.

"Where were they?" Blaire asked, and watched her mother's sudden reluctance.

"I guess you were too young to really remember," Mandy said with a sigh.

"Wally took Ted and a number of their allies," Dan said, "down to a place east of Grants where the last of the Family Elders held a number of people they had captured and collected. They—"

"Captured? Collected?" Blaire interrupted, and stared at her dad. "Like the stories of slavers you used to mention once in a while?"

"Yes," Dan said. "Thad and Betti asked Wally for some help to find their kids, and Wally agreed to try. They came north to Betti's sister's place but had to leave without Sam and Glory. Hasn't either of them talked about those days?"

"No," Blaire said, "they haven't, and I guess I never thought to ask. I was so happy to be here, and I guess I just thought they were too."

Dan nodded. "I guess it was a lot of responsibility that landed on Sam's shoulders, trying to keep Glory safe when he didn't know what would happen next. And I'm not surprised that he might have pushed some of those memories aside to enjoy the eleven quiet years that have followed."

Blaire smiled a weak smile. "So, the dinner was the night they were rescued and brought back to Thad and Betti?"

"Yes," Mandy said in a happier tone. "It was one of those dinners that just seemed to turn into a party of sorts. Thom was up and around after that horrible man, Police Chief Parks from Hawthorne, shot him, and Sam and Glory were back with their folks, and Carole and Eddie fixed dinner for everyone. After dinner, you, Glory, and Sam played board games on the family room floor while the adults sat around and visited. I think that was the night you caught Sam's attention."

Blaire blushed and she quickly picked up the stack of dishes and took them to the kitchen.

"Didn't you see them a lot after that?" Mandy asked as she collected the glasses.

"Yeah," Blaire admitted, her face still feeling warm. "Glory and I would wait for Sam to get out of his last class and then they would walk me home after school almost every day on their way to their aunt's house."

Blaire began rinsing the dishes and Mandy joined her in the kitchen.

"I talked to Wally yesterday," Blaire said as Dan brought the platters and bowls. "He said I'm old enough to apply with the State."

"Apply?" Dan asked sharply and stopped to look at her.

"I thought we discussed this and—"

"And I said I'd think about it," Dan said, and went into the living room.

Blaire watched him for a moment and then sighed and let the moment pass. She saw her mom watching the two of them. "Have you heard anything more about the attacks on the Malone and the Jordan places?"

"No," he said after a long moment of silence. "No leads. Wally said his friends went looking, but they didn't find anything more. At least Wally hasn't mentioned anything if they did."

"Is one of the friends the fellow they call Kyle?" Blaire asked.

"Kiile," Dan said. "Yes, he's one of his friends. You've met him a few times."

"Yeah. I figured he was one of those that helped," Blaire said, set the last of the plates and flatware in the dishwasher, and turned to rinsing the platters and bowls.

⟁

The evening had passed slowly, almost lethargically, Blaire thought as she dressed for bed. She had tried to talk to her dad, but it had simmered down into another evening of meaningless talk on irrelevant subjects. She had discussed more cooking with her mom and had half expected, actually hoped, Sam would stop by at some point. Then she quickly reprimanded herself; their relationship was still very fragile after what she'd done, and a little more than strange, with him being six years older. She had to admit she had taken to his sister Glory first, since she was only two years older, but when Glory had started high school and embraced all of its demands and new opportunities, her time for a younger friend had quickly evaporated.

Sam quietly remained in the background from the first time they met, always dropping off gifts on her birthdays and Valentine's Days, always pleasant to her when they met or passed each other on the streets. She smiled, knowing her mom had noticed his presence and polite conduct early on, but Blaire was ashamed of herself. She knew she had blindly accepted him as the older brother she never had, the friend she could always count on, the boy next door that was always around. She never gave it a thought as to why he acted the way he did toward her.

When he had graduated from college, she was halfway through her sixteenth year and eager to taste and feel all that was new in the life of a teenager. Then in mid-May, Sam had asked her mom and dad if he could take her to the graduation party the evening after his graduation ceremony. For a long time after that, she could only remember her anger and the disappointment of them saying no, feeling it was inappropriate for a girl her age to attend such a party. Blaire had flown into a rage and pouted and sulked for most of a week.

When the graduation came and her parents went and supported Thad, Betti, and Glory in the first college graduation by anyone in their family, she had refused to attend the ceremonies. It was much later in the summer when Glory told her how much it had hurt her brother's feelings that she did not come to the ceremonies. That was the slap in the face that woke her up. She suddenly saw how she had only been thinking of herself, never before considering how her actions were affecting those around her, never before thinking about Sam's reaction, never before thinking about why he had asked her parents if she could go with him.

In the two years that followed, Blaire tried to make amends, though her attempts seemed to be futile at best. She focused on what others needed and how she could help, to give her life some meaning beyond those of instant gratification normally attributed to recent high school graduates. And no matter how hard she tried, she knew the town still saw her as Dan and Mandy's spoiled, ungrateful, self-absorbed daughter.

Thinking about her dad and the deputies she was associated with on a daily basis, she slowly decided what she wanted to do with her life was to become a law enforcement officer, maybe even a special state deputy. But she was completely unprepared and again surprised and disappointed when her dad opposed her decision—a decision that also seemed to sit crossways with Sam.

As she set on the edge of her bed and brushed her hair, her mom's voice gently filled her thoughts.

'But it's what she wants to do. How can it be so terrible?'

'It isn't terrible, Mandy,' her dad replied in a defeated tone. *'It's a matter of time.'*

'The trouble? Is it really starting again?'

'It certainly looks like it,' Dan said. *'The attacks on the Jordan place and the Malone place were for one purpose and one purpose only. Ted, Thom, and I came here to get things back under control after Shara and Jill narrowly escaped the slavers, and now they're targets again. Only now, Shara and Greg fear the children are also in danger.'*

'Which ones?'

'All of them. Sedona, Sierra, Cheyenne, Kayli, Kail, Billie, Alyssa, Ridan, and maybe Blaire and even Glory.'

'All of them?' Concern deeply colored Mandy's tone. *'And he thinks Blaire and Glory?'*

'Unfortunately. They're old enough to bear children.' Dan's tone was full of concern and worry. *'Wally says Greg has started some kind of self-defense training for the older children after the attacks, but he's afraid he waited too long to think about Blaire*

and Glory.'

'*He thinks something is about to happen? Another attack?'*

'*Yes. Kiile rescued twelve captives this morning and captured their twenty-four captors. WL-One passed the information along to us just before dinner.'*

There was a long pause before either said anything.

'*Talk to her, Dan,'* Mandy said. '*She knows something is going on and she wants to learn how to help.'*

'*There's no time, Mandy. We can't train her quickly enough. All we can do now is to try to protect her.'*

Sunday, November 19

"Do you two have Brickle and Strawberry saddled yet?" Greg asked as he helped Brendan with the buckskin.

"Yes, Dad," they answered together.

He looked out of the stall as Sedona led Brickle into the main aisle and Sierra followed.

"Please check your grandma's gear to be sure it's okay for the ride," he added as he unfolded the stirrup and handed Brendan the reins.

"We're on it," Sierra said as Greg turned into Dílis' stall and wiped him down.

When the horses were ready, Sedona led the string out into the yard between the stable and the main house. Shara stepped out onto the back porch and the girls waved. Greg gave Sierra Dílis' reins and angled across the yard to intercept Shara before she reached the three-rail fence and STSX waiting beyond.

He stopped her and kissed her fully, holding her longer than normal.

"Stay alert, Bren," he said softly. "I know you feel it too, something on the wind. I can't identify it yet." He kissed her again.

"I will, Greg," she said with a smile. "You and the girls have a good ride with Coleen and Brendan and we'll be back before you know it."

He smiled and hugged her and then let her go. "Let me know if you have any trouble."

"Who else?" she asked, and then turned to STSX. "Power up, STSX. Let's go and collect our passengers."

▲

Sedona and Sierra looked at each other as their dad hurried across the yard to catch their mom before she left. They listened to the tone of their feelings and glanced from each other to their parents and back again.

'It has to be that feeling we had last night,' Sierra said. *'They're both guarded and concerned.'*

'Could it just be because they are going to be apart?' Coleen asked the girls, hearing their comments.

'No, Grandma. It's more than that,' Sedona said.

'There! They said it!' Sierra said suddenly. *'There's something up. Something serious.'*

'What do you mean, girls?' Coleen asked. *'What did they say?'*

The girls turned and looked at Coleen. *'They have a phrase they say to each other when they are split up and going into trouble. They've used it since just before they attacked and captured Obscure, almost a year before we were born.'*

'How do you know when they started using it if you weren't born?' Coleen asked, confused.

'Dad and STSX told us when we heard them using it,' Sierra said.

'And we asked about it,' Sedona finished. *'They do it without thinking when something serious is about to happen.'*

'We've heard them use it a couple of times since Labor Day,' Sierra said with a sigh.

▲

"Ready, girls?" Greg asked happily as he walked back to the group and took Dílis' reins.

"Yup," they said together and quickly jumped up, each

106

slipping her foot into the stirrup and swinging her other leg over the saddle.

Coleen and Brendan took a moment longer to get up and situated, and when they were ready, Greg swung up onto Dílis' back and started slowly toward the gate to the west pastures.

"I don't know how you girls can get mounted so quickly," Coleen said, smiling hugely at them. "You can't even see over Brickle or Strawberry."

They watched and waved at Shara as STSX slowly lifted from the pasture beyond the fence and disappeared behind his veil.

"Dad?" Sierra asked, and Greg turned to listen to her. "When we went to bring Grandma and Grandpa out, you started calling Mom by her 'C' name, Casi. Why did you do that instead of using her 'S' name, Shara, or her nickname, like usual?"

"Well, actually," he said, "we're always supposed to use our registered names, ranks, and IDs when were on a mission or flying. The people in the Force don't know us by our Terran names or by our Terran IDs."

"So, when we fly on STSX," Sedona continued, "should we be using our 'C' names?"

"We probably should just to get in the habit," Greg said with a smile. "But officially, you two aren't registered yet." He chuckled. "Actually, you're already cadets and I hope you will be pilots before you're registered. That is certain to cause some ripples in the Rings."

"Will that be a problem?" Coleen asked.

"Only for some, Mom," Greg said. "I'm trusting the director will understand our need like he has in the past, but it will be unusual to say the least."

The girls looked at him and smiled, feeling the happy, mischievous rascal in his tone.

"Shara and STSX should only be gone about an hour," Greg said for Coleen and Brendan's sake. "If we pick up the pace, we can make it out to the rock outcropping on the first ridge and have a few minutes there before they start back with Jim, Shelly, and Carrie Anne."

"We're ready, Dad," the girls said in unison.

"We'll try to keep up, son," Coleen said. "Let's go."

▲ ▲ ▲ ▲ ▲

"Where are we going?" Shelly asked as her dad drove past the drive to his place and continued heading east on the country road.

"Just a little farther," Marty said as he slowed and turned into a newer drive leading north through the stand of pines. "Here we are. We're having Thanksgiving at Carole and Wally's this year and we're going to stop there first. They have offered rooms for you if you want to stay at their place, or you can stay with us in your old rooms."

"They've finished the house?" Carrie Anne asked.

Shelly and Carrie opened their windows and watched ahead as Marty followed the slowly winding road into the open pasture and the large log-and-stone house came into view.

"Breathtaking, isn't it?" Marty asked rhetorically.

As he swung around in the circle drive situated to the right end of the wide house, he stopped under the portico.

"They made the main entrance on the garage and kitchen end of the house, so they could keep the view from the living and dining room," Marty explained as he helped Shelly out.

Jim and Carrie got out quickly and stood beside the car, captivated by the broad, unobstructed southerly view across the valley.

"Wow" was all Shelly could say as she rounded the front of the car and followed her dad into the house. They walked up the corridor with three short flights of steps spaced along its length leading up to the living room and the large stone fireplace on the far wall.

"Hey, Shelly!" Carole shouted as she ran from the kitchen to greet them. She caught Shelly in a tight hug and then turned

108

and gave Carrie an equally enthusiastic greeting. "My, my. Just look at you. You are suddenly a right and proper young woman," she said, and hugged her again.

"Hey, Gramms," Carrie said when she saw Rusty following Carole from the kitchen. She hurried and greeted her with a hug.

"Oh, my. Carole is right," Rusty said, and she hugged Carrie. "You are looking very grown up." Then she turned and greeted Jim and Shelly with a hug and a peck on their cheeks. "Shara said you'd be here in plenty of time for lunch. How was your trip?"

"Wonderful as always," Shelly said.

"Even after all of these years of making trips out here with Shara," Carrie said, "the flight is incredible. Mom just told me the first time we flew out here, Jill was with us and Shara actually had an engagement with five enemy fighters."

"That's true, she did," Jim said with a smile. "Her first solo engagement. Greg and I were here working and heard her commentary as it happened."

"Wow," Carrie said softly, and walked over to the front windows and slowly started taking in the grandeur of the great room.

"I can't believe this place," Shelly said as she turned and surveyed the great room, a large living room facing the tall, three-story, fully windowed front wall, curved to capture the complete view from the west to the east. She noted the fireplace on the west wall and the dining room raised slightly behind the living room to protect its view as well. "And your rock outcropping," she said as she noticed the front of the living room encircled the flat rock where Carole and Wally were married, bringing it comfortably into the great room.

"Yes," Carole said with a huge smile. "We had to keep that. We spend a lot of time there with the kids, watching the changing view of the valley, the changing seasons, the sunsets."

"You've done it up very well," Jim said as he studied the other features of the great room. "And I assume the bedrooms are all in the west end of the house."

"They are," Carole said. "The master, the kids' rooms, and one guest room face south and have nice views of the valley. The other two guest rooms face north and have an equally impressive view of the northern rim mountains and the West Gate Post. You may have noticed, we got snow down to about nine thousand feet over the weekend. Nothing heavy, but a sign of things to come." She turned and gestured to the dining room. "Through the back doors, we can go straight to the stables, tack rooms, the feed barn, and the two practice arenas. We're still building the paddocks. Three are done and three to go."

"How many horses do you have now?" Shelly asked.

"We have six of our own and we're boarding and training six more," Carole said as she stepped up into the dining room and kitchen level. "Shara's given me a lot of help laying the place out and getting started."

"She doesn't mind the competition?" Carrie asked as she followed the group into the dining room.

"I guess we see each other as neighbors with similar interests," Carole said, and smiled. "Not as competitors. I hope Dad told you that we have room for you if you'd like to stay here." Carole led them to the hallway into the west wing. "I'll show you the guest rooms and the bedrooms, but if you wish to stay with Mom and Dad, that's fine with us, too."

When they returned to the living room, they settled into the comfortable chairs and sofas and a young woman came into the room and asked if they had any drink requests.

"Oh, sorry." Carole shook her head. "This is Niki. Our head house girl. She also helps me with the kids and cooking when she has time."

"Hello, Niki," Marty greeted, and gave her his choice. "I didn't know Wally let anyone else in his kitchen."

She smiled. "He usually isn't home when the cooking needs to be done." Then she turned to Shelly. "Your choice, ma'am?"

"It's just Shelly, Niki. I'm still family, I think," Shelly said, and gave Niki her request.

Niki took Jim, Carrie, Carole, and Rusty's requests and left for the kitchen.

"What's Wally up to?" Jim asked. "I thought he might still be taking Sundays off."

"Normally, he takes Sunday and Wednesdays off," Carole said, "like we did when we first got married. But this morning Thom called him into the office and I haven't heard from him since he left. Even WLOne has been quiet, which could mean nothing in particular."

⋏ ⋏ ⋏ ⋏ ⋏

"Are you sure Aunt Carole is okay with me staying here with you and Gramps?" Carrie asked when she saw Rusty in the hallway outside of her room.

"Sure she is," Rusty said, and checked the linens in the guest bath. "Besides, you know your way around here and you can ride Buster up to see them if you feel the need."

"Thanks," Carrie said, and hugged Rusty. "Can I wander around a bit?"

"Sure. You just make yourself at home, Carrie," Rusty said. "And let me know if you need anything."

"Thanks, Gramms," Carrie said, and followed the hallway into the living room.

She took the shortcut through the kitchen and crossed the yard to the stables.

⋏

"Hey. Look who's here," Carrie said when she entered the stable and Sam Reeds looked up from his mucking.

"Hey, Carrie," he said, and smiled as she walked down the main aisle and looked into the stalls. "Rusty said you and your folks were going to show up this weekend." He turned back to the stall he was cleaning.

"Got in just before noon," Carrie said. "Stopped up at Aunt Carole's for lunch and I came back to stay with Gramms."

"So your folks are stayin' up there?" he asked. "And I'll bet your mom and her sister will talk the night away."

"Probably," she said as she stopped at a locked stall and looked in. "A boarder?"

"Yeah. That's Morning Star," he said. "She's in cutting training. How's your dad? I missed seeing him the last time you were out."

"He's doing okay, I guess," Carrie said with a heavier tone. "He's up for reenlistment or retirement next summer."

"Wow. A big decision."

"Yeah. A really big one."

Sam stopped and looked at Carrie. She knew he had heard the change in her tone of voice.

"Is there a problem?" he asked.

"Only for me," she said, and turned to look at him as he stepped out and sat down on a hay bale. She walked over and sat down on the bale next to him.

"How's it a problem, Carrie?"

"I know it shouldn't be," she said softly, and leaned forward with her forearms on her knees. "If Dad re-ups, he'll probably be stuck in Lynchburg for another three or four years."

"Would that be bad?"

"I don't know why, but he seems nervous with that option," she said. "Even Mom seems nervous about staying there. But me, I'd just go on as normal, finish high school, and I'd be ready for college when he came up the next time."

"Okay, so it isn't a problem for you if he re-ups?"

She turned her head and looked sideways at him. "It isn't, except I don't know what they won't tell me. I don't know why Dad feels he should retire and move back here."

"I see. So, you don't want to leave your friends when you're about to begin high school."

"Yes," she said, "and no. When he first mentioned retiring, I was upset and I argued that I needed to stay there and finish school. I didn't want to move away from the only home I know, even if it is a government-supplied apartment on the eighth floor of an apartment building."

She suddenly smiled, remembering the many times Shara had come to pick them up and return them home, and they had climbed over that eighth-floor balcony rail to enter or leave her fighter. Seeing Sam's curious look and knowing that she could not talk about what she was thinking, she quickly recomposed her expression.

"The problem is that I like the valley," she admitted. "I always have and I've always wanted to live here, closer to Aunt Carole, Uncle Wally, Alyssa and Ridan, and Gramms and Gramps. I do have friends in Lynchburg, but they are all military and they come and go. If we stay there, there's no expectation that my friends will also stay or be there through high school. If they are, they could be gone within a year or less."

"So, you wouldn't mind moving back here and finishing school?"

"No," Carrie admitted, "and yes. I think moving won't fix whatever Dad is nervous about."

"Aah. I see you have a dilemma. You know you can be happy wherever you end up living, and the valley isn't such a bad place."

"I know," she said, and smiled at herself. "I wasn't born here like everyone else." She turned her head and looked at him again. "But my genes tell me this is home. You might not understand, since you were born here. In the valley, I mean."

"I was," Sam admitted proudly, "and I take your point. I was born down south, and in the years of fear and turmoil before I met Wally and Glory and I moved here to live with my aunt, I thought the north was a foreign land. But it isn't. I know we're still in the same valley and my genes also call it home, but they like the years we've spent in the north."

"Not quite the same, Sam," Carrie laughed. "I remember nothing of the years you remember from your life in the south. Just the many happy ones I've had with many visits back here."

"Okay, back to the subject," he said, and gave her shoulder a gentle squeeze. "Have you just asked your dad what's bothering him?"

"I don't think they know that I know something is bothering them." She looked at him again. "I've heard them talking about it, but I haven't heard enough to know what is specifically happening."

"Well," he said with an expressive sigh. "My humble opinion is that you should tell them you've heard them and that you know they are concerned about something. Ask them straight up what it is." He held her eyes for a moment. "Of course, they may not tell you and you'll be right where you are right now. But they might, and then you'll be one step ahead of where you are now."

"Yeah," she said, and stood up. "I guess I should." She started to look into another stall, but stopped and turned toward the house. "I'd better go. Gramms is looking for me."

▲

Sam watched her in surprise as she walked out of the stable, back toward the house, and wondered if she really knew Rusty was looking for her, or if she was just saying that for an excuse to leave.

Monday, November 20

Blaire finished her hour with Carole in the enclosed arena and asked if she could ride for a while before she returned Carole's horse to the stable.

"I've kept you away from your family too much already," Blaire admitted, nodding to Shelly sitting on a bleacher bench. "Thanks, though, for letting me practice."

"Go on, Blaire," Carole said, then smiled and shooed her toward the door. "Tell Sam hi for me. I'll see you when you get back."

Carole turned, caught Shelly's hand, and headed for the main house, leaving Blaire smiling in the middle of the arena.

▲

114

Blaire reined up in front of the closed stable door and worried for a moment that her arrival might not be welcome, but she quickly forced the notion aside and dismounted. She tied the reins to the post and put her shoulder into pushing the door open just enough for her to slip inside. When she closed the panel and turned, she saw Sam standing in the main aisle watching her, but he was not smiling.

"Hello, Sam," she forced herself to say pleasantly. "I was riding at Carole's and decided to drop down and say hey."

"Hi," he greeted coolly. "Long, cold ride just to say hello."

She slowly walked the aisle toward him. "I wish you weren't still mad at me, but I guess that's just the way it is. I don't know how to apologize more than I already have."

He waited and did not answer. When she stopped in front of him, she took a deep breath and looked him in the face.

"I wanted to talk to you again," she said, holding herself calm against a rising guilty desire to run away and hide, "about my wanting to apply to the state law enforcement academy."

"Why me?" he asked, without encouraging or questioning her motives. "You know you can do whatever you decide to do."

"Please, stop," she said, and took another deep breath. "I thought that out of everyone, you might understand. I know the trouble is starting again. I've heard Mom and Dad talking, and everything changed when the Jordan and Malone places were attacked after Labor Day. Ever since, Dad's been getting more and more concerned, and I want to be able to help somehow. And I can't do anything but be a burden if I don't learn how."

"Who said you were a burden?"

"You know very well that a helpless, self-centered girl is a burden when troubles begin."

He let his gaze drift down to the floor and she wished he was looking at her instead of away from her.

"You haven't always been self-centered, Blaire," he finally said. "But I can't tell you what to do."

"Yeah, I know," she said softly. "Dad won't endorse my application, so I'm going to submit it in the blind and see what happens."

"There's very little chance your application will even be read," he said, surprised, "without an endorsement or a letter of recommendation. You'll be—"

"I know." She turned and braced herself against a stall door. "But I have to learn how to help!"

"Help do what, Blaire?"

"To defend the kids against the slavers!" She spun and looked at him as if he should know. "Dad says they're back. Labor Day, the increasing number of prowlers, and the attacks. Even Wally's mentioned it around the office. It all points to one thing, and I can't just sit around and just wait, hoping to be protected! I need to help! I have to do something! Don't you feel that way?"

He stood and watched her, his expression almost blank. "So you think the slavers are active again?"

"Damn, Sam!" She stopped herself and just stared, forcing herself to calm down. "I thought you knew. You of all people! Damn!" Then half to herself and half out loud, she continued, "Your dad's the deputy down by Grants. I was sure you'd know what I'm going through and would understand. I really thought you'd understand. Damn! I've said too much to the 'wrong' person! Again!" She turned and stomped the length of the aisle floor back to the sliding door. "Damn!"

⅄

She had the panel pushed aside and was astride the horse before Sam could force himself to move, suddenly realizing how hard it had to be for her to come and ask him for his opinion and he had just blown it off. He felt he was the one letting her down this time.

By the time he reached the door, Blaire and the horse were gone.

⅄ ⅄ ⅄ ⅄ ⅄

Jim was reading the newspaper on the monitor in the

dining room when Niki led Bill Woods up the entry corridor and into the living room.

"Hey, Dad," Jim said as he stood up at their arrival.

They embraced, and Jim offered Bill a chair when Niki asked if he would like coffee. Bill nodded, and he sat down and looked around the great room.

"Impressive, isn't it?" Jim asked as he switched the monitor off.

"Yes," Bill said, and looked back to Jim. "I'm surprised at Carole's vision every time I come out here. So much more modern than our older homes, yet very traditional in its layout and construction. An inspiring blend of the two."

Niki stopped and set a cup in front of Bill and poured.

"And how is Niki this morning?" Bill asked as she set the carafe on the table and picked up the one Jim had nearly emptied.

"Very well, Mr. Bill. It's a pretty, sunny day and the family is together again." She smiled and turned to the front windows. "What more could we ask for?"

"Not much, I guess." Bill chuckled, and picked up his cup and watched Niki head back to the kitchen.

"I guess Alyssa and Ridan are in school today," Bill surmised.

"Carole says they get Thursday and Friday off," Jim said, and poured himself another cup.

"And Carole and Shelly are out with the horses?"

"Yup." Jim smiled. "They stayed up talking long after Wally and I went to bed, and they were already up and at it again when I got up. Wally was up early, had eaten, and was off to work before then. Blaire Lupis came for a lesson and then went riding on one of Carole's horses. I thought Carole and Shelly would come back in when Blaire left, but they're still out in the barns somewhere."

"Carole said something about you thinkin' of retirin'," Bill said, not quite a question.

"Yeah," Jim admitted. "End of May. I have to decide before then."

"You thinkin' about moving back here?"

"Certainly," Jim said with a smile. "It's home for Shelly and me and we're hoping Carrie can adjust. She seems to like the visits."

"Things must be windin' down in that job of yours."

"Not really," Jim admitted, and leaned over the table. "More like winding up."

"Then why are you thinkin' about retirin'?"

"I think Shelly and Carrie will be safer here in the valley," he said softly, "around family and friends. The trouble is starting up again and my new superiors won't understand my second job. I think I need to be here."

"So are you goin' to look for a place?"

"Starting this afternoon," Jim said. "Shelly and I have an appointment with the Realtor in town this afternoon. I'm hoping I can get Carrie to come with us."

"You think that might be a problem."

"Rusty said she'd take a measure and try to help persuade her to come," Jim said with a smile. "Nothing like the duplicity of a beloved grandmother to help sway a fifteen-year-old."

Bill chuckled. "Where are you looking?"

"Not sure yet," Jim said, and shook his head. "Need to see what's available."

"Mind if I ask around?" Bill asked. "There are some properties that might be available and aren't listed with the Realtor."

"No, not at all," Jim smiled. "I want a nice piece, forested of course, but with enough open meadow that Shelly and Carrie can ride, and a view for a nice main house. Other than that, I guess it just has to be in the valley near town."

"That piece just across the county road to the south might be available. I'll see what I can find out," Bill said as he spotted a young redhead on horseback as she stopped in front of the stable and dismounted. "That must be Dan Lupis' daughter."

Jim turned and saw her quickly lead the horse into the

stable. "Yes, that's Blaire. Looks like something may have her dander up."

One-Fifteen

Blaire stopped her red, rag-topped jeep at the end of the CW Ranch's drive just before turning onto the east-west country road from the Rockin' H to the main highway north of town. She opened her handbag, found her mother's earpiece, and put it on.

"WL-Two," she said when she tapped the earpiece. "Private connection with Shara Malone, please."

She waited a very short moment and heard Shara's voice.

"Shara, Blaire Lupis here," she greeted. "May I stop by and take a few minutes of your time this morning?"

"Certainly, Blaire. Anything in particular?"

"Yes, but I'd like to explain when I get there."

"Of course."

"I'm leaving Carole and Wally's and will come directly if that's all right."

"I'll see you in a few minutes then. We're in the tack room so park by the bunkhouse," Shara said, and the connection broke.

⚜

Shara was standing in the stable door with one panel slid aside when Blaire walked around the bunkhouse and headed her way.

"Good to see you, Blaire," Shara greeted with a hug. "Come in out of the wind," she continued as she led the way inside and through the first door on her right.

"Hello, Blaire," Greg said as they stepped into the room and Blaire stopped and inhaled the familiarity of oiled leather and the sight of riding gear.

"Hi," she said, and turned to look at him. "Should I still call you Mr. and Mrs. Malone like when I was little?"

"That isn't necessary, Blaire," Greg said. "I know it's easier to call Shara by name, but you certainly are old enough to call me Greg."

"Thanks. I feel like I'm someplace in between and don't know which I should do." She smiled.

"We've been inspecting and repairing leathers all morning," Shara said, and laid a halter aside and sat down. She gestured to a chair for Blaire. "Your interruption is greatly appreciated. What can I do for you?"

Blaire settled into the chair and glanced at Greg and then back to Shara.

"Would you be more comfortable if I left, Blaire?" Greg asked.

"No. No, it isn't that," she said. "I'm trying to think how to start."

"Maybe at the beginning?" Shara proposed.

"Of course, but that's why it's difficult."

Blaire briefly explained her experiences growing up and how she suddenly woke up, seeing how self-centered she had been as a young teenaged girl. She explained how her focus has changed in the past two years and that with her dad's influence in their family, his duties as a deputy affecting everything they did, she began thinking law enforcement would be a good direction for her and would let her learn how to help people and make a difference with her life.

Greg nodded and smiled.

"I tried to talk with Dad about applying to the State," Blaire continued, "but he was not very supportive."

"I'm a little surprised," Shara said, "but I think he'd rather have you close to home for a while and not away in school or training."

"If I read between the lines," Blaire said, "I'd have to agree with that. But after the attack on your ranch and the Jordan ranch, he changed. They've both gotten very cautious..."

Shara waited as Blaire studied the floor, her thoughts flitting from one topic to another.

Shara glanced at Greg without moving her head, and then back to Blaire. *'Blaire, would you please hand me the reins on the saddle rack behind you?'*

"Sure," Blaire said absently, and turned to locate the reins. She picked them up and handed them to Shara.

"Thanks," Shara said, and laid them with the halter she had set aside earlier. "So what brings you to us?" Shara asked, and smiled at Greg.

"I heard Mom and Dad Saturday night talking about the troubles starting up again, and that he didn't think there was time for me to go away and learn how to protect myself." She looked at Shara sheepishly. "I don't want to hide and require someone to protect me. I want to learn how to protect myself and to help protect others. How to be of value when there's a need. Dad said you were training the children—yours and Jill's Cheyenne. He named the other kids, Kayli, Kail, Billie, Alyssa, and Ridan, but I don't know if you're training them or not. He mentioned how I was in danger, and maybe even Glory, because we're older. I was wondering if you could teach me like you are the children."

Shara looked up at Greg. "Where were they when you heard them?"

"They were around the fire pit off the back deck, behind the garage," Blaire said, and looked at Shara, curious.

"And you?"

"I was in my room getting ready for bed," Blaire said. "What is it?"

"So you were diagonally across the house from them," Shara said. "Right?"

"Yeah," Blaire said softly.

"How long have you been able to *hear* them?" Greg asked.

"I...I don't know what you mean," she said, and looked at him.

'Like now and just a minute ago when I asked you to get the reins,' Shara said, and caught Blaire's hand before she could react. "It's okay, Blaire. It's okay."

Blaire covered her mouth with her free hand and stared wide-eyed at Shara. "What's going on?" she asked in a whisper.

Shara smiled and held Blaire's hands. "A very good and very misunderstood gift; a talent has awakened in you, Blaire. Have you told anyone you can *hear* like you just did?"

Blaire slowly shook her head. "I haven't. I didn't know I was. I wasn't sure how I knew things I shouldn't know, and Saturday night I was so mad at Dad that I didn't realize I couldn't be hearing them talking—not in the normal way."

Shara took her time and explained what she suspected, much like she had done with Sedona and Sierra, stressing the necessity for extreme secrecy. Greg gave her the short course on how to focus and control her thoughts so no one else could hear her unless she wanted them to.

"Blaire?" Greg asked when they had reached a suitable place in their explanations. "Would you let us run a test to see how developed your talent is? You already have exhibited enough that I want to start some communications training with you."

"Sure, I guess," she said, and looked from one to the other.

"I need to ask you to keep what we do next completely secret," Shara said, "between yourself and us until we explain who else can know."

"Okay," she agreed.

"Has your dad talked to you at all about what we do?" Greg asked as he led the way out of the tack room into the main aisle of the stable.

"Not really," Blaire said. "I know you and Kiile have helped them, the deputies, in the past, but he's never said how or why."

"That's good," Greg said, and smiled as he led them across the yard toward the three-rail wood fence. "Your dad was handpicked to come here and help Wally. Actually all three of them were—your dad, Thom, and Ted. They have non-military connections to a secret organization we work for known as the Force. Shara and I work for the military side of that organization in our secret life. And you have just stepped into that secret life and will have a few very big decisions to make."

They stepped through the opening in the fence and Blaire stopped suddenly, looking around the pasture.

"What is it?" Shara asked softly.

"There's something here. Something *big*, but I don't understand. I don't see anything."

Shara looked at Greg and shook her head. "I don't believe this, Greg." Then she turned to Blaire. "You're right. There is something *big* here, right in front of you in fact. And I'm very surprised you know. But it *is* okay. It's part of another gift you've been given. Take my hand and step forward with us and you'll see."

They stepped through STSX's veil and Blaire could only stare in disbelief at the open portal and the ramp extending toward them. "What the...?"

"This is Greg's and my ship," Shara said, and led her up the ramp. "Please come aboard and do trust us. It's a lot to absorb suddenly, but this is for real."

Shara led Blaire up the ramp and settled her into the aft double-wide cushion chair. Greg sat down beside Shara in the chair facing her.

"STSX, please meet Blaire Lupis. She is Deputy Dan Lupis' daughter," Shara said in a conversational tone.

"PLEASED TO MEET YOU, MISS LUPIS. MAY I CALL YOU BLAIRE?" STSX asked in a gentle voice.

Blaire's mouth fell open and slowly she nodded. "Y...yes, you may."

"THANK YOU."

"STSX," Greg said. "Please give us an evaluation of Blaire's abilities to *hear* and *speak* empathically. She also has a sense of presence which she demonstrated as we approached."

"YES. BLAIRE'S PERCEPTION OF PRESENCE IS WELL DEVELOPED BUT IT CAN BE REFINED. I WILL NEED TO DETERMINE HER BLOOD ORIGINS." STSX turned his focus on Blaire and said to her alone, *'BLAIRE LUPIS, PLEASE PUT YOUR RIGHT HAND ON THE TABLE IN FRONT OF YOU IF*

YOU HEAR AND UNDERSTAND THIS MESSAGE.'

Blaire looked around the chamber, looking for the source of the voice in her head as she placed her right hand on the table.

'PLEASE FOCUS ON MY VOICE AND THINK TO ME THE WORDS, YES, I HEAR.'

Blaire focused on STSX's feel and his words and repeated the words.

'VERY GOOD, BLAIRE. NOW PLACE YOUR LEFT HAND ON TOP OF YOUR RIGHT HAND IF YOU SEE AN IMAGE IN YOUR MIND.'

She looked at Shara's blank expression and placed her left hand on top of her right.

"WOULD YOU PLEASE DESCRIBE THE IMAGE YOU SAW," STSX asked out loud.

Blaire looked at Greg and then back to Shara.

"I see you, Shara, in a yellow robe, lying on a couch with a transparent cylindrical cover over you, like sealing you in. You seem asleep, but the air is full of tension and a monitor or something above the couch is showing many erratic traces in many colors. There is something with many wires or tubes attached to your left arm.

"In another room, one with three walls of monitor panels, displays of many kinds and lights filling the open spaces between them, I see Greg leaned over two screens. He is very tired and his face is drawn with fatigue and concern. There is something on the monitors he doesn't like, and he keeps asking for something—Medical, he calls it—to try something else."

Blaire looked at Greg and then back at Shara. "There is something wrong with you, and Greg and this 'Medical' are trying to find out what to do. They have been trying for a lengthy amount of time and it seems nothing is working. What was happening, Shara?"

"I was dying, Blaire," Shara said softly, but held Blaire's eyes. "That was two days after Greg found me, rescued me from the slavers in a place called Point Obscure. I was poisoned on the orders of my great aunt, Judge Bernice Reeds, when they captured me. It took Medical and STSX three days to create and administer a suitable antitoxin. STSX says I almost didn't make it."

"How could it create an anti—?"

"With great difficulty," Shara said. "Greg remembered something from one of his assignments and found a scrap of information on toxins and antidotes specifically made to control slaves. They had to figure out the antidote and create it with the limited supplies he had on board."

Blaire noticed Shara was breathing heavily, deeply affected by the memories. "When did this happen?" Blaire whispered.

"I was poisoned on the fifteenth of the October before you and your family came to Riggin," Shara said. "Five days later I woke up here onboard STSX. I was in the Medical couch behind me. In the image STSX gave you, Greg was in the room above us." She pointed to the ceiling as she turned toward Greg. "Greg, would you show Blaire the rest of the ship? She'll recognize things from her image." *'I need a minute.'*

"Sure, Bren," Greg said, and motioned for Blaire to follow him.

When Blaire had gone, Shara closed her eyes and leaned back into the chair's cushions. *'STSX, why did you give her those particular images?'*

'FIRST, NO ONE COULD HAVE TOLD HER ABOUT THAT INCIDENT. ONLY THE COMMANDER AND I KNOW FIRST-HAND WHAT HAPPENED IN THOSE FIVE DAYS. YOU KNOW BECAUSE WE HAVE SHOWN YOU. SECOND, BLAIRE KNOWS SOMETHING VERY SERIOUS IS HAPPENING, BUT SHE DOES NOT KNOW THE DEPTH OF THAT TRUTH. IT SCARES HER. THE IMAGE CONVEYS THE SERIOUSNESS IN NO UNCERTAIN TERMS. WE ALMOST LOST YOU, SHARA MALONE, AND THAT WOULD HAVE BEEN A COMPLETELY UNACCEPTABLE SITUATION FOR ALL OF US—EVERYONE INVOLVED IN THE CAMPAIGN. WITHOUT YOU AND THE COMMANDER, THERE WOULD NOT BE A CAMPAIGN AND THERE WOULD NOT HAVE BEEN ANY RESCUES. WITHOUT YOU, THERE WOULD BE NO COMMANDER.'

'BLAIRE HAS GENUINE TALENT AND DESIRE TO LEARN AND TO HELP. BOTH SHOULD BE FOSTERED AND NURTURED. SHE CAN FEEL HER SURROUNDINGS, EVEN IN A TRANSFERRED IMAGE. SHE IS VERY PERCEPTIVE, MUCH LIKE YOU WHEN THE COMMANDER BEGAN TRAINING YOU. SHE IS ONLY LACKING IN TRAINING ON HOW TO USE THE GIFTS SHE HAS BEEN GIVEN AND HOW TO HANDLE THE NEXT GIFTS SHE MAY RECEIVE.'

'Do you think she can learn the physical skills necessary?'

'SHE IS PRESENTLY AUDITING CLASSES AT THE COLLEGE, UNABLE TO DECIDE ON A FIELD OF STUDY. AMONG THE CLASSES SHE'S AUDITING, SHE'S ATTENDING AEROBIC DANCE, ADVANCED TECHNICAL MATHEMATICS, A BIOCHEMISTRY LAB STUDY, AND A MARTIAL-ARTS-BASED PHYSICAL EDUCATION CLASS.'

'So you think she can learn?'

'YES. SHE HAS ALREADY, INSTINCTIVELY OR LOGICALLY, PLANNED AND BEGUN PREPARING HERSELF.'

Shara took a deep breath and stood up as Greg led Blaire back to the seating area.

"I think we should go in and have a bite of lunch," Shara said, and turned to the aft portal. "It will be more relaxed there and Blaire can ask us her many questions. Coleen and Brendan are out in their apartment and we will have some time before they come in for lunch. STSX, please close the portal after we leave."

Greg and Blaire followed Shara out and down the ramp. When they passed through the opening in the fence, Blaire looked back at the seemingly empty pasture and smiled.

⋏ ⋏ ⋏ ⋏ ⋏

Cheyenne swiped her student card in the cashiering machine slot at the end of the school food counter, collected her tray, and hurried into the seated throng of students in the cafeteria. She had spotted Sedona and Sierra when she got into the line for the counter, seeing them settled at a table in the corner between the only two windowed outside walls. She set her tray beside Sierra and slipped into the chair without pulling it out first.

"Wasn't Saturday night something?" she whispered, looking around to be sure no one else was close enough to hear.

"Sure was," Sedona admitted.

"Mom *felt* the snooper before I did," Cheyenne said, and took a sip of her drink. "I guess I was too focused on her roast and Dad talking about the barn repairs. Mom was up and out the back door before I *felt* him. She had him with the first throw."

"Aunt Jill is really good with those throwing darts," Sierra said.

"And Kiile and his men were there seconds after," Cheyenne said, a little awe showing on her face.

"Well," Sierra said, "and I don't mean to sound disrespectful, but after Labor Day's performance, he should be a lot more prepared."

"He was," Cheyenne said, and spooned a mouthful of casserole. "Where's Tayn?"

"He's coming," Sierra said. "He had to discuss a math problem with his teacher. He thinks the book's answer may be wrong."

"I'm finally getting a handle on the darts," Cheyenne said. "Mom says my fingers are almost too short."

Sierra laid her hand on top of Cheyenne's and compared the length of their fingers. "If they are, it's not very much. They're shorter than mine, but only a little."

"Mom thinks another six months and I won't remember they were short." Cheyenne giggled and took another bite. "You're doing okay with them."

"Pretty good," Sedona said, and smiled. "We'll all try them tonight at practice."

"That'll be fun," Sierra said, and looked across the room.

"There's Tayn, and it looks like he was right."

Over lunch, Blaire met Coleen and Brendan and Meara when they came in and joined them. Greg finished ahead of the rest of them and excused himself, explaining he had to meet Kiile and discuss the next supply shipment.

Shara knew there were new students arriving along with the normal assortment of necessities from uniforms to equipment, from non-Terran food staples to a few hard-to-get delicacies. She actually looked forward to the selections of non-Terran side ingredients she had ordered, having fallen in love with the flavors and taste sensations she had experienced on her trips to and from the Rings.

When Greg had gone and the meal had settled into small talk, Shara asked Meara if she would accompany her and Blaire to the practice room.

"This is where the children train and practice," Shara said as she led the way into the room just inside the southeast entrance to the enclosed arena. "We run through their self-defense drills every night before we move to the other areas of their training."

"This is better than anything we have at the college," Blaire said absently as she looked around the room.

"Meara," Shara continued, "I'd like you to watch Blaire as I explain and then run through a few basic drills. Blaire, please take your jacket and riding boots off" —Shara pointed to the bench beside the door they had come through and the hooks on the wall— "and join me in the middle of the mat."

Shara spent nearly two hours explaining the fundamentals of the techniques, the reasons behind using one countering move over another, showing Blaire how to use her sense of presence to stay ahead of an opponent or assailant. As their session progressed, Blaire settled into the routine, an eager, enthusiastic student intent on learning everything her teacher had to give her.

Shara asked Blaire to give her examples of the dances she had learned in her dance class. Then she showed Blaire how to dissect the movements and apply pieces and parts of them to her defensive movements, giving her more options and additional twists to further increase her advantage in the face of an adversary.

Shara finally called an end to the session and handed Blaire a towel and another cup of water.

"This probably wasn't as strenuous on you as it is on this old body," Shara said with a smile, "but I admit it always feels good to spar every now and then."

"What? You're not old." Blaire stopped wiping her face and stared at Shara.

"Maybe not, Blaire." Shara smiled and took a long sip of water. "But sometimes the body tells me otherwise."

"It's eleven years of having little to do," Meara said with a chuckle. "Other than to chase two girls around the ranch and train horses and riders. No real exercise to speak of."

Blaire laughed at the put-on scowl Shara gave Meara. "I do appreciate the time you've taken with me today." Blaire smiled at both of them. "When I called this morning, I wasn't sure where I was going. I needed to talk to someone, but you make me feel like maybe I am welcome and trainable."

"You are welcome here and you are trainable," Shara said firmly. "We just need to see what makes sense now and how quickly we can make sense of it." Shara looked up and smiled. "Greg's back. He'll want to explain a few things before we finish for the day."

⋏ ⋏ ⋏ ⋏ ⋏

"Afternoon," Greg said as he entered the practice room and turned to Shara. He pulled her to him and gave her a quick kiss, and then turned to face Blaire and Meara. "I understand you've had a thorough session this afternoon, Blaire. Do you have any questions?"

"Lots. But I think I should listen and let my mind stop

spinning," she replied. "I want to thank you for your time, the lunch, the practice session—everything."

"You're welcome," he said, and smiled. "Put your boots on and let's go in by the fire and I'll explain the choices you have as I see them. STSX should be able to give me your measure by then."

Greg turned to Shara, put his arm around her shoulders, and led them out of the arena to the main house.

"Would you like coffee or tea?" Shara asked as they entered the back door.

"Tea would be fine," Blaire said, and Shara turned to the kitchen.

Greg led Blaire into the living room and offered her the overstuffed chair by the fire. He sat down on the loveseat across from her and waited for Shara to join them. Meara settled onto the end of the long couch nearest Blaire.

"Greg?" Blaire asked when Shara sat down beside him. "Where are these gifts coming from? Why am I suddenly getting them? Am I becoming something—?"

"No, Blaire, you're not becoming some kind of a freak," Shara answered for Greg. "These gifts come from your bloodline. I got mine from my uncle Paul's bloodline and some from my mother's bloodline. Greg got his from both his parents as well."

Matti stepped into the living room with a tray of tea and greeted Blaire as she poured. They exchanged pleasantries and Matti returned to the kitchen.

"What makes their bloodlines different?" Blaire asked, leaning closer as if to keep others from hearing.

"It's the origin of our bloodlines," Greg said, "as much as the hereditary talents the bloodline carries. My mother has a very strong talent for *hearing* and my father's line does too, though he never developed his gifts. There was no one to teach him about them or how to use them. It was really quite a shame."

"So you're saying my folks, or one of them, have these talents?" Blaire asked.

"Yes, to some degree. I don't know if they know or can use them," Greg said. "You might try to talk with your dad about their bloodlines and how he was recruited by the Force. His answers might be surprising."

"I'll bet they would be," Blaire said, and smiled.

"Now, Blaire," Greg said, changing his tone. "I want to explain that you have a couple of choices to think about. The first is to train and become an Agent for the Force, sort of similar to your dad, where you would work alone for the most part and live two lives. One life would be what people see, like your dad being a deputy, and the other would be a secret life where you would report things you find out or discover to someone assigned to you in the Force. Second, you could enlist in the Force as a cadet and learn the ways of becoming what we call a Shadow.

"As a Shadow, you would work in a team, like Shara and myself now, or like Cheral and I were when we came here looking for the slavers." Greg let his words settle a moment, and then continued. "Teams are assigned based on a number of reasons—skill sets, capabilities, or even so the older, more-seasoned member can help train the younger team member in the ways of being a Shadow. Anyway, a team is set up for a specific period of time, or for a specific mission, to any of many other sets of requirements."

"As a Shadow, you have two options," Shara added. "You can train to work assignments as they are handed out, be placed on site to do your work and then be extracted when the task is completed." She smiled and looked at Greg. "Or you can take the next step and learn to become a fighter pilot. Greg's past partner, Cheral, took the latter path, as did Jill, Nick, and myself."

"Shara excelled in her training and became a Shadow and quickly got her pilot's ribbon." Greg smiled back at Shara. "With that distinction, she and I can choose our assignments, or in this case, lead the others in this assignment."

"So there are two choices, and one has two choices within itself?" Blaire asked to be sure she understood.

"Yes," Shara agreed. "You'll have to decide which path you are interested in before we know which course of training to start you on."

"Wow," Blaire said softly. "What's enlisting involve?"

"For normal cadets, it requires a four-year commitment to serve the Force while you're learning," Greg said formally, "and the cadet pays the Force back a small amount for their training out of their pay. Since I run a school to train cadets much faster than the Academy—the director allows me to offer a three-year commitment instead. Three to five months of training and the rest in service to the Force, and I usually get a big vote in who is assigned where for their service."

"And you'll get to train here," Shara said with a wide smile, "and not at the Academy."

"If you want to train to be a fighter pilot," Greg continued, "you will also get flight pay on top of the regular cadet pay, and my students get reduced charges toward the cost of a fighter. Since we're in a combat environment, the Force picks up a big chunk of the costs for training and for the fighters."

"Stop. Please," Blaire said, and put her hands on both sides of her head. "My head is spinning. How can I ever digest all of this and make a decision like this?"

"Tell you what, Blaire," Shara said. "You have the general idea of the choices. Take them and think about them. Ask me any questions that come to mind." Shara touched the side of her head. "I'll be listening for you, and I'll try to answer them. Come back tomorrow and we'll figure out what you feel is best, short and long term, and then we'll choose."

"When you decide if this is what you want to do," Greg added, "we have some history to give you and then we'll take a tour of our secret world."

Shara turned serious. "Blaire? Will your folks agree to your doing this?"

"I hope so, Shara," Blaire said. "But if not, I will probably go ahead. I don't want to go against their wishes, but I *am* almost nineteen. Three more weeks, on the twelfth."

"Try to explain to your folks what you want to do and why," Shara encouraged. "My mother tried to manipulate my life for hers and the slavers' benefit and I never had a chance of getting her approval of my desires, so I know how it feels to move forward knowing they don't agree. I don't wish that on anyone. Please try to talk with them."

"Okay," Blaire said softly, then finished her tea and stood up. "I need to think on this, a lot. Thank you for taking so much of your day for me. I didn't expect to dominate all of your time."

"You're very welcome, Blaire," Shara said, and led the way to the back door. "The kids will be getting here soon from school and our day will begin in earnest. It is very good to see you and help you understand what's happening. Tomorrow, we'll talk about why we're here and what we're facing. All of us, together."

"Thanks," Blaire said, then threw on her jacket and stepped outside.

Shara and Greg watched her as she crossed the yard and disappeared between the apartments and the bunkhouse.

"Maybe we ought to have Jill and Rose here when she comes back," Shara said absently, watching the now empty yard.

"Might help at that," Greg said, and squeezed her shoulders. "Let's go in and enjoy that fire. We have about a half an hour before the kids arrive."

Shara herded Tayn and the girls out to the practice room and Greg stopped in the tack room on the way. He turned his thoughts and asked, '*STSX, please conduct a search of the archives and historical records in the Rings. I want any information you can find on the family planetary origins and blood origins of Deputy Dan Lupis, Deputy Thom Baine, Deputy Ted Marks, and Marshal Wally Lima or Limanski. Also collect any information available on Mandy Lupis—I don't know her full or maiden name—and for Eddie Baine, Collier.*'

'*SEARCH COMMENCING.*'

135

'Thanks. I am hoping with that information, you and Medical can help us enhance the children's gifts as they begin to develop and be prepared if the worst happens.'

'UNDERSTOOD.'

Greg stepped out of the stable's back door, *hearing* the children competing with the dummy throwing darts, and saw Kiile's young Corporal and Meara as they entered the arena. He hurried to catch up.

▲ ▲ ▲ ▲ ▲

Shara slipped into bed and snuggled close to Greg as he wrapped the sheet and quilt over them. "Almost time for the fleece sheets, love," he said as he drew her close and kissed her.

Jill had taken Cheyenne home around nine and Tayn and the girls had turned in shortly after that, tired enough to not protest the going. Greg and Shara turned in as soon as Coleen, Brendan, and Meara had left and the house was quiet and Matti had things settled for the night.

"I've got you," Shara chuckled. "Why do I need fleece sheets?"

"Maybe you don't," he said, and gently tickled her. Then he slowly calmed her wiggling and cuddled. "STSX says Tayn and the girls are about as far along as age and size allows them to go in defense training. Does Meara agree?"

"Yes," Shara said with a little heaviness in her voice.

"Yeah," Greg said softly. "I'm sorry too. They should've had more time as kids before having to grow up."

"They still look and sound like children," Shara admitted, "until they're put to the test. Then they are very serious and determined. Did you see them practicing the darts? All of them had trouble with the traditional feather darts, barely able to hit the target, until Sierra spun around and snapped one like our throwing darts."

"I was impressed," Greg said. "Even Cheyenne is nimble and spot on, every time."

"They're just as capable with the Kaasprs and the

Brekshiirs," Shara said.

"Talking with Blaire and the unexpected appearance of her *hearing*," Greg said, "makes me think we should evaluate all of the other children—Kayli, Kail, Billie, Alyssa, and Ridan—before we overlook one of them."

"So? Speaking of Blaire," she said after a few minutes and a couple of long kisses. "What does STSX say about her?"

"I thought you might've heard him."

"I was busy with the kids," Shara defended, "and left those details to you."

"Well, I think it's obvious he likes her and is pleased with her abilities," Greg said happily. "She's old enough to finish what she starts, and he gave a very good measure of her current abilities. He says she did very well following your instructions and techniques."

"She was very competent," Shara admitted. "She caught on quickly and was able to repeat what I showed her. I think her studies these past two years have helped a lot."

"That's what STSX says," Greg agreed. "And as she learns to use her perception and sense of things around her, she could become defensibly very able."

"Which way do you think she'll choose?"

"Did you ask Jill and Rose if they can break away from work and come out when she arrives?"

"Yes. They said they can come."

"With their examples, I'm expecting her to try for it all."

"Really? That's a little presumptuous, isn't it, Mr. Malone?" she asked, and poked his ribs. "That's what I think too." She kissed him quickly and then said, "Now, love, I have something to discuss with you and I need your full attention." Shara slipped her arm under him, squeezed him tight, and rolled onto her back, pulling him with her.

One-Sixteen
Tuesday, November 21

It was nearly nine o'clock Tuesday morning when Sam stopped his truck in front of the Lupis' house and got out. He knocked on the door and waited, and after a moment Mandy opened the door, greeted him, and let him in.

"Good morning, Sam. It's good to see you again," Mandy said. "It's been a while. Come in. Can I get you a cup of coffee?"

"Thanks, but no," he said as he stopped just inside the door. "I was just wondering if Blaire was here. I stopped up at Carole and Wally's place but she isn't scheduled to ride today, so I thought I'd stop by while I was here in town, picking up some things for Marty."

"I'm sorry, Sam," Mandy said. "She left half an hour ago to run some errands. She had to go by the college and then I don't know where else."

"Do you know when she'll be home?"

Mandy shook her head. "I have no idea, Sam. She said she might be late, but I don't know how late."

Sam took a deep breath, feeling he deserved to be disappointed after the way he had treated her. "Thanks. Would you mind telling her I came by when you see her?"

"Surely," Mandy said. "You know I'll let her know."

"Thanks," he said, and stepped out onto the small porch.

"Mrs. Jordan, Mrs. McIntire? I'm sorry," Blaire said as she followed Shara through the dining room and into the living room. "I didn't know I was interrupting anything."

"You aren't." Shara gestured to a chair and sat down in the overstuffed chair by the low fire. "I asked Jill and Rose to come and talk with you when you came."

"Please, call me Jill," Jill said as she settled at one end of the loveseat.

"And I'm just Rose, Blaire," Rose said with a chuckle. "Enough with the 'Mrs.' stuff. We already know we're married with kids."

"Thanks," Blaire said, "but why?"

"To help you decide," Rose said, "and to let you know we each faced the same questions and sudden awareness to the secret lives we now share."

"I didn't know you two were—"

"Of course not," Rose said with a wide smile. "No one knows unless we tell them."

"Okay, some introductions before we get started," Shara said, then looked at Blaire and gestured to the carafes and cups. "Tea or coffee?"

"Oooh, coffee please," Blaire said. "It's too early for me for tea."

Shara poured and handed Blaire a cup. "Please take one of Annie's sweet breads. Now, for introductions. You might know the scandalous secret around Riggin is that Jill is Greg's half-sister. It really isn't scandalous, since Jack was not married to Amy when Greg was conceived. They have the same father and different mothers. You've met Coleen, Greg's mother, and you probably know Jack and Amy."

Blaire nodded. "I'd heard Jill was Greg's sister when I was much younger."

"And I'm just a homegrown, longtime friend," Rose said. "I was born here, raised here, schooled here, and work here. Until I became friends with these two" —She gestured to Shara and Jill— "I had seldom gone anywhere. Maybe over to the Capital once or twice."

"Jill and Rose are both captains in the Force," Shara explained, "and they are decorated fighter pilots. And so are

Nick and Doug. I want them to answer any questions you might have about what we're offering and help you decide *if* this is what you would want to do."

"Okay," Blaire said, and looked at Jill. "I guess I'll start with a question about the enlistment and the commitment to serving."

"Serving is what it's all about, Blaire. To help defend others, their rights, their freedom," Jill said, her smile turning serious. "I was in the same boat you find yourself in. I had no plans, no future—except to be Nick's wife if he ever asked. I put up a reasonable front, but I was unable to defend myself and scared of my own shadow most of the time. But when I found out that Greg and Shara had led Doug, Rose, Nick, and Jim Woods into the slavers' complex to rescue me and the other five captives, I realized what I wanted to do. When I found out I could *hear*, I told Greg and Shara I wanted to learn what they knew and do what they do. That was twelve years ago, and it seems like yesterday."

"Most of the time," Rose said, "our jobs with the Force are watching and listening, looking for things hidden in the fabric of our society, searching for those loyal to the slavers. But our normal lives are just like everyone else. We have jobs, raise our kids, and keep our homes. Things have been calm and thankfully allowed time for our kids to grow enough so we can be ready for this new phase of our war."

"I thought I was having a nightmare when your ranches were attacked," Blaire said softly. "I didn't know otherwise until a couple of days after when I overheard Dad mention something about it to Mom."

"You *heard* the attacks?" Shara asked, surprise coloring her expression.

"Heard? I was seeing double," Blaire said, glancing from one to another. "I was overwhelmed. I thought I was going crazy."

"I guess so," Shara said. "I know we can help you with that."

Their conversation continued until Blaire ran out of immediately significant questions.

"Were you able to talk to your parents about this?" Shara asked.

141

"Yes," Blaire said, and smiled. "That actually went better than I expected. I tried to rehearse what I was going to say, but after dinner Dad asked if I was still planning on sending in my application to the State. He almost smiled when I said I had a better offer and that I had already started the evaluation process. I teased him a little, seeing him smile for the first time in a long time, and he was very surprised when I told him I had spent the day with you and Greg. They're okay with it if I enlist."

"That's wonderful, Blaire," Shara said happily. "It means a lot to have your family behind you. Did you talk about your ancestry?"

"Yes," Blaire said. "I thought he was kidding, but I think he's actually serious."

"About what?" Jill asked.

"About where his family lives." She looked at Shara. "You won't believe this, but he said his parents were born into a long family line that lives in a small town near a place called Casimir—"

"That's Franni's hometown," Rose interrupted. "Sorry. We have a friend from there."

"Casimir? You know someone from there?"

Jill and Rose nodded slowly and Shara chuckled.

"It truly is a small universe," Shara said. "Okay, what else did he say?"

Blaire studied the three of them for a moment and then slowly continued. "He said his parents immigrated here and he was born just outside Louisville, Kentucky. He said he's full-blooded Betollean, whatever that is." She sighed. "Mom said her parents were born in a small town outside of a place called Daneubois." She saw Shara's face light up. "She says it's a city of universities and schools of higher learning."

"Then she's Ferannian," Shara said, and smiled.

"Yes. That's what she called herself," Blaire admitted. "How do you know?"

"My cousin Cheral," Shara said, "Uncle Paul's

granddaughter, is from Daneubois. Her grandparents are professors in one of the universities, and her parents own and operate a minerals reclamation business in Aleemill, a short shuttle flight from Daneubois."

Blaire just stared at Shara for a long moment. "So it's true. We're from someplace...out there?" She absently looked up at the high, trussed ceiling.

"It seems the talent comes from our non-Terran bloodlines," Shara admitted.

"Then all of you—"

"Have non-Terran blood," Jill said.

"I'm a half-blood," Shara said, and chuckled, "in more ways than one. I'm half Native American and I'm half Ferannian and Kyddellan, though my Ferannian bloodline is stronger and goes back to Rygonian origins. It's the same as Greg's, but he's full-blooded."

Blaire looked at Jill.

"Yeah, that makes me a half-blood also," Jill admitted. "I found out after all of this started, and I met Greg, that my father is Rygonian, same as Shara's half and Greg. My mother is a local Terran mix."

"And I'm a Terran mix with just a little Betollean blood dribbled in to make things interesting," Rose said.

"Really?" Shara asked. "You never said. How much?"

"Medical says about an eighth, maybe a little more." Rose smiled. "We're not sure about Doug."

They laughed, and Shara saw Blaire relax a little with Rose's implied double meaning.

"The training then?" Blaire questioned softly. "Are the children developing talents as well?"

Shara nodded. "We still have to finish an evaluation, but it's very early to expect anything from the eight- or nine-year-olds. But development in ten- and eleven-year-olds was a big surprise."

"So, it seems," Jill said, "we have another full-blood in our midst."

Shara raised her cup of tea and looked at Blaire. "Let us be the first to congratulate you. Those are two very honorable bloodlines."

They sipped and then Rose asked, "Have you decided whether you want to join us and train to be part of the Ladies' Brigade?"

Blaire smiled and sipped her coffee. "I think I have. I've only flown once before, but if I do well enough, I think I'd also like to learn that part too."

"Wonderful," Shara said. "I will have you sit with STSX for a history lesson upload and then we'll meet Greg at Obscure for lunch in the Mess and a tour of the captured slavers' facility turned Shadow Base." She looked at Jill and Rose and stood up. "How long can you stay? Can you join us at Obscure?"

"Yes," Jill said, and nodded vigorously. "I told Father what was up."

"I have the week off," Rose said smugly, and nodded as she followed Shara and Blaire through the dining room and outside. "Until school lets out. Looks like a girls' day out."

▲ ▲ ▲ ▲ ▲

Sedona and Sierra stopped beside the swings and waited for Cheyenne to catch up. They had been playing tag during the lunch recess, and Tayn was across the playground talking with Billie. When Cheyenne stopped beside Sedona, she bent slightly and brushed her dress off, slowly looking around the playground before straightening.

"Do you feel him?" she asked softly. "Across the street in the gray pickup."

"Yeah," Sedona said, still looking at Tayn and Billie.

"He mentioned the 'dark-haired twins and the redhead' a minute ago," Sierra said, and looked at Cheyenne as she turned and led them to the merry-go-round.

They each took a place near the center and leaned back on the handrails radiating out to the edge. Cheyenne gave it a push as she got on and started it spinning slowly so they could scan the playground and the streets without being obvious.

'Six, get the license plate numbers on the gray pickup,' Sierra said, *'and check with Wally to see who he is.'*

Sedona looked for Tayn and did not see him or Billie. She *felt* for him. "Tayn and Billie have gone back inside."

'Mom, Dad,' Sierra closed her eyes and said. *'Everything is okay, but we are being watched by a man in a gray pickup. Six got the license, a picture of the man, and contacted Wally, and I'm giving you an image for reference. Cheyenne and Sedona are with me on the playground and Tayn and Billie are inside.'*

A short moment passed and Shara answered, *'Has he made any kind of a move? Do you need us to come?'*

'No, Mom. He's been talking with someone but we can't tell who. He mentioned the dark-haired twins and the redhead in a conversation and made us feel uncomfortable.'

'Does he know you've spotted him?'

'No. We haven't looked at him, but we know he's there and he has that feeling about him.'

'Okay. Stay together after school, and if he's still there when you're ready to leave, let us know. Does Billie walk home?'

'Yes. Usually by herself. That isn't good, is it, Mom?"

'No. I think you four should start walking her home after school and keep Six close by. I'll start meeting you with the truck at Eddie's and bring you four to the ranch. Do Kayli and Kail ride the bus?'

"Yes, Mom. Alyssa and Ridan take another bus up to their place. We'll walk Billie home. Tayn will like that.'

'I'll be listening for you. Let me know if you have any trouble.'

Sedona looked at Sierra and smiled.

'Who else, Mom? See you at Billie's.'

"Wow," Sedona said as the recess bell rang and they started back to the building. "Can you believe she said that?"

"That's the best thing she's said to us in a long time," Sierra said. "Just like her and Dad when they know there's danger."

⋏⋏⋏⋏⋏

"UPLOAD COMPLETE," STSX said out loud, and Blaire shook herself to relieve the tension she felt in her shoulders. STSX continued to her alone: *'BLAIRE LUPIS, THE HISTORY UPLOADS WILL BE MENTALLY ACCESSED WHILE YOU SLEEP AT NIGHT. EACH NIGHT FOR THREE NIGHTS YOU WILL DREAM A PORTION OF THE STORY. YOU ASKED THAT THE STORY BEGIN WHEN GREG AND CHERAL CAME TO THE VALLEY AND BEFORE THEIR ATTACK ON THE SLAVERS' COMPLEX. THAT PORTION WILL BE YOUR FIRST NIGHT'S DREAM, AND IT WILL OCCUR TONIGHT. THE SECOND AND THE THIRD PORTIONS ARE CONTINUATIONS OF THE STORY, BRINGING YOUR UNDERSTANDING TO A TIME AFTER THE DELIVERY OF SHARA AND JILL'S CHILDREN. A SUMMARY IS INCLUDED TO COVER THE YEARS OF THE CHILDREN'S GROWTH TO THE PRESENT TIME.'*

'Thank you, STSX,' Blaire said, and stretched as she stood up. *'What will happen if I wake up during the night?'*

'THE STORY WILL STOP UNTIL YOU ARE ASLEEP AGAIN. NO DATA WILL BE LOST.'

'Thank you.'

"Blaire?" Shara asked from STSX's upper deck.

Blaire turned to the opening in the ceiling. "Yes?"

"Are you hungry yet?" Shara asked, and Blaire knew she knew she was.

"Famished," Blaire said. "May I come up?"

"Yes," Shara replied. "I've called Jill and Rose. They'll be here in a moment."

Blaire climbed the ladder rungs set into the central chamber's wall and emerged in the chamber behind the cockpit and forward of the navigation and communications compartment. She turned at Shara's voice and saw her sitting in the cushioned pilot's chair, facing her.

"Take the right-hand jump seat," Shara said, and unfolded the seat attached to the right cockpit wall.

"We're in," Jill said from the lower deck.

"STSX, please close the portal and retract the ramp," Shara said as Blaire sat down.

Shara had Blaire strapped in by the time Rose slipped through the floor opening and started unfolding the left jump seat. Jill followed her in and took a place behind her, backed up against the aft cockpit bulkhead.

"I'll use the handholds," Jill said as Rose buckled in.

"Okay, you know the drill," Shara said, and swiveled her chair to forward facing. "Blaire, I'm going to power up STSX now."

Shara ran her fingers down the two armrests, throwing appropriate toggles as she went.

"Ignition ready."

"IGNITION IN FIVE SECONDS."

"Systems check."

"CLOAKING ON, SENSOR BLOCKING ON, SHIELDS ARE FULL, PASSIVE SCAN INDICATES NO LOCAL TRAFFIC. IGNITION. ALL SYSTEMS ARE MISSION READY."

"Please lift and hover at two hundred feet," Shara said, and STSX put her command into action.

Blaire grabbed the arms of the jump seat and Shara turned to be sure she was all right. Blaire's wide smile and bright green eyes greeted her silent inquiry.

"Now I see why you named your ranch the Flying M's," Blaire said. "Inside joke."

Slowly Shara advanced the thrust levers at the end of the left armrest and pulled STSX's nose up gently with the lever on the right. She turned with a smile and watched Blaire looking over the canopy rail.

Shara let STSX drift north over the Rockin' H and then the Lazy D, giving Blaire time to recognize the familiar places below. East of the Lazy D, she turned south and drifted down the east side of Riggin. Shara rolled STSX so she could see the school, but the pickup Sierra had told her about was gone. She gently *listened* to Sedona and Sierra and was satisfied they were in class and concentrating on the subject and the teacher's presentation. Tayn, Billie, and the others, with the exception of Kail, were equally engrossed in their classes. Kail was talking to a friend and Shara laughed when the teacher noticed.

"As we drift south," Shara said, and pointed ahead on the right, "you'll see the Double J and Jill and Nick's place on the cliff overlooking the river."

"I see it," Blaire said, "and look at how big the buttes are."

"A very pretty valley, Blaire," Rose said. "And worth everything we have to give to keep it safe."

Shara slowly drifted closer to the Saddle Horn rock formation and said, "STSX, alert Shadow Base we are arriving."

"OUR USUAL PARKING SPOT IS AVAILABLE. CONTROL SAYS THEY ARE PLEASED TO SEE US."

"Thank you, STSX," Shara said, and started their descent toward the forest.

Blaire stiffened, expecting an impact as they approached the unbroken sea of trees.

"The landing clearing is hidden behind Shadow Base's cloaking veil, Blaire," Shara said. "We won't hit anything."

Blaire exhaled as STSX slipped through the veil, and the clearing in the trees around the edge of a huge half moon opening in the ground stared back at them.

Shara settled STSX to one side of the clearing, near the hatchway beside the open maw, and waved to Greg standing beside it.

"We're down," Shara said, and turned her chair to aft facing and smiled at Blaire. "Nice enough?"

"Oh, yeeaah!" Blaire gushed. "Don't pinch me. I don't want to wake up."

Shara chuckled and made sure Blaire was unbuckled. She gestured for Blaire to follow Jill and Rose through the floor opening and then she followed.

At the aft portal, Blaire stopped her and asked, "Do you always talk to your ship like a person, a friend?"

"Yes." Shara smiled back at her. "STSX is as close to artificial intelligence as it comes, and sometimes he doesn't seem artificial at all. He is courteous, caring, and very protective of me, Greg, and the girls. He is our closest friend and companion. When we travel, he is our world, literally. Without his titanium, ceramic, and many other metals hull and his incredible intelligence, we couldn't do all the things we do. He is as much of us as we are of him. And I have always found that if you treat your friends and companions with understanding, courtesy, and civility, they will treat you accordingly."

"Wow," Blaire said softly. "I'm glad I took your lead and spoke nicely to him."

Shara nodded and led Blaire down the ramp. "STSX, please close the aft portal."

Greg stepped up and caught Shara's shoulders in a gentle hug. "How was the flight, Blaire?"

"Wonderful," Blaire said. "Incredible. Just amazing."

Greg chuckled. "I'm glad you liked it." He turned and led the way into the hatchway, and began giving Blaire a description of the facility as they went. He tried to prepare her for the view when they turned and stepped into the launch bay, but smiled, knowing there was no way. Blaire stopped dead in her tracks and stared at the huge chamber with the half-open roof.

"Almost two football fields across," Greg said softly, and Blaire nodded without saying anything or closing her mouth. "This way," he said in a normal voice, and started across the chamber to the door in the north wall. "We'll get some lunch before we take a tour. STSX tells me you worked up an appetite."

"Yes, I...did," Blaire said softly, and quickly followed Greg and Shara. Jill and Rose fell in behind her.

▲

"Good afternoon, Commander," Kiile said as he joined them and greeted Greg. "Captains. And who might this young lady be?"

"Marine Captain Kiile," Greg said formally, "please meet our newest cadet, Blaire Lupis."

"Very good to meet you, Cadet Lupis," Kiile greeted with a handshake. "Would that be Deputy Lupis' daughter Blaire?"

"Yes, sir," Blaire said smartly. "Thank you, sir. I know you don't remember me, but I remember you."

"Kiile, Cadet Lupis has had a full morning and has worked up a serious hunger," Greg said calmly. "Would you select a table and join us while we gather a suitable quantity of rations?"

"Certainly, Commander," Kiile said, and smiled. "With pleasure. This way please. And I do remember you, Blaire, from when you first moved to Riggin."

Kiile led them to the food counter and Blaire followed Shara through the line, selecting small portions of things she recognized. Occasionally, Shara would point out something and suggest she try it, and she took a sampling. When her tray was full with her main dish, a drink, and a dessert, she followed Shara to the table Kiile had picked to one side of the eating area.

"Blaire," Shara began to explain when they started eating, "Squad Leader Kiile—he prefers squad leader to captain—is the Officer in Charge of this launch facility. It's officially known as Obscure, though we have nicknamed it Shadow Base because it houses all of our local Shadows and fighter pilots, the fighter squadron, and all of Kiile's marines."

"He calls Greg 'Commander,'" Blaire said curiously, "so is Greg the Officer in Charge of all of this?"

"Yes," Shara said. "Greg and I are responsible for every man and woman assigned here as a cadet, trainee, or combatant, plus a number of off-world fighter squadrons and the campaign to stop the slavers. Colonel Kooich commands

Fighter Operations and Colonel Mooren and Franni are the campaign wing commanders under Colonel Kooich. Once you have completed your preliminary physical training, you will be identified as a cadet pilot trainee. Once you have soloed, and when you're not training, you will report to Colonel Mooren for mission assignments during your free time."

"For approximately the four weeks following this holiday weekend," Greg continued, "you will be billeted here. You'll eat, sleep, work, and practice here in the complex. The Force supplies your uniforms and all of the services and equipment you'll need. I hope this isn't going too fast for you, Blaire, but we try to not waste time. If you're going to train to fly fighters, I need you upstairs" —he pointed toward the ceiling— "as soon as I can get you there. Shara, myself, or both of us fly with the cadets often, so we'll see you a lot."

"If you have any questions, or need girl-talk time with your friends," Jill said, and tapped her forehead, "just talk to us. I'm available and Shar's usually available. Unless things get busy for some reason."

Blaire finished eating her main course and was about to get up for more to drink when a man and a woman stopped beside the table and greeted Shara and Greg.

"Colonel," Greg said, and stood up. "Please meet our newest cadet."

"Colonel?" Blaire asked absently. "You're Tayn's mom and dad. Sorry, sir," she continued, and hurriedly stood up.

"Blaire," Greg said. "Colonel Kooich, Leeana, and Tayn are billeted at the ranch in one of our apartments."

"Very pleased to see you again, 'Cadet' Lupis," Hench said, warmly stressing her title as Blaire took his hand in greeting. "The commander talked to us about your evaluations last evening. Very impressive. I'm sorry we missed seeing you, but I'm sure that will change."

Leeana smiled. "So I see you've decided to join our ranks. I'm glad."

"Thank you, ma'am," Blaire said. "I'm still a little overwhelmed."

151

"That will pass quickly," Leeana said. "Possibly we'll see you at the ranch over the weekend."

"Possibly," Blaire said, and watched as they turned, walked out of the Mess, and turned the corner into a corridor. Blaire sighed and sagged back into her chair.

"Blaire," Shara said, sensing Blaire's rising concerns. "You have no problems talking with Wally, right?"

Blaire shook her head.

"Think of Greg and me like you do Wally. He's the head man in the local Law Enforcement and Greg and I are the head men in this facility and Campaign. It's the same. You know Colonel Kooich—Hench—and Leeana, just by their informal names. They and Colonel Mooren and Franni are like our deputies.

"We'll watch and guide you, and when it's time, we'll evaluate your progress. But rest assured, there is no hidden agenda. We want you to succeed! If you succeed, we succeed. It's just that simple. Learn and ask questions when you don't know or don't understand. Ask us if you need help."

Blaire nodded and smiled. "Thanks. I will."

Greg and Shara sat quietly in their living room watching the fire in the large stone fireplace. Shara had settled in her customary manner on Greg's lap with her legs draped over the arm of the chair and Greg's arm around her, holding her gently to him. They *listened* to the children in the practice room with Meara and Kiile's corporal and assured themselves that all was well.

"Did I tell you Blaire found out about her ancestry?" Shara asked softly without moving.

"No, but I did have STSX do a little research on all of the deputies."

"Turns out Dan Lupis' family," Shara began, "family name Lomr, is from a small town near Casimir on Betolle, and her mother Mandy's family, maiden name Cumers, family name Cmrai, is from a small town outside of Daneubois on Feranni. Blaire is a full-blood."

"That certainly explains a lot," Greg admitted.

"Jill admitted Jack is Rygonian," Shara said, "and Amy is a Terran mix, making her a half-blood also."

"And you know Nick's mom Darcy was a Reeds, full-blood Kyddellan," Greg continued, "but did you know Bob is a half-Terran and half-Rygonian mix?"

"So Nick's three quarters and Jill's half," Shara said, thinking out loud, "making Cheyenne more than a half-blood."

"Yup."

"And you'll never guess," Shara teased, "but Rose revealed she's slightly more than an eighth Betollean herself. She doesn't know about Doug, but she will ask him tonight."

"My, my," Greg said. Then after a long moment, he continued. "Well it seems STSX found out that Doug McIntire's family line comes from Zeupa, a renowned educational city on Somstri in the Botuni System. He's also a full-blood."

Shara sat up and looked at Greg. "That makes Kayli and Kail more than half. Do you know if their bloodline is known for any particular talents?"

"I'm glad you're sitting down, Bren," Greg said, and smiled. "Telekinesis."

"Wow," Shara whispered. "Do you think that's why Doug has such a knack at fixing things? I know he's very well liked at the mill because of it."

"Possibly, Bren. Possibly," Greg said, and pulled her back to him.

"What about Alyssa and Ridan?"

"Wally is a half-blood," Greg admitted. "Family name Lmkii, his father came from Rygon while his mother is a Terran mix. Carole is the other way around. Marty is a Terran mix with a little Somstri mixed in, and Rusty is full-blood Ferannian. That's why Carole felt Wally when he was wounded in the attack east of Grants twelve years ago."

"Then their kids are half-bloods," Shara said.

"Yup." Greg smiled. "And Deputy Ted Marks is a half-blood from Antheria. Another heavy-worlder like us."

"That could be handy," Shara said absently, and Greg nodded.

"I also found out that both of Thomas Baine's parents immigrated as children from Istlar on Tanjera in the Ambali System. He's a full-blood. And Eddie's father Daniel, family name Calr, immigrated as a child from Teligr and her mother is a normal Terran mix. She's a half-blood."

"So, Billie too," Shara said, thinking of the number of Talents they were producing. "This is going to be hard to keep secret."

"I'm thinking so, too," Greg said, and looked up as Sedona and Sierra came through the back door followed closely by Cheyenne, Jill, Meara, Coleen, Brendan, and Henry.

"Where's Tayn?" Shara asked without getting up when the girls settled on the loveseat and Jill and Meara took places in the chairs and proffered the long couch to Coleen and Brendan. Henry found the overstuffed chair by the foyer.

"He went with the lieutenant to talk with Hench and Leeana," Sedona said.

"Here, Bren," Greg said, and helped her turn around to face Jill and Meara. She settled with her legs draped over the other arm of the chair and Sedona and Sierra smiled at each other. "How was the session?"

"Good," Cheyenne said. "Meara says we're doing very well in our physical and defense routines."

"They have mastered all of the routines we've given them," Meara said, and smiled at Jill. "I think Cheyenne is doing very well at keeping up with the others."

"I got Tayn twice tonight," Cheyenne said, and tapped her chest with her thumb. "He said that was very good."

"Yes," Greg said. "I suppose it is. What's the plan for tomorrow night?"

"No session tomorrow night," Meara said. "I figured the

kids need a quiet evening before the Thanksgiving excitement. They could use the time with their grandparents."

"You're probably right," Shara said.

"Dad?" Sierra asked, patiently waiting to get his attention.

"Yes, love," he said, and turned to hear her.

"Will you tell us what you found out about the man in the gray pickup?" she asked.

"I was going to talk about that later," Greg said, "but this is as good of a time as any. I take it he was gone when you walked Billie home."

"Yes," Sedona said. "He felt like he was far away to the south, but I couldn't tell how far."

"Okay," Greg said. "Wally said the truck was registered to a Jack Wilton of Hawthorne, one of two remaining men from the original Family Council which supported Judge Bernice's Council of Elders. But the man in the image from Six suggests it was Steve Wilton—Jack's son—that was driving."

"He knows who we are," Sierra said softly. "Do you think he'll be back?"

Greg steeled his expression, trying to maintain his composure and control his fears. "Sierra, I'm sure he, or some he sends, will be back. Our fear is that they may think it'll be easier to catch you kids than to catch Mom or Jill."

"That's why I asked you to start walking Billie home," Shara said, "so she won't be alone, and why I said I'd come and pick you up. If I need to, I'll pick all of you up at school."

"Wally called his deputy in Hawthorne, Bill Trent," Greg said, "and he'll keep a watch on the pickup and let us know if it heads north again."

"But Uncle Greg," Cheyenne said. "There are so many of them. Marshal Wally needs to watch all of them."

Greg looked down at Shara and then at Jill. "I know, Cheyenne. There are a lot of them, and we have to find and stop their leaders."

Wednesday, November 22

Eddie opened the kitchen door and waited as Shara parked the double-cab pickup in front of the furniture shop and got out.

"Hey," Shara greeted with a wave as she crossed the drive and stepped up onto the porch. "Just stopped by to pick up the girls and Tayn."

"Billie said they walked her home yesterday," Eddie said, and gestured Shara inside. "She said something about someone in a gray pickup was watching them."

"That's what we know," Shara said.

"With school dismissing early before the long weekend, I figured I'd come home and fix us some lunch," Eddie said as she took a couple of plates down from the cabinet. "She'll enjoy nosing around the flower shop while I work this afternoon."

"I heard you were back working part-time with Mary," Shara said. "How's that working out?"

"All right, I guess," Eddie said, and checked whatever she was baking in the oven and then stirred the pot on the stove. "I only work three days a week—mornings on Mondays and Fridays and all day on Wednesdays. I've set a couple of afternoons aside and am teaching Billie sculpting."

"That sounds nice. Does she like it?"

"Yes. Very much," Eddie said. "She likes the clay, though she hasn't settled on any specific subject. She likes to make all sorts of things, then she wads them up and starts on something else."

"Do you fire your work?"

"Yes. Thom bought me a good-sized kiln last Christmas and I still have the flat one for glass and other flat works."

"How's your dad?" Shara asked, hoping it wasn't a bad question.

"Basically, he's doing okay," Eddie said with a sigh. "You know he never really bounced back after they rescued him, but he knows where he is, who he is, who we are, and he delights in Billie's company. Those eight years of captivity probably aged him twenty, if one. A couple of years ago I tried to get him to move in here with us, but he wants to stay in my old house. Even though I have most of Mom's furniture here and bought new for him, he says he likes being where Mom lived for a while. The house is paid for and Thom wouldn't let me sell it when we got married, so it worked out well for him. We see each other nearly every day, and he gets out and comes by the shop on the days I work."

"I'm glad, Eddie," Shara said, and watched her as she went into the family room and looked out the back door at the street through the trees. "I wonder what's keeping the kids," she said. "They should already be here."

Eddie turned and saw the startled expression cross Shara's face.

"They're in trouble!" Shara shouted and turned for the kitchen door. "Sedona says four men came out of the woods after them! Call Wally!" Shara swung the door open, and dashed off the porch and ran down the drive toward Walnut and the school.

Eddie swung through the kitchen, snapped the stove and oven off, picked up the earpiece, and hollered for Wally as she followed Shara out and up the street.

One-Seventeen

"It feels like the same man," Sedona said as she pushed the elementary school's front door open and glanced up and down Ester. "There's more than one."

"They feel like big men," Sierra said.

"Can you hear them saying anything?" Tayn asked as Sierra led them across the street and started west on Spruce. "I'm not hearing them."

"A while ago," Cheyenne said, "but not now. I think they're in the woods beside Walnut."

"Billie," Sedona said, "you stay in the middle. Keep us around you as we go."

"Okay," Billie said, and Sedona felt her nervousness.

"They're a problem," Tayn said softly to Billie, "but we'll take care of you."

Sedona and Sierra walked side by side with Billie behind them. They led them west two blocks before turning south on Amos to meet up with Walnut. Tayn and Cheyenne followed side by side behind Billie, *feeling* and *listening* for the men. As they turned onto Walnut, Sedona scanned the wooded trace behind them and in front of them.

"They're close—" Sierra started to say when the four burly men sprang up from the verge and started running toward them, each carrying a rope in one hand and a large cloth sack in the other.

Cheyenne and Tayn quickly stepped up beside Sedona and Sierra, forming a line between the charging men and Billie.

'If they get past us, Billie, run like a scared horse!' Sedona shouted in her mind, and focused on one of the men.

'I will! Be careful,' a new voice said in Sedona's head, but she

had no time to think about it.

Tayn caught the closest man's arm and spun, twisting it and throwing the man forward. He was on the man's back before he hit the ground, then grabbed a handful of hair and smashed the man's face against the street. He repeated the move each time the man tried to get up.

When Tayn moved, Cheyenne jumped up and planted both feet squarely in the second man's face as she flipped and landed back on her feet. She bounced forward and charged as the man fell backwards and slammed onto the ground. He rolled over to push himself up and Cheyenne vaulted onto his back, caught his head and snapped it sideways. The man went limp and she turned to help Tayn.

Sedona and Sierra dove under their two men; each grabbed a leg and jerked them out from under them. The men spun off balance and slammed into each other. Sedona grabbed a handful of hair on her man and Sierra grabbed a handful of her man's and together they smashed their faces together. Sedona looked at Sierra and shoved her hand out for Sierra to take. When she did, they turned to the two staggering men and, still holding their hair, looked deep into both men's eyes. Their focused, concentrated shriek exploded in the men's minds; they grabbed their heads with both hands, stumbled backwards, and collapsed.

Sedona and Sierra turned quickly and saw Cheyenne smiling from where she knelt beside the unconscious body of Tayn's man, juggling a large rock.

Sedona glanced at the men, looked up, and saw her mom and Eddie running toward them.

"Dad and Wally are coming," Billie said, hearing the patrol car's siren coming closer.

⋏

Shar and Eddie slowed and stopped in the middle of the street and surveyed the scene; four large men incapacitated in seconds by four children. Marine Twelve and three other marines materialized at the edge of the street beside the men.

"I'm not sure I believe this," Eddie said softly. "I know

you've been training them, but..."

"Yeah, me too," Shara said as Sedona and Sierra ran forward and hugged her, and Billie hugged Eddie.

"We're okay, Mom. We kept Billie safe," Sedona said with her face buried in Shara's jacket.

Shara reached out and gestured for Tayn and Cheyenne to come to her, but Cheyenne came slowly, almost reluctantly.

"What's the matter, Cheyenne?" Shara asked, and knelt down to face her.

"I think I may have listened to yours and Mom's history too many times," she said as her eyes filled with tears. "I don't think that one's going to make it."

"Why do you say that?" Shara pressed.

"I watch Mom practice with Dad and she says when it's real, you have to fight to win." Cheyenne leaned forward and hugged Shara. "I knew this wasn't practice, so I fought to win and I won."

"Yes, dear, you did." Shara tightened her embrace and held Cheyenne for a long moment, wondering if they had gone too far, too fast. Then she looked around and smiled. The four children were unharmed and had prevailed against very serious opposition. *No,* she told herself, *we did this one right!*

"Captain," Twelve said as he looked up from the man Cheyenne referred to. "This one's dead. Broken neck."

"These two are unconscious," one of the marines said as he checked the men Sedona and Sierra had overpowered.

"Same here," another marine said when he checked the last man.

Shara, Eddie, and the children turned as Wally's jeep stopped by the curb and Thom and Wally got out. Thom rushed to Eddie and Billie and listened as Shara quickly explained what had happened, recounting the encounter the children had the previous day. Twelve confirmed the portions of the children's story that they saw.

"Six should have a complete video," Sierra said. "It was following us, but since the men did not have weapons, and we didn't call it, it didn't engage."

"When she finished with her man," Tayn said to Wally, "Cheyenne came and helped me knock that one out. I had him down, but she hit him with a big rock."

"We'll take them and get IDs and extract any information we can from them," Twelve said. "Marshal, what information do you need for your incident reports?"

Wally looked around again, stepped closer to Twelve, and then separated themselves from the group as they talked.

"Mom?" Sedona and Sierra asked together.

"Twelve won't be able to get anything useful from those two men," Sierra said.

"They're...sort of...vegetables," Sedona added.

Shara stood up and looked at her girls. "And just why do you say that?"

"We...sort of...figured out how to scramble someone's mind," Sierra said sheepishly.

"But this time I think we may have overdone it, as scared as we were," Sedona said. "I don't think their minds will heal."

"You were scared?" Shara asked, and looked at them closely. "I didn't detect any fear from any of you. I felt extreme focus and determination from each one of you—Billie included." She turned and looked at Billie and then at Eddie. "You may want to keep a close watch on Billie in case she starts developing early."

'She already hears and speaks, Mom,' Sedona said. 'I told her to run if we couldn't stop the men, and she answered that she would.'

"Really?" Shara asked, but not meaning it as a question. "Eddie, Thom. We need to talk before I take these four home. Wally? Do you need the kids any longer?"

"No, Shar," Wally said. "Twelve and his men will help me from here. Let me look at Six's videos sometime."

"Okay," Shara said, then turned her four charges and started walking back to Thom and Eddie's place. She looked at Eddie.

"I think you two have suddenly gotten your hands full."

⋀ ⋀ ⋀ ⋀ ⋀

"Abe? Nikle here," Don said when the voice on the other end of the phone connection said hello. "Have you seen the Copper boys?"

"Hey, Don," Abe said, his voice slightly garbled.

"Are you eating?"

"Yeah," Abe said, and his voice cleared as she swallowed. "Just getting started. It is that time of day and no, I have not seen the Copper boys. Are they supposed to be in town?"

"Yeah," Don said, instantly frustrated by Abe's reply. "I sent them up there to pick some things up for me and they have not returned."

The connection remained silent for a long moment.

"Are you there, Abe?"

"Yeah," Abe finally said, stretching his word out in exasperation. "Don, I do not want to know anything about what you are doing. You know the Copper boys would not come by my place, and I do not want to know why they were in town."

"Do not take that tone with me, Abe."

"It is not a tone, Don," Abe said sharply. "I have not seen them and I do not expect to see them, and I will not look for them."

"I want you to go down by the elementary—"

Don stared at the phone console when the connection light went out. He quickly rekeyed Abe's number and the phone rang without answer. He hung up and tried again.

"Damn you, Abe Brownly! You do not hang up on me! You will pay for this!"

Thursday, November 23
Thanksgiving

"Blaire," Mandy called as she slipped her coat on. "Are you riding with us or driving yourself?"

Blaire opened her bedroom door and stepped into the hallway.

"Actually, Mom, I'm going to have Thanksgiving dinner this afternoon with the Malones and their friends. I'm sorry I got in late last night and wasn't able to mention it."

"Aah. That was nice of them to invite you," Mandy said. "Will you stop by the Limas' later? At least to say hello and wish them a happy day?"

"Of course, Mom," Blaire said with a bright smile, and gave her mom a quick hug.

"Do the Malones host a big dinner?" Mandy asked as she led the way into the living room where Dan was waiting.

"I'm not sure," Blaire admitted, "but I suspect they do. Shara said there were going to be a number of people there that she wanted me to meet. I'll see after I get there."

"Okay, dear," Mandy said as Blaire put her coat on and grabbed her purse. "You have a good time and we'll see you when you stop by later."

"See you then," Blaire said as they stepped out and she locked the door.

⋀ ⋀ ⋀ ⋀ ⋀

Blaire took a side trip on her way and stopped her red jeep in the wide driveway of a large but modest ranch-style home at the west end of Birch. From her visits when she was younger, she remembered the beautiful view of the river framed in pine trees from the family room and deck on the back of the house. She stepped up onto the wide front porch and rang the door chime.

"Good morning," Blaire said when Sam's aunt opened the door and smiled, recognizing her. "I'm sorry to bother you on Thanksgiving, but I was wondering if Sam was around."

"Oh, I'm afraid he's gone at the moment," the woman said. "He didn't say where he was going, but I can take a message for you, Blaire?"

Blaire turned and studied the yard for a moment. "I wanted to be the one to tell him," she said, "instead of him hearing it from someone else, but I guess I really don't have much choice." She looked at Sam's aunt and smiled. "Please just let him know that I stopped by and wanted to tell him in person. Tell him that I'm going to be away for a while. I guess I may have gotten my wish, sort of."

"Your wish?"

"He'll know what I mean. Just tell him I'm sorry for everything. I didn't mean for things to work out the way they have. I'll see him sometime when I'm back."

"Will you be gone long?" Sam's aunt asked as Blaire turned and stepped down onto the sidewalk.

"I'm not sure," Blaire said, and smiled. "Maybe."

Sam's aunt was still watching her, and waved as she got into her jeep and backed out of the drive.

⋏ ⋏ ⋏ ⋏ ⋏

When Shara opened the heavy wooden front door and greeted Blaire, there were already a number of guests there. Shara quickly led her in and hung Blaire's purse and coat on a hook on the foyer wall.

"You look absolutely beautiful," Shara said, and smiled approvingly at Blaire. "Glad you wore a dress. There won't be many chances to wear one after this weekend."

"Thank you," Blaire said in return. "You look rather stunning yourself. Your dress, boots. I wouldn't have thought about doing feather tails like you did in your hair."

"Something my dad taught me to do," Shara said, referring to her hair. "I only get to wear a dress and dress up for holidays and special occasions," Shara said. "Greg still gets all goofy when I do."

"I can see why," Blaire giggled.

"Okay," Shara said as they stepped into the living room. "The important stuff. The necessary is down the hall on the left, between the girls' rooms, and the libations are on the buffet in the dining room. If you don't see what you like, ask me or catch Matti in the kitchen. Annie figures dinner will be ready around three, and other than that, mingle and have a good time. Give me a minute to check on the girls—get yourself something to drink and then I'll introduce you around."

Blaire watched Shara as she turned and went into the hallway, and then made her way to the buffet along the wall in the dining room opposite the kitchen. She smiled at the wonderful, teasing aromas spilling into the room as the house girls slipped in and out of the kitchen to manage the needs of their guests. She scanned the offerings and settled on a chilled white wine.

"Hello, Blaire. You look very pretty," Greg said as he stopped beside her with a warm greeting. "We're very pleased you could make it. Have you found everything you need?"

"Yes. Thank you. And thank you very much for the invitation." Blaire smiled. "But I am wondering—under the circumstances, am I supposed to start calling you commander?"

"Only when we're in formal company or on duty," he said, continuing to smile. "I know it seems a little confusing, but you are a personal and family friend and you may call us Greg and Shara when we're off duty or in private. Once you report for duty, I'll have to become your commander, like everyone else's, when we meet in training, meetings, or in official situations."

"I hope I can remember which to use when," Blaire said, concerned she might embarrass herself—or worse, Greg and Shara.

"You'll do fine," he said, and turned her to look around the room. "I know Shara will introduce you to everyone, but to help start, see the couple by the fireplace?" When she nodded, he continued. "That is Colonel Mooren and his wife Franni. He is in charge of my fighters under Colonel Kooich. Franni is Captain Mooren, a nav-com officer and a fully qualified pilot in her own right. She flew Shara's wing in most of the early campaigns, up until Shara's pregnancy advanced enough to take her out of the cockpit."

"She flew and fought while she was pregnant?" Blaire asked, surprised. "How long?"

"Yes, she did. Couldn't keep her on the ground, Blaire. She flew and fought up until her last month, when Meara told her she was starting to stress the babies." Greg chuckled. "She is a very strong willed and sometimes, determined woman."

"I know," Blaire said, and smiled at him. "I've assimilated the first two parts of the history upload STSX gave me. She is a rather unbelievable woman." Blaire took a deep breath. "Okay, you were saying. Colonel and Captain Mooren are your wing commanders. Who's next?"

Greg pointed to various other couples and individuals, giving her their names and ranks, and generally explained their function within his command. When he pointed them out, she saw the familiar faces of Doug and Rose; their two children, Kayli and Kail; the grandparents, Coleen, Brendan, and Henry; Colonel and Captain Kooich and their son Tayn; Meara; and Squad Leader Kiile. When he identified the four new flight cadets, she looked at Greg.

"They look so young. Am I too old to be starting this?"

"Blaire, you're not, but the new group is young. The youngest is fifteen, the same age that I was when I started flight training." He looked around the room and, seeing the woman he was looking for, he caught Blaire's elbow and led her into the formal part of the living room.

"Blaire," he said when they stopped in front of a seated woman that quickly stood up and faced them. "I would like for you to meet Captain Ani Tigs. Captain Tigs was your age when she came to us as a cadet for flight training. Captain Tigs, Cadet Blaire Lupis."

Ani greeted Blaire warmly and quickly introduced Blaire to her friends.

"Thank you, Ani," Greg said. "I'm going to introduce Blaire to a few others and then I'll let her mingle. Perhaps you can get to know each other a little then, and maybe let her know what she's gotten herself into."

"Yes, sir," Ani said, and smiled with a wink at Blaire. "I would love to."

Greg stopped at another couple, introduced Blaire, and made small talk before he moved on to another. They were about to move to another couple when Blaire saw Greg's smile as he glanced at the hallway. She turned and saw Shara leading the twins out to greet their guests.

"There they are," Greg said with a huge smile, and stepped forward.

Blaire waited beside him and smiled at the beautiful girls, nearly as tall as Shara, wearing matching dresses of the same cut, length, and fabric as their mother's, the same low-topped boots, jewelry, and hair feathers. Except for slightly longer hair and matching, subtle differences in facial features that she attributed to Greg's additions to their genetics, they were gorgeous young copies of their mother. Almost embarrassed, she saw Greg was beaming when he looked at Shara.

'Are you two trying to play tricks on our guests?' Blaire heard Greg ask the girls.

'No, sir,' they answered together. *'They do that all by themselves.'*

Greg chuckled and Blaire smiled, pleased to be allowed to eavesdrop.

"Well, I must say," Greg said as he reached out and caught one of each's hands, "you two look as beautiful as your mother. Let's go show you off."

⋏

Sometime after noon, Coleen, Brendan, and Henry,

in search of a little time away from the energetic crowd of guests, left the group and went out to the stable. They were not displeased or upset or lonely, but actually the opposite—filled with the happy enjoyment of every minute with their children, their grandchildren, and their many friends and associates— but they also enjoyed the moments away, to allow the energy to settle a little, to assimilate and reinvigorate their souls. And to fulfill that need to happily reflect on their blessings before the house girls called everyone to the banquet, they saddled the three horses they usually rode and spent some quiet time in the lower pasture to the west of the main house and ranch buildings.

Shara and the girls visited with one group and then another, slowly making sure they spent some time with everyone that came. Blaire enjoyed time with Ani and Emli and Barba, two of the other female pilots, talking about life in the valley and how lucky Blaire was that she could come and go into town as she pleased. Ani and her friends talked about how they still felt like the town saw them as strangers, out-of-town visitors when they ventured in to shop or grab a meal away from Obscure. Blaire mentioned that maybe having a 'local' go with them might make the excursion more enjoyable, and the women agreed.

The sudden rapping of the striker on the wood front door startled Blaire and she saw Shara casually get up and go to the door to greet whoever was late in coming. She watched as Shara opened the door and stopped in surprise and then firmly embraced a taller woman in a blue-black flight suit and holding a carrysack.

"Cheral!" Shara greeted loudly. "When did you get back?"

Shara stepped back inside and the woman followed her in. A second woman in the same uniform, also with a carrysack, followed Cheral in.

"Just a few minutes ago," Cheral said. "I hope you don't mind, but I decided to land here before we went to the base. Do you have a place where two weary space-farers can clean up and change into clean party clothes?"

"Certainly," Shara said, and started toward the hallway. "You can use our room."

"This is my nav-com, Lieutenant Keli Quil," Cheral said as they followed. "Keli, this is my cousin and our host, Shara."

Blaire leaned closer to Ani and asked, "Cousin? Is that Cheral Haak? Where has she been?"

"Yes it is," Ani said, and sipped her drink. "Captain Haak left Sunday to pick up her new fighter. I understand she was assigned a Q-Ship."

"Sorry—a Q-Ship is like the commander's ship and the big ones at Obscure?" Blaire asked.

"Right," Ani said. "She took flight training with my cadet class and finished flying a Class 2 patrol fighter like mine. And it looks like she got promoted, wearing major's lapel insignias. I'm told she was the commander's nav-com, a three-year rookie when they came to the valley."

"Yes," Blaire said, remembering the assimilated history information. "She was shot multiple times, badly injured in Pennsylvania when they were trying to find out where Point Obscure was."

"Really?" Ani looked at Blaire with a questioning expression.

"Yeah," Blaire continued as she absently watched Shara come out of the hallway and go back to the group she had been talking with. "Took her nearly eight months to get back on her feet and back to work. While she was recovering, her teammates brought her data as they collected it and she analyzed it, finally agreeing with the commander's opinion that Obscure was somewhere around here. She worked undercover here in town as a waitress and he as a college student until he found the complex. That was just before his sister Jill and Shara were both captured by the slavers."

"They were captured?" one of Ani's friends asked.

Blaire nodded. "The commander—major then—rescued Shara and treated her for the poison they gave her. Days later, when she had recovered, she demanded she be included in the attack on the Complex and the attempt to rescue Jill before the slavers shipped her out as a slave. Without her, I believe their mission would have failed."

"I didn't know that part of the history," Emli said.

"From what I'm learning," Blaire said softly, "the commander's wife is not one to take lightly. Especially in a fight."

"I know," Ani said. "Her combat kills are a record that still stands. She's broken her own record, twice, for the number of personal kills in a single engagement. And it's a treat to fly with her in combat."

"Seventeen still says she can replace any of his marines anytime she feels like it. The marines agree." Emli explained the story of Kiile's successful first attempt to stop a slaver's freighter from taking captives off planet and how Shara had taken out a sentry when he spotted them, by herself and barehanded.

"How long have you known the commander?" Ani asked. "It's obvious you're a close friend of the family."

Blaire pondered the question, trying to remember when she had actually first met them. "I guess since I was seven. I don't remember when we actually met, but they've been our friends since my mom and I moved here, almost twelve years ago. It really doesn't seem that long."

"It's also obvious," Ani said, "they think you're pretty special, and we'll help you get through your 'boot camp' as easily as possible."

"I'm not special, Ani," Blaire argued quickly. "I'm just someone they know."

"We were all just someone they got to know, Blaire," Barba said. "But they made us special to them and they've made you special to them as well. We'll certainly help anyone they think is special."

"Welcome to the Force and soon-to-be member of the Ladies' Brigade," Ani said, and raised her glass in a toast. "Lead us on a sortie to the buffet, Blaire. We need to acquire refills for these empty glasses."

▲ ▲ ▲ ▲ ▲

Stuffed from the huge Thanksgiving feast and very melancholy from the few drinks she had, Blaire relaxed and enjoyed the warm camaraderie of Ani and the other women pilots, the colonels and their mates, and the unexpected inclusion in Shara and Cheral's conversation about her trip to the Rings, her meeting with the director, and her promotion to major. Blaire felt like she was special, being included when Shara invited Lieutenant Quil to join the conversation and she talked about her three years of training at the Academy, how she wished she had known about Greg's school, and how thrilled she was when Cheral had selected her as her nav-com.

When Shara and Greg left with the girls to visit the Thomases, Blaire decided that was an appropriate time for her to also slip away to visit the Limas. Her head was still spinning from the evening as she turned up Carole and Wally's drive and drove up to their impressive house, literally a beacon, lit up on the brow of the long, sloping meadow that wended among the many stands of trees, extending up into the northern rim mountains. Blaire parked among the other cars, entered through the heavy, double wood doors under the portico, and hung her purse and coat on a wall peg.

"Blaire," Carole said, louder than normal, when she saw Blaire enter the living room. Carole greeted Blaire with a hug and asked if she wanted anything to drink or eat. "Make yourself at home," Carole said when Blaire replied "Maybe later."

Blaire walked over to the front window and found herself studying the lights of the town, how it lay with the land, and in the moonlight saw the higher ground between Saddle Horn and Cantle Ridge, realizing that was near the place where Shara had taken them Tuesday. She smiled, knowing she knew it was there when most did not.

"Pretty, isn't it?" Carrie said as she stopped beside Blaire. "Hope I'm not interrupting anything important or bothering you."

"Not at all," Blaire said, bringing herself back to the moment. "Did you have a good dinner?"

"It was wonderful," Carrie said expressively, "and so nice to be here with Gramms and Gramps and Uncle Wally and Aunt Carole."

"I think they're glad you're here too," Blaire said. "And for me, it's nice to see you again. Sorry I had to miss dinner with all of you."

"Dad said you were eating with the Malones," Carrie said, and Blaire nodded. "He says that over the years he's spent a lot of time with them, and with Mr. Malone before he got married. Something about work."

Blaire held her smile, knowing Jim Woods was a big part of the first two parts of the history STSX had uploaded to her.

"Was it nice?" Carrie asked. "Their dinner?"

"Yes, it was very nice," Blaire admitted simply. "I see the deputies came." Blaire noted her dad, Ted and Thom from the original group of deputies, and Bill Day, Scott Plumen, and Harvey Saulter, the new group that came to Riggin just after she and her mom had.

"Yes," Carrie said as she turned and looked around the room. "They're nice, but...I don't want this to sound too awful, but you're the only one that comes that is close enough to my age to talk to. Billie is too young, and even though you're almost four years older, I feel like I can talk to you."

"I know," Blaire said. "Billie has Alyssa and Ridan to talk and play with, but we're at that awkward age in the group."

Blaire saw Carrie stop and look at her. "Aunt Carole said she'd tell you, but Sam came by looking for you this afternoon before dinner."

"Did he want anything in particular?" Blaire asked.

"I didn't hear what he said to Aunt Carole," Carrie said, "but they talked for a few minutes. He had just finished dinner with his sister, his mom, and his aunt. I don't think his dad came up from Grants."

"That's a shame," Blaire admitted. "He was always close to his dad, but the last few years have been more difficult for him."

"Are you two an item?"

Blaire looked at Carrie, smiled, and shook her head. "No. I made Sam very angry a few years ago and he hasn't forgiven me. I think we could've been, but not now."

Blaire looked around the room and spotted the buffet table to one side in the dining room.

"Come on. I think I need a glass of wine after all." Blaire led the way across the living room, weaving through the chatting clusters of people. Then, with a glass of wine in hand and Carrie following with a glass of Carole's homemade lemonade, Blaire led them toward a corner of the living room to a couple of closely set chairs framed by the dining room steps on one side and the stone fireplace wall on the other. As they settled into the chairs, Blaire overheard Deputy Scott Plumen talking with Ted Marks.

"...Harvey and I worked the late shift last night and didn't hear anything about it until I read the incident listings this morning," Scott said to Ted. "Were the kids okay?"

He had Blaire's full attention.

"Yes. I understand," Ted said, explaining what he knew, "four big fellas with ropes and burlap sacks tried to take the five of them as they walked from school to Thom's place."

Blaire wanted to jump up and start asking questions, but restrained herself. She did not want to interrupt their train of thought or cause them to stop talking.

"What happened?" Scott pressed. "Harvey and I read the report, but Wally just wrote that the men were subdued and the children were unharmed."

Ted glanced around quickly and leaned closer to Scott. Blaire listened harder.

"It seems the four older ones—the Malone twins, the Jordan girl, and the Kooich boy from out at the Malone place— protected Thom and Eddie's daughter. Took the men down before they could get halfway across the street. The Jordan girl broke one man's neck and then helped the Kooich boy with his, knocked him out while the boy held him down. Wally found the other two men lying on the ground, muttering incoherent nonsense. They could barely walk and had lost all of their eye-hand coordination."

"What does that mean?" Scott asked.

"I don't know for sure," Ted admitted. "Wally just shook his head and said they had bloody faces, one had a broken nose, and beyond that they were simple, blathering idiots."

"Wow," Scott said in surprise. "How'd they do that?"

Ted shrugged. "Don't know. Mrs. Malone and Eddie got there in minutes. Said they heard the girl's screams but it was already over when they got there," Ted continued, gesturing with a shrug. "I sure wish I'd've been there to see it. You know, the fly-on-the-wall sort of thing."

Scott nodded with a smile. "I noticed they weren't in the jail. I suppose Wally's *friends* took them for interrogation?"

Ted nodded and absently tried to take a sip of his empty glass. He looked at the glass and motioned to the buffet and the two of them walked away. Blaire could not hear anything more without 'eavesdropping,' and turned back to Carrie instead.

Carrie was watching and Blaire knew she was waiting patiently.

"Sorry, Carrie," Blaire said. "I heard Ted and Scott talking about some trouble the children had yesterday."

"That's okay," Carrie said. "I heard Dad talking with Mom about it last night after I went to bed. Little Cheyenne was upset, but they were okay and unharmed."

"Upset? Because the man that attacked her died," Blaire surmised, sensing the pain and guilt a ten-year-old might feel after such an experience.

"Yeah," Carrie said softly. "I think that would be tough for someone that young. But Dad said Wally said she was a precise and skilled defender, no lost motion, no uncertainty, no hesitation. How he knows how she fought, I don't know, but Dad said she fought to win and to keep the others safe. She succeeded. I guess they all did." Carrie leaned closer and giggled softly, breaking the solemn mood that was developing. "Dad told Mom that Eddie pleaded with Thom and they finally asked Shara if they would train Billie like they did the older kids."

Blaire smiled. "That would only leave Alyssa, Ridan, and the McIntire twins," she said, softly to herself, thinking about the earlier discussion on bloodlines.

"Huh?" Carrie asked, barely hearing Blaire's comment.

"Nothing. Just thinking about the other young ones," Blaire said, and changed the subject. "Do you know when you're heading back?"

"Not until Sunday," Carrie said, sounding happy. "Mom and Dad are looking at land. We went out both Tuesday and yesterday looking at what's available, and Grampa Bill says there are a number of tracts that the Realtor doesn't have listed. I think we're moving."

"That's wonderful," Blaire said, quickly covering a sudden yawn and stretching her arm and shoulder. "Oh, my," she said, embarrassed. "I think I'm being told that I ate too much and did too much today. Can we go riding tomorrow? I think the weather is going to hold off."

"Sure," Carrie said, and smiled. "I'd like that."

"How about around ten?" Blaire asked as she stood up and finished her wine.

"Sounds great. I'll be here."

▲ ▲ ▲ ▲ ▲

"Hi, Grandpa," Sedona and Sierra said together when the Thomases' house girl let them in, took their coats, and they saw Greg's dad coming toward them.

"Hi there, yourselves," Jack said as he crossed the living room and gave them each a hug. "My, my. Don't you two look beautiful? Grandma and your aunt are in the kitchen. You're just in time for a late dessert."

"Thanks," they said, and hurried through the room, headed for the kitchen. "Chy? Grandma?"

"Hello, Dad," Greg said as he took Shara's coat and hung it on a peg beside the children's.

"How are you two doing?" Jack asked as he hugged Shara and then led them in.

"Managing," Greg said, and extended his hand to Nick. "How're the Jordans?"

"My head's still spinning," Nick said as they sat down in the spacious living room and he sat down beside his dad, Bob. "Thanks for letting Chy train with the others."

"We're all thankful we made that decision," Shara said softly. "Anyway, how're the new barn and the horses?"

"The main barn's been up for a number of weeks now," Bob said. "We repaired the damage to the feed barn in the first two weeks and replaced the damaged feed shortly after that. The horses are back under a permanent roof, which they seem to like better than the lean-tos and canvas tents we had to put them in."

"Yeah," Shara said with a chuckle. "They certainly do seem to have their preferences."

"Have you decided if you're going to add more hands?" Greg asked.

"I was looking around to see if anyone was interested," Nick explained, "but Dad decided to wait until spring. He feels we can manage through the winter with what we have. Winter is usually a lot less active."

"And Mom and I are going to help exercise the horses on weekends," Cheyenne said as she walked in, carrying a tray of iced tea glasses. "I hope this is okay. I chose tea for everyone since dinner was sooo good and we all ate waaaay too much. If not, I can get what ever you want."

"Aah," Greg said as he took a glass and handed it to Shara. "I didn't realize you were in training to be the next house girl."

"I like to keep my options open, Uncle Greg," she said

without skipping a beat. "Would you like dessert? It's a strawberry and lemon mousse stuff, all swirled up with nuts and whipped cream on top."

"Wow." Shara smiled and winked. "And a waitress too."

She smiled brightly, and when everyone accepted her offer, Cheyenne hurried back to the kitchen.

"I'm so glad to see she's happy," Shara said, and looked at Nick. "I'm sure yesterday still bothers her."

"Some," Nick admitted. "We sat on the deck by the fire last night and had a long talk about it. I think she knows we are very proud of her and of her ability to be a part of the team and help protect everyone. She felt better knowing Sedona and Sierra had to get tough too. Jill fussed over her a lot, talking about her own first fight and how she had to be tough to be part of your team and pointed out things from the history. It'll always be with her, but I think she has a handle on it now. She just has to remember when it's okay and when it isn't."

Shara nodded, smiled, and sipped her tea.

Only a few minutes passed before Cheyenne followed the house girl carrying a tray of dessert plates back into the living room. Jill came in and took a seat beside Nick, and Amy settled beside Jack as Cheyenne helped pass the plates around.

The conversation was happy and pleasant. Jack was pleased with work at the mill and praised Jill's accomplishments often. Sedona and Sierra talked about the horses and a test they had in school, and Amy gave them an update on the preparations for the Fall Flower Show scheduled for next week, hopefully before the snow started.

Finally, the evening started to get late and Greg silently asked Shara if she was ready to go. She was, and Greg told the girls it was time. They collected their glasses and took them to the kitchen as Greg and Shara got up and thanked Jack and Amy for the time with them. Jill hugged them both, and when Shara and the girls got their coats, Cheyenne stopped beside Greg.

"I want a hug from my favorite uncle," she said, and smiled at him.

Greg bent down, caught her around the waist, and picked her up in a tight hug.

"Thank you for saving Mom and being my uncle," she whispered in his ear.

He squeezed her a little more. "Thank you for being my favorite niece."

When he bent and set her back on the floor, she looked at him and her expression sobered. "I heard that Mr. Nikle last night, Uncle Greg. He was not happy. He called someone named Abe, and after, he was very upset and said a lot of very bad words."

"Thank you. We'll try to do a better job of watching out for him and those he sends," Greg said, and smiled. "Like you said, there are a lot of them and we have to watchful. Talk to me," — and he touched her forehead— "whenever you hear something you think I should know or have something you want to tell me, or if you just have a question. Okay?"

"Okay," she said with a wide smile.

As he stood up, he held her eyes and in a normal voice, he said, "We have three days of this weekend left, so you need to get your mom or dad to bring you to the ranch in the morning. Your physical and defense training scores are excellent and your navigation test scores were very good, young lady, so now it's time for you to learn the equipment."

"Really?" Cheyenne squeaked in disbelief, and looked at Sedona and Sierra's smiles.

"When have I ever given a cadet an order and not meant it?" Greg asked, and smiled at her.

One-Eighteen
Friday, December 1

"How do you two feel about your week?" Greg asked Sierra, who was sitting on his lap. After a light dinner and a visit to the stables to check on the horses, he and Shara had settled on the loveseat in front of the fire with the girls on their laps.

"Oddly enough, I think I'm getting the hang of the navigation stuff," Sierra replied.

"Oddly?" Shara asked. "What's odd?"

"Well, we both know how to read maps and stuff like that," Sedona said. "We can figure distances and times to places."

"But the maps in the training are all digital, three-dimensional, and sometimes very strange," Sierra continued. "And before we began to understand what we were seeing, you split us up."

"Don't get us wrong," Sedona said, "we like Leeana and all, but she explains things a lot differently than you two do."

"So?" Greg asked. "You didn't like spending one session with Leeana and then the next session with your mom?"

"It wasn't that, so much," Sierra said. "Though we do work better when we're together."

"It was the differences between Mom and Leeana," Sedona said. "Like, when you explain going to a particular place—"

"We can *feel* what we need to do to plan and plot the course," Sierra said, continuing Sedona's explanation. "We can *see* which programs we need to call up, which routines we need to pick, the inputs we will need to start the process. You know."

"It *feels* almost intuitive," Sedona said, and waited.

"Am I giving you too much information?" Shara asked, puzzled. "Am I absently telling you what the answers are? How to solve the problem?"

"You're supposed to tell us 'how' to solve the problem, Mom," Sierra said, and the girls chuckled. "I don't think you're giving us the answers, but I think we just know you better and we communicate differently than we do with Leeana."

"Physically by voice and in our minds at the same time," Sedona said with a firm nod. "We can *hear* Leeana, but we're not linked like we are with you."

"Maybe it's the mother-daughter, father-daughter thing. It's more emotional," Sierra said softly. "As long as we can remember, we've sort of known what you would say next, or do next. Not like seeing a future or anything like that—"

"But like a spilt second before you say things," Sedona finished for Sierra. "When we started *hearing*, we figured it out. And I think that's what's helping us when you teach us."

"We don't have that with Leeana," Sierra admitted. "She still teaches us okay, just different."

"She's like our teachers in school," Sedona admitted. "Knowledgeable, but the subject is just a subject to be taught and learned."

"But when you show us something, Mom," Sierra said, "it seems like the subject interests you, it seems important to you. You make us want to learn it. And I like that."

"Thank you," Shara said, and felt her face warm. "I would never call myself a teacher, but I'm glad that whatever I'm doing helps you understanding what you need to learn."

"Dad?" Sierra asked, changing the subject. "We noticed there are two styles of simulators. The one we use is like STSX. What's the other one?"

"It's a preflight console for the patrol fighter pilots," Greg explained. "The pilot uses it to preselect the information he or she expects to use on a mission, making it available during the mission without the delay of having to search for it on the fly. In flight, all inputs are through a small navigation terminal in the cockpit."

"So cadets training to fly the patrol fighters use it," Sedona confirmed.

"Yup," he said. "There is no verbal or empathic communications between the pilot and the patrol fighter. It's all done mechanically and electronically."

"But the hows and whys are all the same?" Sierra asked.

"Yes, for the most part," Shara said. "You're using the Q-Ship simulator because you, Cheyenne, and Tayn will be learning in STSX and KKLC."

Sierra smiled at Sedona and squeezed Greg.

"When will we actually start training on board STSX?" Sedona asked as she tightened her arm around Shara.

"Soon, I think," Greg said, and smiled at them and then suddenly turned to look past the fireplace.

Shara and the girls also felt the wave of urgency and saw the images of many men charging out of the dark woods, firing projectile weapons.

"Deputy Reeds is in trouble!" Shara shouted, but they all already knew.

⚔ ⚔ ⚔ ⚔ ⚔

"Good evening, Thad," the middle-aged woman behind Hector's Half Acre Café's pie counter said as he stepped in and glanced around the dining area of Community's only public eating establishment.

"Evening, Clara," Thad said. "How is Hector these days?"

"Fine. Doing fine. He is in the back fixing the dough for tomorrow's bread and rolls," Clara said, and picked up a menu. "You looking fer dinner? Or just something to drink?"

He caught her glance at his deputy's uniform and smiled. "Since I am still on duty, I will have dinner and a glass of your fresh-brewed tea."

Clara led him to a table near the back of the dining room and offered two specials as he sat down.

"I think the fried chicken," Thad said. "Dark meat, mashed

potatoes, and the green beans sounds good, and some of your giblet gravy."

He spread the napkin from the flatware on his lap and glanced around the room as Clara turned in his order and came back with his tea.

"Things seem a little more tense than they were on Wednesday, Clara," he said softly. "Hear of anything going on?"

Clara made a show of setting his tea on the table along with the basket of biscuits and a dish of butter pats.

"Seems some think Nikle is stirring the pot again," she said in between her motions. "I do not know what he is up to, but people are nervous, especially since he took that group on a hunt after Labor Day and he is the only one that came back. Too much like the old days."

"Yeah," Thad said with a nod, remembering Wally's incident reports on the attacks Nikle had perpetrated on the Malone and the Jordan ranches. He could not tell Clara what he knew, but hoped they could pin Nikle down before he caused more problems. He looked at Clara and said, "Let me know if you hear anything you think I should know. Call that number I gave you, anytime night or day."

She nodded and went back to check on her other customers.

Thad was watching two men seated near the front door when Clara brought his dinner and refilled his tea glass. The men seemed nervous, glancing at him numerous times after he sat down. As he ate, Thad noticed they continued to glance his way and he began to wonder if they were the nervous ones or if they were trying to make him feel nervous instead.

He finished his dinner, settled with Clara, and said he would see her and Hector on Monday, then he stepped out and casually walked the short main street of Community. The two men from the café left after he did and went the other way down the street.

Thad visited with the local merchants and many of the village folks as they ended their day. He knew most of them had homes scattered in the wooded lands around the village while a few had settled within the unincorporated boundaries of the town, and almost all of them he knew personally from his youth, having grown up there and raising his family in the nearby area. Many were surprised when he had come back as a deputy a year after Wally's big raid to release the captives Don Nikle had accumulated for a feeble bid at restarting Judge Bernice's slave-trading business. But in the years since, the townsfolk had come to accept and even seemed to enjoy the peace and security his and Deputy Willy Carle's presence brought.

Finally, Thad stopped at the hardware store and caught Walter as he was closing up for the night. He thanked Walter, as he usually did, for letting him park his jeep beside the store while he was walking around town. When Walter had gone on his way, Thad got into his jeep and started slowly through town, waved back at a few people that waved at him, and then he headed west on the road back to Grants.

About six miles from town, where the road turned south, away from the lake, WL-Two broke the silence.

"DEPUTY REEDS, THIRTY-THREE PERSONS ARE IN THE WOODS AHEAD! THEY ARE ARMED! FIFTEEN ON THE EAST AND EIGHTEEN ON THE WEST."

Thad stomped on the brakes and slid to a stop in the middle of the road, halfway through the curve. Suddenly the men rushed out of the forest, each shining a hand lamp in his direction. The jeep's windshield shattered and Thad threw the jeep into reverse and tried to back away. Bullets peppered the jeep as he swerved and careened into a ditch. A sudden pain burst in his side as he dove out into the darkness.

He rolled and returned fire through the space under the jeep; a man fell for each shot he fired. With only one more nine-cartridge clip in his pocket, he knew there were too many of them, but he focused and fired. Again and again.

⏶ ⏶ ⏶ ⏶ ⏶

"I'm seeing a number of infrared targets gathering east of

the little town," Franni said as she double-checked the monitor on the right-hand console of the nav-com compartment to confirm her sensation. "They are all men and they are armed with long guns, projectile weapons."

"Do you think they are hunters?" Colonel Mooren asked.

"I don't think so," Franni said firmly. "They have the same feel of intent as the men that attacked the commander's and Captain Jordan's places. Casi reinforced that feeling in the briefing at the first of the week when she told us that man Nikle was up to something."

"Better have Kiile put his troops on standby," Colonel Mooren said.

"I did, Crem," Franni said, and smiled.

"Where's the deputy?"

"He's walking along the main street on his way back to his vehicle," Franni said without having to look at the monitor.

"He'll be going back to Grants, won't he?"

"That's what he did Wednesday after he said goodnight to the man in the hardware store."

"Then he'll have to go past that group of men," Crem surmised, half out loud. "Franni, I don't think I like this. Can you tell if that man Nikle is with the group of men?"

"No. I don't have his particular sense so I can't tell," she admitted. "The commander or Casi might be able to tell."

"I know, but I hate to bother them with something we should be able to handle," Crem said with a sigh. "If we take precautions, we might be able to round them all up if they try anything. Then we can see who's there."

"The deputy is leaving town," Franni announced. "And the men on the road have split into two groups, one on either side of the road at the big curve nine miles east of the town."

"Drop three of the remotes and let Kiile know if the *feel* of the men goes hostile."

"TTYF, position remotes Three, Four, and Five around the cluster of men I am monitoring," Franni said to their ship. "Arm weapons for possible defense. Crem, bring us down closer."

"Closing," he said, and let TTYF8 drift down along the north side of the road, over the south shore of the lake.

"They're definitely hostile," Franni said. "I sense some sort of short-range communications in use. Someone in town must've told them when the deputy left town. TTYF, request Kiile's immediate ground support. Contact Colonel Kooich and request a patrol fighter for backup."

Franni and Crem watched the jeep as Thad drove along the lake and suddenly slid to a stop as he entered the curve turning away from the lake. They knew his remote had alerted him. The men in the forest charged out when they saw the jeep back away.

"Remotes, fire!" Franni shouted when the men fired on the jeep and the deputy began returning fire. "TTYF, all remotes, defend the deputy. Fire! Surround and restrain the attacking men. The deputy has been hit! Contact WL-One and the marshal!"

▲ ▲ ▲ ▲ ▲

"STSX," Greg said as he stood Sierra up and got up himself. "Hover behind the main house. We'll board from here."

Shara turned and looked at him and then quickly at the girls, waiting, watching their parents, unsure of what they expected of them.

"Girls, get your Blues," Shara said, and ran to the bedrooms. "You have one minute to dress." She turned and saw Greg was right behind them. "STSX, alert Kiile and the marshal. We'll pick the marshal up as we leave."

They changed quickly and Shara and Greg were in the dining room before the girls caught up. Sierra was clasping her utility belt as she came out of the hallway.

"SQUAD LEADER KIILE IS ALREADY EN ROUTE WITH A TRANSPORT AND THIRTY TROOPERS."

"STSX, Ignition ready," Shara called as she ushered the girls through the door. "Greg, take this leg. I'll have the girls watch the planning."

"Close the aft portal," Greg said as he hurried ahead and climbed the ladder to the cockpit.

He was in his chair and strapping himself in when the girls climbed through the floor portal and turned aft to the nav-com consoles. Shara slid into the cushioned chair and asked for system status.

"IGNITION READY. CLOAKING ON, SENSOR BLOCKING ON, SHIELDS FULL, PASSIVE SCAN IS CLEAR."

"Systems are ready," Shara said as she strapped in.

"Lift two hundred feet," Greg said. "Secure?"

"Everyone's secure, love," she replied. "The girls are on the pullout jump seats. Let's get Wally."

Greg swung STSX around to the northeast and pushed the thrust levers forward.

"COLONEL MOOREN SAYS DEPUTY REEDS HAS BEEN SHOT IN THE ATTACK. HE RETURNED FIRE AND NEUTRALIZED TWELVE OF HIS ATTACKERS. TTYF8'S REMOTES NEUTRALIZED SEVEN ATTACKERS WHEN THEY RESISTED. THE REMOTES HAVE CONTAINED THE REMAINING FOURTEEN."

"STSX, tell Wally we will be beside his ranch house in less than three minutes," Shara said, and switched on a number of screens, quickly explaining to the girls what she was doing and why.

When she felt STSX start down and the ranch getting closer, Shara turned to Sierra. "Please go down and bring the marshal on board. Give him a choice of a cockpit jump seat or one of the seats below."

"Sure, Mom," Sierra said, and hurried down the ladder.

Shara felt the marshal waiting as STSX settled near the circle drive and the aft portal opened.

Sierra greeted him, asked STSX to close the portal, and offered the marshal his choice of seats. As she had expected, he chose a cockpit seat where he could talk to them.

"Thanks," Wally said as he turned to the cockpit. "Can we grab Thom on the fly?"

"Sure," Greg said. "Should we land in the shop parking lot or the field to the south?"

"If you hover, he said WL-One can bring him up," Wally said. "I can bring him aboard if you like."

"Thanks," Greg said as he swung STSX south and accelerated.

⏶

"Okay," Shara said, and looked at the girls. "What would you plot to get there quickly?" Shara put their destination on the three-dimensional display.

"Vertical departure," Sierra said.

"Then skim along above the thicker air, maybe twenty-five miles up, and drop straight down when we get there," Sedona added.

"Why?" Shara asked.

"Mother," they both said together.

"The shock wave!" Sierra said. "We don't want anyone to hear us—"

"And at twenty-five miles up, we can go a *lot* faster. There isn't enough air to cause much noise," Sedona finished.

"Right you are," Shara said, and listened as Wally brought Thom on board. "STSX, secure the airlock, please. We need to hurry." Then Shara nudged Sedona.

"Dad," Sedona said as she turned forward, "we have a flight plan laid in to get us there as quick as possible."

"I see it. Thanks," Greg said. "Thom, Wally, grab a seat down there until we get back to level and stabilized."

"Okay," Wally said loudly. "We're ready."

"STSX," Greg said, and passed his warm thoughts to his girls. "Let's follow the plan and get there." He shoved the thrust levers forward and pulled STSX's nose up to follow the girls' green line.

▲ ▲ ▲ ▲ ▲

"Do you see anyone else in the forest, Franni?" Crem asked as he maneuvered TTYF around the scene below, watching Kiile's troopers as they herded the last nine attackers into a cluster beside the road.

"Not close by," Franni said. "TTYF, send one of the remotes to check out the pair of figures I sense on the ridge about three miles above the lake. Due north. Keep Cloaking on. Kiile has Deputy Reeds on board his transport and in Medical, Crem."

She focused on her sensation and TTYF acknowledged.

"There are two people on a rock outcropping," Franni continued. "They could be watching."

"They'd have to have night-vision equipment to see anything," Crem said as he swung around to the south of the scene and looked across the dark lake. "TTYF, bring up an enlarged view of Franni's sensation. Can we see anything visually?"

"INFRARED AND ULTRAVIOLET ENHANCEMENT SHOWS TWO PERSONS," TTYF said as the enhanced image coalesced in front of Crem.

"Both are male," Franni said, "and I estimate one to be in his fifties, Terran years. The other is younger. They do appear to be watching for something. Do you suppose someone was supposed to provide a signal when they succeeded?"

"Most likely," Crem said, and had a thought. "TTYF, ask Kiile if he can rig a fire to simulate a jeep burning."

A short moment passed and then TTYF said, "SQUAD LEADER KIILE SAYS YES. GIVE HIM A MOMENT TO PREPARE."

"The commander is descending, Crem," Franni said. "He has the marshal and Deputy Baine with them."

"Tell him what's up and that we think the scene is being watched," Crem said.

Franni focused her mind and connected with Shara, giving her the complete synopsis and explaining what they were about to do.

"REMOTE THREE HAS SENT ENHANCED IMAGES OF THE MEN ON THE RIDGE. THEY ARE WAITING, WATCHING WITH A LONG-RANGE TELESCOPIC VISUAL DEVICE. THREE ASKS IF IT SHOULD DETAIN THE TWO MEN."

"Franni," Crem said. "Ask Casi if she can tell anything about the two men and if they want us to detain them."

Franni connected and smiled.

"Casi says the older one is the man Nikle," Franni said. "She says she will ask Kiile to take a small squad and encircle them, night vision and cloaked. She is sending their remotes Nine and Ten to lend support to our Three. Once they are in position, Kiile will wait to see what they do when the marines set the fire."

The few minutes it took to get everyone situated seemed forever, but finally Three reported Kiile and ten marines were in place, and Three, Nine, and Ten were equally spaced around the men and their farm truck.

⚓

Don was looking through the monocular telescope and smiled when he saw the fire slowly begin and grow beside the road on the south shore of the lake.

"They must have had a little trouble getting the deputy," Dan said to the man beside him.

"They may have winged him and had to hunt him down," the man said.

"Maybe," Dan said, and straightened up. "But that's one down. Now we need to get up to the ranch and plan for the next one. Buddy will be there by the time we get there."

Don unscrewed the base of the telescope and handed the optical unit to the man and then bent to collect the tripod. He froze when Kiile shouted.

"Hands on your heads! Do not try to run!"

The man with Don dropped the optical unit and sprang for

the truck. The darkness exploded in a fiery burst of brilliant white light and the man slammed into the truck and bounced, falling back in a lifeless heap.

Don spun toward the disembodied voice, drawing his Greymn in his turn. Suddenly a brilliant flash erupted where his hand held the Greymn and another threw one leg out from under him. He tumbled aside, screaming in pain as an unseen marine knelt beside him and administered an anesthetic. When Don slumped to one side, silent and limp, the rest of the squad reported success to Kiile.

"Well done, lads," Kiile said. "Cleanse the site and let's get them loaded. The commander will be waiting. He'll be pleased with the fruits of our hunting."

⁂

With the transport positioned beside the road, hovering above the lakeshore, Kiile stepped out through the wide aft portal and down the extended ramp. He stepped through the veil and greeted Shara and Greg as they stopped in the middle of the road, surprised to see their girls close beside them.

"May Wally and Thom go aboard to see Thad?" Greg asked as he took Kiile's extended hand.

"Yes, sir," Kiile replied. He turned with a nod and the marine beside him led the marshal and deputy through the veil and up the ramp. "We also have your Mr. Nikle on board."

"That's what I hear," Greg said with a smile. "I understand Franni sniffed him out, and when we got here the girls confirmed he was there."

"The girls?" Kiile asked, and looked from one to the other with a wide smile. "You two're getting to be as valuable as your mom and dad."

"Thank you, sir," they said together.

"Commander," Kiile said, and turned his attention back to Greg. "We'll interrogate Mr. Nikle and get all we can when he wakes up, but we heard him tell the other one that someone named Buddy would be up at the ranch by the time they got there. I figure we need to be there to greet Buddy when he arrives."

"I think that would be a great idea, Kiile," Greg said.

"I'm thinking the ranch is the Niles Reeds Ranch east of Hawthorne," Kiile continued. "It would take them a couple of hours to get there by truck."

"Come by the ranch tomorrow sometime and give the Colonel and me a briefing," Greg said. "Do you need our support any longer?"

"TTYF8 is covering us from above and they have a patrol fighter with them, so I think we're covered adequately."

"Okay," Greg said. "I'll go and see what Wally needs. He may want to go with you instead of going back with us."

"Yes, sir." Kiile smiled and turned to another marine. "Seventeen, organize some men and get the deputy's jeep on the transport."

Saturday, December 2

"Time to get up, sleepy head," Shara said as she entered Sedona's room and gently shook her daughter. "Cheyenne's going to be here any minute and you need to get dressed and get some breakfast. Do you know what you want?"

"Do I have to?" Sedona mumbled, and rolled over.

"Yes. Right now," Shara persisted, and shook her again. "What do you want Annie to fix?"

"Cereal," Sedona mumbled, and threw the covers off.

Shara stepped out and opened Sierra's door, and was halfway to the bed when Sierra muttered. "I heard you, Mom. I'm getting there." She threw the covers off, but did not push herself up. "Cereal and toast."

"Okay. In your clean Blues and bring your soiled ones with you," Shara said, stopping to look into Sedona's room. "We'll clean them while you're having your lessons."

"All right, Mom," they said together, and Shara headed for the dining room.

She poked her head into the kitchen and told Annie what the girls wanted, and then went to the back door. She turned and looked at Greg.

"I'm going to get STSX ready," she said. "Jill, Nick, and Cheyenne are almost here."

"Okay, love," Greg said. "I'll keep the girls moving."

He watched Shara as she left and then *followed* her as she walked with purpose out to STSX in the west pasture. By the time she reached him, the girls had made it down the hallway and into the dining room.

"I see we kept you two up way too late last night," he said, and smiled.

"Yeah," Sedona said, and yawned

"Is Tayn with Hench and Leeana this morning?" Sierra asked as she slid into her spot at the table.

"Yes," Greg said. "They finished breakfast over a half an hour ago and Leeana is going to take Tayn up in KKLC this morning. You two, if you can wake up, are going with Cheyenne in STSX. Juice?"

Sierra nodded and Greg filled glasses for each of them as Annie brought a carafe of milk and a bowl of yogurt and set them on the table. Kym set a cereal bowl in front of each of them and Sierra and Sedona thanked them through unexpected yawns.

They had just started eating when Cheyenne ran between the main house and the east apartments, across the back porch, and in through the back door. "You're still eating?" she asked in surprise.

"Yeah," Sierra said while Sedona chewed her mouthful. "We had a very late night."

"I heard," Cheyenne said. "Mom told me what she saw. Was it exciting?"

"The flying was," Sedona said. "But the rest was just trying to stay out of the way. We stayed close to Mom and Dad, not sure if any of the men still had guns."

"Wow," Cheyenne said softly, and looked at Greg. "Sorry,

Uncle Greg. I know it was scary, but it still sounds exciting."

"Just don't let it go to your heads," he said to all three of them. "It might sound exciting, but it's no fun when someone shoots at you and wants to stop you—or worse, kill you. If you do something wrong and they succeed, it messes up everything you had planned to do next."

Cheyenne stared at Greg. "Yes, sir. I'll remember."

Sedona and Sierra nodded quickly when he looked at them.

"Good. This is serious," he said, "so don't forget and think of it as a game. We certainly don't want any of you to get hurt or worse. That would ruin the rest of our day too."

He held their attention a few moments longer and then looked up as Jill and Nick opened the back door.

"Morning, Greg," Jill greeted. "Sounds like you had a night full."

"Yes, we did," Greg said, and glanced at the girls. "We just had a few comments about that." He looked at Sedona and Sierra. "Finish up. Mom's waiting for you."

"Shar's out in STSX?" Jill asked, though she quickly confirmed where she was.

"Yes," Greg said with a nod. "She wants you to go with her and the girls and I need Nick to sit in on a briefing when Kiile gets here."

"We're ready," Sedona said, and stuffed the last spoonful into her mouth, and Sierra swallowed the last of her juice. Sedona got up, grabbed her soiled Blues, and started for the door, but stopped and quickly ran back to Greg. "Thanks, Dad," she said as she threw her arms around his neck and squeezed him tight. "We won't forget."

She waited for Sierra to hug Greg and then they hurried out the door with Cheyenne and Jill close behind.

"Morning, Aunt Shara," Cheyenne said as she climbed

through the floor portal and stood to one side of the central compartment.

"Morning to you too," Shara said, returning the greeting as Sedona and Sierra followed her up. "I want you, Cheyenne, in the nav-com chair, and you two" —she gestured to her girls— "up front in the jump seats. Jill, you can stand in the cockpit or use one of the pull-out seats. Your choice."

Cheyenne quickly strapped herself into the nav-com's chair and the girls went forward. Shara checked the chair straps and then stood up beside Cheyenne.

"I want you to calculate and plot a course from here to the earliest rendezvous with the space station S.S. QuickSilver. Display all time points and any course change points you calculate and provide a duplicate display on the cockpit three-dimensional display."

"Yes ma'am, Aunt Shara," Cheyenne agreed with a wide smile.

"And where are we, Cadet?" Shara asked in a sharper voice.

Cheyenne looked up, her expression contrite. "On an official mission, aboard a heavy fighter in the service of the Force, Aunt, er, Captain Casi," Cheyenne said in a rush, remembering the change in protocol.

Shara softened her poise with a smile. "Thank you, Cheyenne. We need to remember."

"Yes, ma'am," she said, and turned to the monitors on the three walls of the compartment.

"STSX," Shara said as she turned toward the cockpit. "Hover at two hundred feet. Ignition ready. Systems status, please."

She caught the grab rails in the central compartment as STSX lifted, and in a fluid motion she dropped into the pilot's chair and swung it to forward facing as she secured the straps. Casi quickly glanced at Sedona and Sierra's wide smiles and asked "Everyone secure?"

"Secure," Jill answered.

"CLOAKING ON. SENSOR BLOCKING ON. SHIELDS FULL. AIRLOCK SEALED. SYSTEMS ARE MISSION READY.

IGNITION ACTIVE," STSX said as he leveled above the ranch and its shield dome.

"Departure one hundred sixty-five degrees and elevation eighty degrees," Cheyenne announced as the three-dimensional translucent globe coalesced in front of Casi and to her right, suspended in the otherwise vacant space between her and the forward cockpit wall. "Course plot coming up, Captain Casi. Rendezvous in ten point six minutes. Mark."

Casi pushed the thrust levers forward and smoothly but aggressively pulled STSX's nose up to follow Cheyenne's course line on the display. She *felt* Cheyenne look up through the transparent nav-com compartment ceiling and knew she could only see the darkening sky. Casi slowly rolled STSX so the receding landscape was visible to her and she heard Cheyenne's sigh of pleasure in response.

Casi studied the course data as they began to push over and the effects of gravity began to lessen, and smiled at Cheyenne's thoroughness. Cheyenne had displayed the calculated speeds along with the altitude and lat-long positions for each of the small course-change points, showing the necessary increases in speed STSX would need to hit in order to ensure a smooth rendezvous.

"Rendezvous in six point four minutes," Cheyenne announced, sounding completely official without any traces of her age other than the timbre of her voice.

"IFF on. Contact QuickSilver Apache Watch," Casi said. "Let them know we are joining up and will be in formation for a little while. Give them the position you have plotted for us."

"Yes, ma'am," Cheyenne said softly, and then turned to the task. "QuickSilver Apache Watch. Apache commander joining you in left echelon, eight o'clock high, closing to two miles."

"Apache commander. Good morning. Apache Watch has you twenty out and closing," the surveillance officer's feminine voice replied. "Is there anything we can do for you this morning?"

'*Anything you need?*' Cheyenne asked.

'*No, Cheyenne,*' Casi answered. '*Thank them and explain our*

197

mission.'

"Thank you, Apache Watch," Cheyenne said. "Nothing today. We are training new cadets in the finer points of precision navigation and in clear and effective communications."

Casi chuckled and Jill smiled at Cheyenne's paraphrasing of the syllabus description.

They heard the surveillance officer's mirth as STSX settled into position slightly behind and above, two miles to the station's left.

"We hope you have a good mission, Apache commander," the surveillance officer said.

"Thank you, Apache Watch," Cheyenne said, and switched the coms to standby.

"Very nicely done, Cheyenne," Casi said. "We have arrived on time and in the correct position without causing distress or concern for the station's crew. Thank you. Any comments?" She looked at Jill.

"No, Casi," Jill said, her pride showing in her voice.

"Mom?" Cheyenne asked, turning her seat to face her. "Do I have an official mission name, like Aunt Sha—I mean Captain Casi?"

"Not yet, dear," Jill admitted. "Not until you're registered."

"Caiti and Coli have theirs already," Cheyenne argued. "Why—"

"We need to talk about this after the mission," Jill said sternly. "I promise we'll talk with your aunt and uncle about it then."

Cheyenne turned back to the consoles. "STSX, please store the content of the navigation exercise," she said, and then waited in silence.

"Cheyenne," Casi said softly, pushing her warm feelings to her. "Please trade places with Coli. You did very well and now Coli needs to do an exercise."

The girls switched places and Casi turned her attention

back to the mission.

"I want you to locate Shelly Woods and plot her location on the three-dimensional display," Casi said as Coli secured the seat straps.

Almost before Casi finished with the request, a single green dot appeared on the display.

"Shelly Woods is presently grocery shopping," Coli said. "Carrie is with her and they are discussing ranch property they looked at across the road from the Lazy D."

Casi smiled and Jill turned to look at her niece, surprised at her quick retrieval and detailed response.

"Calculate and plot the most direct course to a position over their present location," Casi said, taking note of their own position.

Coli bent to the task and a blue line appeared on the display, arcing over the north, polar region from their position over central Asia. "Estimated time en route is fourteen point eight minutes at normal cruise speed, er velocity."

"Let Apache Watch know we're leaving," Casi said.

"Yes, ma'am," Coli said. "Apache Watch. Apache commander is breaking formation."

"Roger, Apache commander," the surveillance officer said. "It was nice to speak with you. Have a good mission. Apache Watch out."

"Thank you. Apache commander out," Coli said, and returned the coms to standby as Casi pushed the thrust levers forward and STSX drifted out of position.

~

After Caiti finished her exercises, Casi rolled STSX inverted and started a slow cruise across Europe and snow-covered northern Asia, along the Aleutians and down across the wintery western Yukon and northern US to the valley.

"Looks like that winter weather is going to drift across the valley today," Casi said softly as they slipped over the edge of the cloud bank approaching the valley from the northwest.

"Doesn't look like the snow showers we got last week," Jill admitted. "This one looks like it could be our first serious snow this fall."

"Caiti?" Casi asked. "What does the scanner show for a snow density?"

"Do you want moisture content or estimated snowfall?" Caiti asked in reply.

"Snowfall," Casi said, smiling.

"Presently, about three inches per hour," Caiti said. "Forecast indicates more in the valley after the storm passes the Rim Mountains. Possibly up to five per hour by midnight. The storm should last until tomorrow, mid-afternoon."

"Okay," Casi said. "Let's get down, have some lunch, and get ready for the afternoon session."

⋏ ⋏ ⋏ ⋏ ⋏

"I certainly hope today is better than last night seemed to be," Nick said as Greg listened to the girls and Jill as they walked out to STSX.

"I hope so too," Greg sighed. "Maybe now we can stop the attacks and the raids, at least here in the valley, and we can begin again to focus on other places."

"Did Jill have it right that Wally's deputy was wounded?" Nick asked, and followed Greg into the living room where Greg sat down in his favorite overstuffed chair by the fire.

Greg sat the carafe of coffee on the end table and gestured to Nick, asking if he wanted a cup. "Thad was hit twice in his right side as he tried to back away from his attackers."

Nick nodded as he sat down and passed a cup for Greg to fill. He looked up as Hench entered through the back door and stuck his head in the kitchen to get a second carafe of coffee. He grabbed a cup and joined Greg and Nick in the living room.

"Is he okay?" Nick asked as Greg handed the filled cup back. "I assume Kiile put him in Medical."

"Morning, Nick," Hench said as he settled on the long couch and poured himself a cup. He set the carafe on the end table.

"Morning, Hench," Nick said.

"He did," Greg said. "Kiile will give us an update, but STSX confirmed Kiile's Medic was able to remove the bullet that didn't go completely through."

"Glad he's going to be all right."

'*SQUAD LEADER KIILE HAS ARRIVED,*' Two said as Kiile's transport settled onto the west pasture.

"Kiile just landed," Greg said out loud. "We'll get an update in a moment."

Nick nodded. "How are the girls doing?"

"Shara's flying a course Cheyenne plotted to rendezvous with the space station," Greg said after a quick check. He smiled at Nick. "It seems to be a good course and very thoroughly planned out."

"I'm glad she can settle down and rise to the challenge," Nick said. "She's very smart and capable, but sometimes her youth gets in the way."

"Certainly," Greg agreed. "We just need to keep working with her without taking that youthfulness away. She can still have both, but just needs to learn how to move from one to the other at the right times." He turned to Hench. "How're Tayn's exercises going?"

"Good, I think," Hench said, and smiled. "A little less youthful spontaneity, maybe, but he is still young and easily distracted."

"Aaah, here's Kiile now," Greg said, and looked up as the back door opened and Kiile walked slowly through the dining room and stopped at the edge of the living room.

"Coffee?" Greg asked. "Grab a cup from the table."

"Yes, sir," Kiile said, and stiffly picked up a cup and returned to the living room. "Thank you, sir."

Greg looked at Kiile, recognizing his disappointed manner and contrite air from their long association.

"Okay, Kiile," Greg said, and poured the coffee. "What's the problem? What's happened now?" He handed Kiile the cup.

"I'm glad you didn't ask what I've done now, sir," Kiile said, and tried to smile. "But the truth is that it's my fault and I will assume full responsibility for the incident."

He had their attention and stood rigidly at the end of the loveseat.

"I've lost Nikle." Kiile's face went completely ashen as he stared at Greg.

Shara and her extended family's journey continues in
Paladin Shadows Series Book 11,:
Garda Nua Part 2: When a planet is stolen.

Riggin Town Map

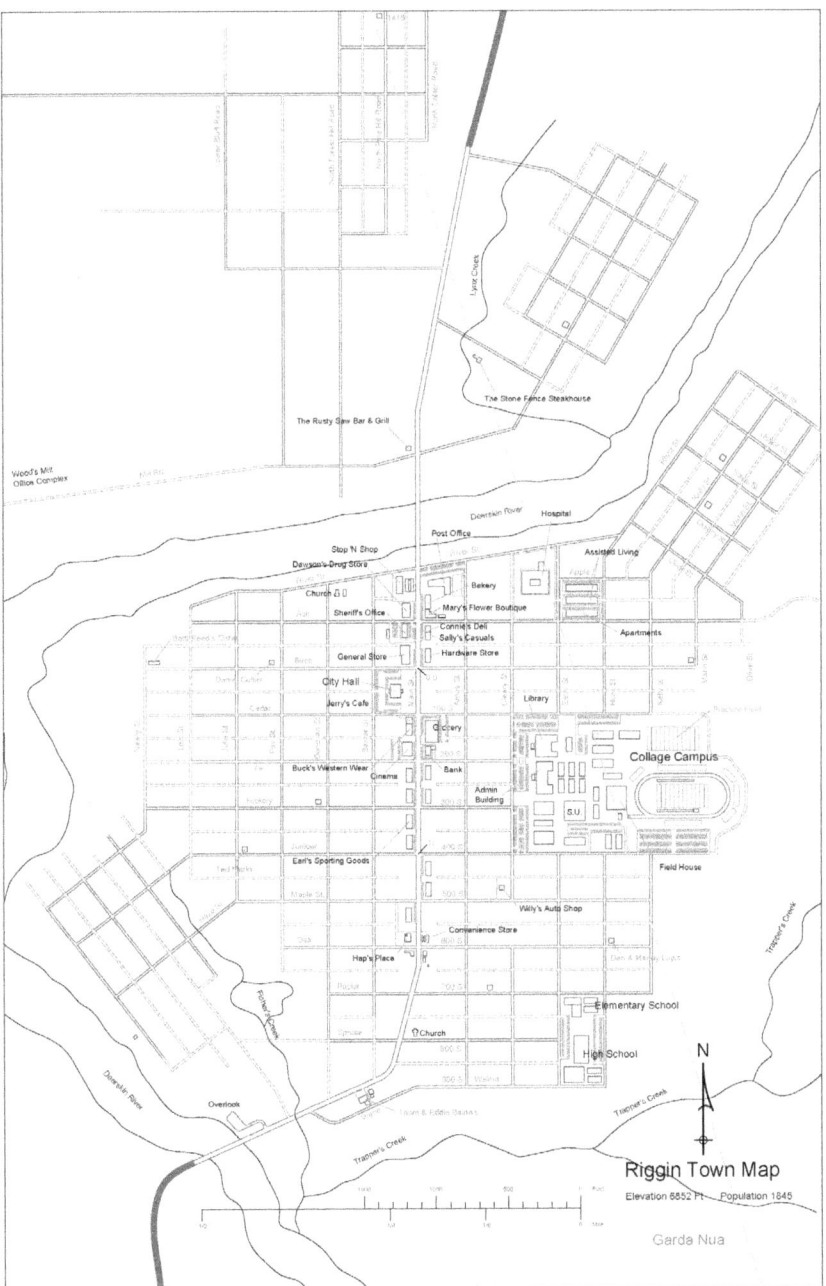

The Stone Fence Steakhouse

The Rusty Saw Bar & Grill

Woof's Mit
Office Complex

Downish River   Hospital

Post Office

Assisted Living

Stop N Shop

Dawson's Drug Store

Church

Bakery

Sheriff's Office

Mary's Flower Boutique

Connie's Deli

Sally's Casuals

General Store

Hardware Store

Apartments

City Hall

Jerry's Cafe

Library

Grocery

Collage Campus

Buck's Western Wear

Cinema

Bank

Admin
Building

S.U.

Earl's Sporting Goods

Field House

Willy's Auto Shap

Convenience Store

Hap's Place

Elementary School

Church

High School

Overlook

N

Riggin Town Map
Elevation 8852 Ft   Population 1845

Garda Nua

Riggs Valley Map

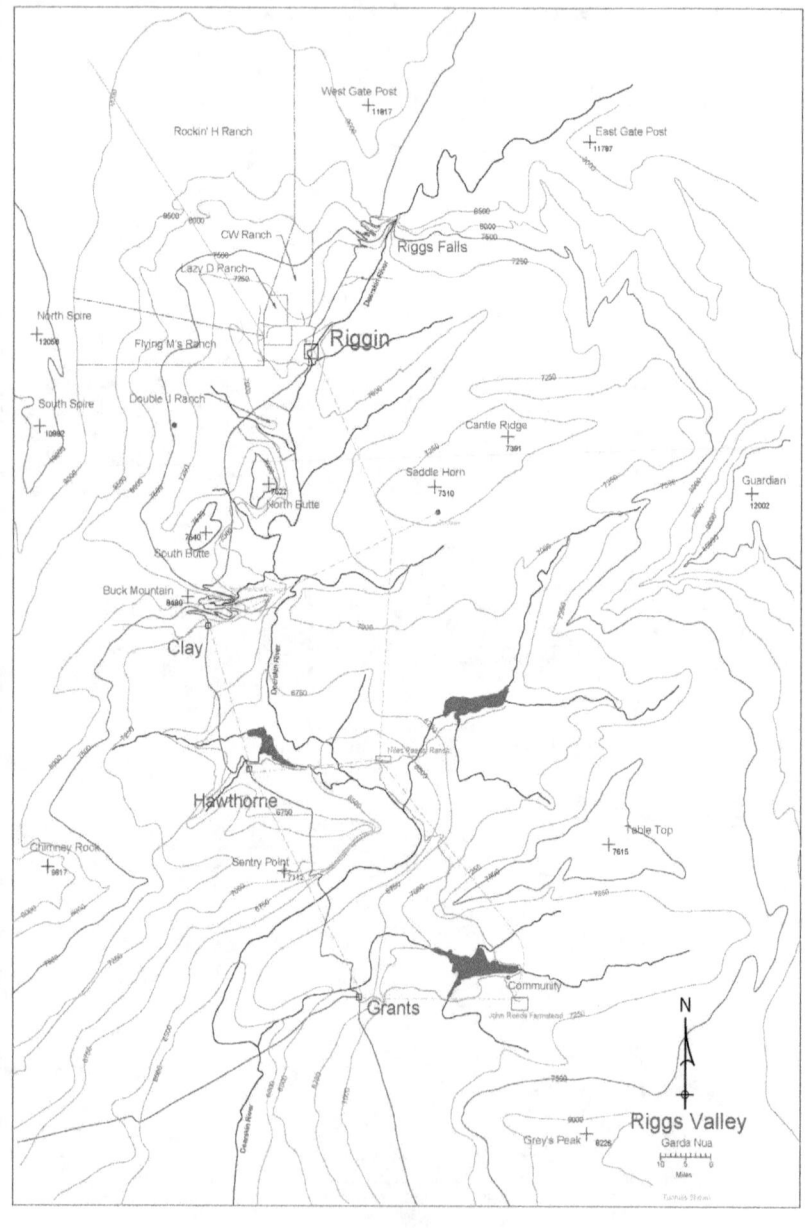

Glossary

Characters:

-A-

Annie	Cook at the Malone's Flying-M Ranch.
Anthor of Marit	Neila's grandfather. Living in Belimoor on Somstri.

-B-

Baine, Thom	State Deputy assigned to Riggin under Marshall Wally Lima. Father of Billie.
Baine, Eddie	Thom Baine's wife. Maiden name: Eddie Collier. Married on Dec 31, C.3482.750, age 35 yrs. Mother of Billie.
Baine, Billie	Daughter of Thom and Eddie Baine. Born on November 10, C.3483.429. Age 8 yrs old.
Beeli, Kiile	Captain, a Marine Squad Leader in the services of the Galactic Peace Force. Commandant of Marine base at Point Obscure. GPF Terran ID: USL15-EFM. (Kiile pronounced quickly Kī-īle.) ¬
Bren	Short version of Greg's nickname, 'BrenCara,' for Shara. Meaning: "Special Raven Haired Friend."
Brickle	Sedona's favorite horse. Named for her mottled caramel coloring.
Bucky	Cheyenne's favorite horse. Named for his buckskin coloring.

-C-

Cadet Pilots	Cadet students training in the art of space combat.

Apache Patrol Two:	Cadet Huml
Apache Patrol Three:	Cadet Milik
Apache Patrol Four:	Cadet Ilistr
Apache Patrol Five:	Cadet Lupis, Class 2 Fighter
Apache Patrol Six:	

Camerso	Gentleman's Gentleman to Prince Lukré. Previously the Gentleman's Gentleman to the late Prince Kiese.
Cara	Second house girl at the Malone's Flying-M's Ranch.
Cassel, Brendan	Coleen Malone's second husband, mate. (GPF Terran ID: IAL01 SS3)
Cassel, Coleen	Husband/mate to Brendan Cassel, second marriage. Previous marriage: Coleen Reese. Maiden name: Coleen Malone.
Chairman Sorgat	Principal Officer in the Trader's Union
Coleen Malone	See Malone, Coleen
Coleen Reese	See Reese, Coleen
Collier, Eddie	Floral Arranger at Mary's Flower Boutique. 24 yrs old when she married Thomas Baine. Daughter of Daniel Collier. No siblings.
Collier, Daniel	Eddie's missing father. Non-terran family name is Calr.

-D-

Dnar, Cera	Jill Jordan's GPF name (Pronounced: Key + ¬¬ray; Means: Fiery Red). A Captain and pilot in the GPF.

Dnar, Jadn	Bob Jordan's non-terran name.
Dnar, Jesi	Nick Jordan's GPF name. A Captain and pilot in the GPF.
Dnar, Keely	Cheyenne Jordan's GPF name.
Danny	Shara's 15 yr old black stallion. Retired from competition.
Davis, Carole	Waitress at Hap's Place. Shelly's younger sister by one year. 23 yrs of age when Wally was assigned to Riggin.
Davis, Marty	Husband of Rusty Davis. Father of Shelly, Carole and Todd Davis.
Davis, Rusty	Wife of Marty Davis. Mother of Shelly, Carole and Todd Davis.
Davis, Shelly	Raised in Riggin, wife of Lt. Jim Woods. 36 yrs of age. Mother of Carrie Anne Woods.

Deputies, Special

In Riggin:

Thom Baine. See Baine, Thom.

William (Bill) Day See Day, William

Dan Lupis. See Lupis, Dan.

Ted Marks. See Marks, Ted.

Scott Plumen See Plumen, Scott

Harvey Saulter See Saulter, Harvey

In Hawthorne:

Bill Trent

In Grants:

Thad Reeds Rural Support

Willy Carle

Dílis	Shara's 15 yr old black-faced roan. Greg's favorite and named by him. (Pronounced Jee + lus)
Director, Peace Force	Identification AGL36Q

-E-

Elders, The Family	Brian Woods	(deceased)
	Harry Woods	(deceased)
	Harold Danley	(captured)
	Malcolm Clotter	(captured)
	Charley Clotter	(captured)
	Dave Barns	
	Don Nikle	

-F-

Family Council	Support council for the Council of Elders, the nearly extinct governing body of the southern Riggs Valley. Normally ten members, only remaining members:
	William (Bill) Copper
	Jack Wilton

Fighters, Apache Squadron

Apache One: Q-STSX1

Apache Two: Q-KKLC14

Apache Three: Q-TTYF8

Apache Four: Q-STSX12

Apache Five: Q-LTVC21

Apache Six: Q-MKCC5

Apache Seven: Q-KVWC33

Apache Eight: Q-LLRT12

Apache Nine: Q-KCMM9

Apache Ten: Class 2 Patrol Fighter – Ani Tigs

Apache Eleven: Class 2 Patrol Fighter – Emli

Apache Twelve:	Class 2 Patrol Fighter - Barba
Apache Thirteen: McIntire	Class 2 Patrol Fighter – Rose
Apache Fourteen: McIntire	Class 2 Patrol Fighter – Doug
Apache Fifteen: Dnar	Class 2 Patrol Fighter – Cera
Apache Sixteen:	Class 2 Patrol Fighter – Jesi Dnar
Apache Seventeen: Lupis	Class 2 Patrol Fighter – Blaire
Apache Eighteen:	(Unassigned)
Apache Nineteen:	(Unassigned)
Apache Twenty:	Q-QRTT7
Apache Twenty-One:	Q-JCCV4

-G-

Geaardt, Stran	A Shadow. An undercover agent. A Commander in the Galactic Peace Force. Pilot of Q-STSX1. GPF ID: HQZL09-ES. Pronounced "Gee (as in Geese) + art."
Geaardt, Casi (Casey)	A Shadow. An undercover agent. Stran Geaardt's partner, wife. A Captain in the Galactic Peace Force. Pilot of Q-STSX1. GPF ID: HQZL09-ES2.
Geaardt, Caiti	Registered name of Sedona Malone. GPF ID: HQZL09-ES2.1 assigned on her eleventh birthday.
Geaardt, Coli	Registered name of Sierra Malone. GPF ID: HQZL09-ES2.2 assigned on her eleventh birthday.
Geaardt, Moira	Registered name of Coleen Malone
Gpada	Means Grandfather, in the cultural language of Nevar.

Gpama	Means Grandmother in the cultural language of Nevar.
Greg Malone	See Malone, Greg

-H-

Haak, Cheral	Captain/Major in the Galactic Peace Force. Pilot of Apache Patrol Ten, Class 2 Patrol Fighter as a flight student. Advanced to Major and assigned Q STSX12 with Nav-Com Lieutenant Keli Quil. Granddaughter of Paal Haak. Mated with Kiile Beeli on C.3486.738 (Cheral Haak-Beeli).
Haak, Paal	Commander, Galactic Peace Force Academy, Tactical Strategies Instructor, Retired. Grandfather of Cheral Haak.
Hank	Forman at the Smallwood Ranch.
Hawkins, Paul	Brother of Andrew and Nancy Hawkins. Grand Uncle to Shara Smallwood. (aka Paal Haak.)
Hawkins, Clea	Unplanned daughter of Andrew Hawkins and Katherine (Reeds). Married to Henry Smallwood. Mother of Shara, and surrogate to two other daughters. (Deceased.)

-J-

Jordan, Robert (Bob)	Owner of the Jordan Double-J Ranch. Nick's father.
Jordan, Darcy	Nick's Mother. Darcy Reeds married to Ben Jordan. (Deceased.)
Jordan, Nicholas	Aka, Nick. Husband of Jill Thomas. Father of Cheyenne Darcy Jordan. A Captain and Fighter Pilot in the Galactic Peace Force. Pilot of Apache

Sixteen, Class 2 Patrol fighter. GPF Terran ID: IAL36 SS.

Jordan, Jill — Nick Jordan's wife (Jill Thomas) for 11 yrs. Age 34 yrs. Married May 17; C.3482.522. Red Headed mother of Cheyenne Darcy Jordan. A Captain and Fighter Pilot in the Galactic Peace Force. Pilot of Apache Fifteen, Class 2 Patrol Fighter. GPF Terran ID: IAL36-SS2.

Jordan, Cheyenne Darcy — Red headed daughter of Jill and Nick Jordan. Age 10 yrs. Born July 10, C.3482.941. Favorite horse is Bucky. GPF Terran ID: IAL36-SS2.1. Familiar Nickname: Chy (Pronounced Shy)

-K-

Kiese, Prince — Warlord Prince of Knobaal (deceased).

Kiile — See Beeli, Kiile.

Kooich, Hench; Major — Colonel in the GPF, Commander of Q-KKLC14. GPF ID: RWKR17-SC.

Kooich, Leeana — Major Kooich's mate (wife). Captain in the GPF, Nav-Com officer and pilot on Q KKLC14. GPF ID: RWKR17-SC2.

Kooich, Tayn — Son of Hench and Leeana Kooich. Age 11 yrs old. Born September 30; C.3482.658. GPF ID: RWKR17-SC2.1.

Kym — Third house girl at the Malone's Flying-M's Ranch.

-L-

Lima, Wally — State Marshall, 37 yrs old, permanently assigned to Riggin. GPF

	Terran ID: IAL05-SS.
Lima, Carole	Wally Lima's wife, 34 yrs old. (Carole Davis.) Married January 29; C.3482.413. GPF Terran ID: IAL05-SS2.
Lima, Alyssa	Daughter of Wally and Carole Lima. 9 yrs old, born April 22; C.3483.227. GPF Terran ID: IAL05-SS2.1.
Lima, Ridan	Son of Wally and Carole Lima. 8 yrs of age, born May 16; C.3483.616. GPF Terran ID: IAL05-SS2.2.
Lukré, Prince	Replacement for Prince Kiese.
Lupis, Blaire	Daughter of Dan and Mandy Lupis. 18 yrs of age. Redhead. Joins the Force through Greg and Shara and begins training to be a Shadow and to fly Fighters.
Lupis, Dan; Deputy	State Deputy assigned to Riggin under Wally Lima. Wife Mandy. Daughter Blaire. (Registered Family name: Lomr.)

-M-

Malone, Coleen	Married to Tom Reese (1), and to Brendan Cassel (2). GPF Planet-side ID: IAL01-SS. Registered Moira Geaardt.
Malone, Greg	Husband of Shara Malone. 40 yrs old. Born March 17, C.3471.868, married to Shara Smallwood Nov 13, C.3482.336. Married for 12 yrs. GPF Terran ID: IAL02-SS. Father of Sedona and Sierra Malone. Great Nephew to Gary Woods. Son of Coleen Reese (Malone).

Malone, Shara (Shar)	Wife of Greg Malone. 40 yrs old. Born June 20, C.3471.963, in the same year as Greg Malone. Mother of Sedona and Sierra. GPF Terran ID: IAL02 SS2.
Malone, Sedona	dentical twin daughter of Greg and Shara Malone. Age 11 yrs, born August 18, C.3482.615. Favorite horse is Brickle. GPF Terran ID: IAL02-SS2.1.
Malone, Sierra	Identical twin daughter of Greg and Shara Malone. Age 11 yrs, born August 18, C.3482.615. Favorite horse is Strawberry. GPF Terran ID: IAL02-SS2.2.
Marks, Ted; Deputy	State Deputy assigned to Riggin under Wally Lima.
Matti	Head house girl at the Malone's Flying-M Ranch.
Meara Wrth	See Wrth, Meara.
McIntire, Doug	Husband of Rosalee (Mitchell) McIntire. Married June 6, C.3483.272. Married for 9 yrs. A Captain and Fighter Pilot in the Galactic Peace Force. Pilot of Apache Fourteen, Class 2 Patrol fighter. Father is Tom, aka Tor of Anthor, mother is Karyn, aka Canri of Lomsi; both from Somstri, living in Greely, CO.
McIntire, Rosalee (Rose)	Wife of Doug McIntire. A Captain and Fighter Pilot in the Galactic Peace Force. Pilot of Apache Thirteen, Class 2 Patrol fighter.
McIntire, Kaylie	Daughter of Doug and Rose McIntire. Age 8 yrs. Born Sept 2, C.3483.725.
McIntire, Kail	Son of Doug and Rose McIntire. Age

	8 yrs. Born Sept 2, C.3483.725.
Mosl, Corporal	GPF Marine Squad Leader, Thirty-two. Assigned to Lieutenant Kiile's Battalion protecting Obscure and supporting the Terran Campaign. (Pronounced: Moh-sul)

-N-

Neila	Kiile's daughter, Neila of Kiile (Neila Beeli). Born and raised in Turell on Nevar. Grandfather lived in Belimoor on Somstri. Blonde haired, blue eyed. (Pronounced: Neil + ah)
Niki	Head house girl for Wally and Carole at the CW Ranch.

-P-

Pada	Means Father, in the cultural language of Nevar.
Pama	Means Mother, in the cultural language of Nevar.
Piper	House girl and cook at Jill and Nick Jordan's home on the Jordan Ranch.

-Q-

Q-STSX1	Commander Stran Geaardt & Nav-Com Captain Casi Geaardt. Campaign Commander for Terran Campaign and Apache Squadron's Flight Training School. (Apache One.)
Q-KKLC14	Colonel Hench Kooich & Nav-Com Captain Leeana Kooich. Campaign's lieutenant and Flight Operations Commander under Commander Geaardt. (Apache Two.)
Q-TTYF8	Colonel Crem Mooren & Nav-Com Captain Franni Mooren. Campaign

	Wing Commander under Colonel Kooich. (Apache Three.)
Q-MKCC5	Major Aillx Romaan & Captain Colbee Donnr. Wing Second under Major Mooren. (Apache Six.)
Q-KVWC33	Major Daaws Miiles & Nav-Com Captain Meecia Miiles. (Apache Seven.)
Q-LTVC21	Major Neel Glean & Captain Debira Glean.
	- (Apache Five)
Q-LLRT12	Major Deni Bradg & Nav-Com Captain Mri Bradg. (Apache Eight.)
Q-KCMM9	Major Pti Fila & Nav-Com Lieutenant Lori Tam (Apache Nine.)
Q-JCCV4	Major Ronl Bids and Nav-Com Captain Emly Bids. Joined Apache Squadron after supporting the attack of 4 January and getting repairs done at Obscure. (Apache Twenty-One.)
Q-QRTT7	Major Amel Clef and Nav-Com Captain Pela Clef. Apache Squadron B-Group Wing Leaders. (Apache Twenty.)
Q-STSX12	Major Cheral Haak and Nav-Com Lieutenant Keli Quil.
	(Apache Four)
Quil, Keli, Lieutenant	Major Cheral Haak's Nav-Com Officer on Q-STSX12.

-R-

Ranch Hands	At the Smallwood Ranch: Jimmy, Tom (Tommy), Billy and Dusty.
Reeds	Terran family name of the controlling Family in southern Riggs Valley.

Reeds, Glory	Daughter of Thad and Betti Reeds. 21yrs of age, living in Riggin, attending Riggin College.
Reeds, Sam	Son of Thad and Betti Reeds. 25 yrs of age, living in Riggin. Finished college studies at Riggin College. (Registered as: Donl Jst.)
Reeds, Thad & Betti	State Deputy out of Grants. Living in Grants with his wife and working for Marshall Wally Lima. Son Sam and daughter Glory.
Reese, Coleen	Married to Tom Reese (1), mother of Hew and (by an Affair) of Greg Malone. Maiden name: Coleen Malone.
Reese, Tom	First husband of Coleen (Malone). (Deceased.) Distant relation of Gary Woods.

-S-

Shara Malone	See Malone, Shara
Smallwood, Shara (Shar)	Unplanned daughter of Henry and Clea (Hawkins) Smallwood. Youngest of three. 40 yrs old. Born June 20 (solstice), same year as Greg Malone.
Smallwood, Henry	Full blooded Apache, American Indian. Married Clea Hawkins, father of Shara Smallwood.
Stial, Sergeant	GPF Marine Squad Leader, Forty-two. Assigned to Lieutenant Kiile's Battalion protecting Obscure and supporting the Terran Campaign. (Pronounced: Steel)
Strawberry	Sierra's favorite horse. Named after her pinkish coloring; a strawberry

roan.

STSX	Q-STSX1 is a late generation, Shadow Class Corvette, nicknamed as a type as Q ships, operated under the command of Stran Geaardt. The latest in the long evolution of the GPF's Shadow ships. The name is synonymous with the ship's central computer system ID.

-T-

Taam, Crl	Jack Thomas' non-terran name.
Thomas, Jack	Married Amy Woods, daughter of Gary Woods. Father of Jill. Financial Officer at the Woods Lumber Mill. (Father of Greg Malone by pre-marital affair with Coleen Reese.)
Thomas, Jill	Daughter of Jack Thomas and Amy Thomas (Woods). Six years younger than Shara Smallwood and Greg Malone.
Tigs, Ani; Cadet	Cadet Pilot of Apache Patrol Three, Class 2 Patrol Fighter.
Tmn, Officer	One of Prince Lukré's Intelligence Officers.

-W-

Wardly, Anne, Lt.	Staff Assistant and Aide to Admiral Baker, space station S.S. QuickSilver.
Woods, Harry	Son of Horace Woods. Longtime head of the Woods Lumber and Mill (Retired). Father of Gary, James and Brian.
Woods, Gary	Son of Harry Woods. Father of Bill Woods.
Woods, James	Son of Harry Woods. Father of Amy Woods.

Woods, Brian	Son of Harry Woods. Unmarried. Current head of the Woods Lumber and Mill.
Woods, Bill	Son of Gary Woods; no siblings. Father of Jim Woods, Lieutenant (USAF).
Woods, Jim, Lt.	Son of Bill Woods; no siblings. Married to Shelly Davis, father of Carrie Anne Woods.
Woods, Amy	Daughter of James Woods. Married to Jack Thomas, mother of Jill Thomas.
Wrth, Meara; Captain	Galactic Peace Force Marine Medic. Terran age 47. (Meara, pronounced: MYAR + ah). Attending Medic for Sedona and Sierra's birth, for Tayn Koovich's birth and for Cheyenne Jordan's birth. Retired from the Force on 3482.698 at the age of 35 Terran years. Hired by Shara and Greg on 3482.701 as their resident Nanny.

Places and Things:

-A-

Aleemill	A mining colony on Feranni, 30 degrees North of West from Daneubois.
Angrilat	A Principal commercial complex in the Kyddellan System
Antheria	Major Commercial Planet in the Tunst System. Known as a Heavy World with a gravity index of 2.02 times Galactic Standard.
Aridont	City on Listera, cite of water rioting.

-B-

Baile	Planetary system of the planet

Rygon.

Belimoor | Major import and export city on Somstri. Home of Neila's maternal grandparents.

Betolle | Planet in the Daneets System. Home planet of Lieutenant Franni Kaal and her hometown of Casimir.

Botuni | Planetary System of agricultural planets Nevar and Somstri.

Brekshiir | A wrist mounted laser weapon, consisting of one or multiple optics and fired by a unique sequence of mental commands. Specifically designed for the GPF Shadows.

Brekshiir 170 Single Optic wrist Unit, 50 pulses with a range of 300 yds in air.

Brekshiir 490 Wrist Clusters is the most common in the GPF, consisting of 4 laser units, 50 pulses each with a range of 300 yds in air. Individually fired or in combination.

Brekshiir 710 Wrist Clusters, upgrade of the 490. 70 pulses with a range of 300 yds in air.

Brigstoan, Patrol Cruiser | GPF Patrol Cruiser designed for interception and boarding of suspect transports. Operated with a standard pilot crew, fifty aerial marines, a separate pilot crew and a Medical staff.

-C-

C.Date | A date referenced to the galactic calendar. A galactic year is comprised of one thousand galactic turns.

	Example: C.3482.329 is the 329th day of the galactic year 3284. It is also the 310th day of the current story year, November 6th.
Caldite Throwing Dart	A coveted and highly guarded GPF tool, used to inject a sedative or toxin upon impact.
Casimir	City on the planet Betolle, home town of Franni Kaal.
Cellystoan	Planetary system in which the Warlord Prince's home planet, Knobaal, orbits.
Centipar	One hundredth of a par. Similar to a terran minute.
Chain	A terran unit of measure. 66 ft. or 22 yds. or 100 links or 4 rods. There are 10 chains in a furlong and 80 chains n a statue mile. An acre is 10 square chains (that is an area of one chain by one furlong), (or 43560 sq. ft.).
Clay	Town in central Riggs Valley, 93 highway miles south of Riggin.
Colbr	Planetary System with three agricultural planets: Copus One, Two and Three.
Combassa Beans	A vegetable from the agricultural planet Somstri, usually prepared as a paste, high in fiber and nutrients. Prescribed to Casi by STSX to ease the tensions of their missions.
Corsecain	Planet in the Gashii system. Prominent for numerous bloody battles in the Moulit Wars.
CW Ranch	Carole's Ranch: Carole Davis' 65,000 Acre (101.5 sq. mi) ranch above her

dad's Lazy D ranch. She named it 'CW Ranch' when she married Wally Lima.

-D-

Daneets System — Planetary system of the planets Betolle and Feranni.

Daneubois — City of Universities & Higher Learning on the planet Feranni in the Daneets System. Cheral Haak's Home Town.

Dangcee — Mining colony on the fourth planet of the Greel system.

Double J Ranch — A 43,138 Acre (67.4 sq. miles) horse ranch owned by Nick's father, Bob Jordan, situated between the North Butte and Riggin.

-E-

Ematl — Space Port and major City on Nevar.

Envirocube — Shipping container with independent life-support systems for transporting personnel through space in the unpressurized holds of freight carriers.

EVA — Extra-Vehicular Activity. Working outside a satellite, space station or shuttle, in the vacuum of space.

-F-

Flying M's Ranch — Horse ranch belonging to Shara Malone (Smallwood). 209,275 Acres (approx 327 sq miles) split off of Paul Hawkins' larger ranch to its north. Situated West of Riggin. (Previously known as the Smallwood-Hawkins Ranch, Shara renamed if after she married Greg and before the girls were born.)

-G-

Galactic Peace Force	Galactic policing organization headquartered in the Gridelin Rings.
Galactic year	Equivalent to 1000 terran days, or 2.7397 standard terran years. See C.Date.
Gillot	A unit of measure roughly equivalent to a terran ounce.
Grants	Town at the south end of Riggs Valley, 186 highway miles south of Riggin.
Greel System	Planetary system in which the Pico Mining Company has established numerous mining colonies.
Greymn	Major Industrial complex on Omerai Two, renowned for its weapons manufacture. Model 40 is hand weapon most widely used by the Trader's Guild.
	Greymn Model 40: 40 destructive pulses with a range of 400 yds in air.
Gystrom	Manufacturing source of the GPF's Mark Series Cloaking Transmitters, based in a secret location in the Gridelin Rings.

-H-

Hawthorne	Town in central Riggs Valley, 128 highway miles south of Riggin.

-I-

IFF	Identification, Friend or Foe. An identification system to determine if an entity, craft or forces are friendly, and to determine their bearing and range from the interrogator. The

	system is capable of transmitting a hail to another system on command.
Issl	A root tuber, high in minerals and vitamins, from Copus Two in the Colbr System. Translated as Bread Root.
Istlar	Major City on Tanjera. Home city of Thomas Baine's parents.

-K-

Kaaspr	The standard issue brand of hand laser weapon for the Galactic Peace Force. Model 106 is the current standard laser hand weapon used in the GPF. Replaced the previous standard, Model 88.
	Kaaspr Model 106: 50 destructive pulses with a maximum range of 350 yds in air.
Knobaal	Home planet and seat of the Royal Throne of the Warlord Prince Kiese. Located in the Cellystoan planetary system.
Kyddel	System in which Angrilat's home planet resides.

-L-

| Lazy D Ranch | Martin Davis' 15,455 acre ranch (24.15 sq miles). |

-M-

| Millipar | One one-thousandth of a par. Similar to in concept but equivalent to 3.456 terran seconds. |

-N-

| Navigationmate | A ship's crewman assigned the duties of navigation and Astronavigation. |

Nevar — Farming Planet in the Botuni System. Home planet of Kiile.

Nuth — An icy planet in the Sadth System. Site of the Galactic Peace Force's Prison for Exiles and Prisoners of Importance.

-O-

Omerai Two — Industrialized planet in the Kyddel system, noted for its arms manufacturing.

-P-

Par — A fundamental galactic unit of time. Twenty-five pars in a Galactic Standard Turn (Day). Similar to a terran hour.

-Q-

QuickSilver — Planet Earth's multinational, manned orbital space station. (S.S. QuickSilver.)

Q-Ships — Nickname for the Galactic Peace Force's two man Recondite Corvettes. Specifically used by Shadows in their various roles of information gathering, defense and protection.

-R-

Riggin — A small college town in the northern point of Riggs Valley, western United States, planet Earth.

Rockin' H Ranch — A 1,263,950 Acre (1975 sq. mile) horse and cattle ranch belonging to Paul Hawkins and Nancy Hawkins (deceased), situated NW of Riggin.

Rygon — Home planet of the very old Geaardt family name, located in the Baile

System.

-S-

Shadow — Undercover agent of the Galactic Peace Force with specialized training and abilities in clandestine operations and information collecting, generally thought to be able to hide in plain sight.

Somstri — Agricultural planet in the Botuni system.

Sora root — A plant grown on Nevar, Somstri and Copus One and Two. Used as a spice or herb. Side effect and primary use is to reduce female fertility, a natural contraceptive.

Smallwood-Hawkins Ranch — Horse ranch belonging to Shara Malone (Smallwood). 209,275 Acres (approx. 327 sq. miles) split off of Paul Hawkins' larger ranch to its north. Situated West of Riggin.

-T-

Tanjera — Planet in the Ambali System.

Teligrin — From or of the planet Teligr.

Teligr — Manufacturing site for many GPF used toxins and chemical weapons. Home planet of Eddie Collier's father, Daniel. Family name Calr.

Tissl — Mining colony on the third planet of the Greel system.

Trader's Union — The Stellar Merchant's Guild's black market and slave trading business arm.

Tunst — Planetary system of Antheria.

Turell — Kiile's home village on Nevar.

Turn	A Galactic Standard day, consisting of twenty-five pars. Essentially the same duration as a terran day of twenty-four hours.

-V-

Vidcom	A video communication device.
Vidscreen	A video display screen.

-W-

Wiibsa	A small town northwest of Turell on Nevar.

-Y-

Yarrol Fruit	A light flavored, tart fruit from the agricultural planet Somstri served warm, high in minerals and nutrients. Prescribed to Casi by STSX to ease the tensions of their missions.

-Z-

Zeupa	Renowned agricultural city on the planet Somstri in the Botuni System.

Books by Aidan Red

Paladin Shadow Series
Terran Assignment Triptych
Book 1: Things are not as they seem.
Book 2: When luck is not enough.
Book 3: Fate has a different idea.
Terran Recruits Triptych
Book 4: In the wake of chaos.
Book 5: Terran Talents join forces.
Book 6: New rules of engagement.
Operation Retribution Triptych
Book 7: The training phase.
Book 8: Taking the fight off-world.
Book 9: Luring the Prince into the open.
Garda Nua Triptych
Book 10: The proliferation of Talent.
Book 11: When a planet is stolen.
Book 12: Right does not ask permission.
Assignment: Casha-Six
Book 13: No Warning
Book 14: The Best Laid Plans
Book 14: A Change of Heart

Eight's Warning
Book 1: The Past Hunts.
Book 2: The Past Attacks.
Book 3: The Price of Escape.

More Books by Aidan Red

Keeper and His Tiger

Book 1: An Unexpected Complication.
Book 2: Deadly Undercurrents.
Book 3: The Trap.

Fearin' the Banshee

About the Author

Aidan Red's passion for aviation and aircraft design, engineering, and a deep interest in space and space travel go back many years. An avid reader from an early age, Aidan, with great trepidation, ventured into the world of writing during college. With real world experience in business aviation, Aidan's creative side led him to create an alternate world where the beautiful Riggs Valley was born and Shara's life became chronicled in his epic science fiction series, Paladin Shadows.

Paladin Shadows consists of the five triptychs (three-part works), *Terran Assignment, Terran Recruits, Operation Retribution, Garda Nua* and *Assignment: Casha-Six*. In between the Paladin triptychs, Aidan has penned two, three book series, *Keeper and his Tiger,* and *West's Ghost Ranch* and a novel, *Fearin' the Banshee.*

Unpublished books in his various series are scheduled for release on a regular basis in the coming months.

Visit *www.RedsInkandQuill.com* or *www.AidanRedBooks. com* for more information on Aidan Red's books and where to purchase them.